A Palm Beach Love Story

By

Vicki and Rick Angelini

Chapter 1: Robert

It had been a whirlwind love. Robert discovered Leslie Devereaux working at an investment firm as an executive assistant in Boca Raton. He sent Leslie flowers every day. He wrote Leslie passionate letters. He took her to the best restaurants in Palm Beach. At first she found him handsome and attractive, then entertaining and interesting. At thirty-eight he still had an athlete's physique. His six foot, two-inch frame hung on powerful broad shoulders with the chiseled facial features of a warrior.

Within two months Leslie accepted Robert's offer as a private assistant in his firm. He was charming, gentle, and masculine. She found herself yearning to be with him and no one else. They fell completely in love. There were weekends with intimate friends, private cruises, and candlelit dinners.

One evening, he spoke of marriage on a friend's yacht. It began with an intimate catered dinner for two. A string quartet serenaded for the evening. After dinner, they were completely alone on the boat, anchored in the middle of the lagoon.

The lights of the city in the distance filtered through the silk curtains. Gentle slapping of waves on the hull and the soft rocking side to side had created a fairy-tale glow. He took her, firmly, insistently. Tenderly, he pressed his lips to hers, his hips to hers, his heart to hers.

"Do you feel the soft slapping of the waves?" Robert asked softly, looking into her hazel green eyes, "They're for you." Together they drew into each other with the rhythm of each gentle wave. He lifted her petite, 30 something form up, released her long blonde hair to fall in surrender around her ample breasts, and pressed her to him until she felt locked into his being. Then, with the softness of a cloud, she lay under him. "Oh, that this night could last forever," Robert whispered.

Leslie searched his deep brown eyes, looking for a sign, a hint of falsehood, or any sign of simple lust. But she only found a hope, a fulfillment bigger than any others, begging to be answered in her. He was in need, and so was she.

He gently kissed her lips, neck, and shoulders. "Your perfume," he whispered, as he kissed her breast, "intoxicating." He followed her tensing body down her quivering hips. Starlight glowed on her curves. He paused, lowered his head to her smooth abdomen and for a moment seemed as a child to her. Leslie cuddled his head in her arms. She felt him sigh. He continued kissing down her body. "I want you, I need you, I must have you," he whispered, as if afraid others would hear as he made his insistence clear. Each wanting, each receiving, together they tumbled into love. He offered her his true emotion which she willingly accepted, hoping the moment would never end.

Afterwards, Leslie found some cheddar cheese and a bottle of red wine. Added water crackers made a feast at two in the morning.

"Would you ever marry, Leslie?"

"Would you?"

His face became darkened at the question. He said, "It can be good for the right people. Do you think I am the right people?"

Then, holding a comb across her upper lip to imitate his mustache, she teased: "I'll let you know after I analyze it, Robert. You know how important an analyses is to the business of decision making, don't you?"

He laughed and replied, "Please inform me as to your outlook to the possibilities at your earliest convenience," keeping the silly moment.

Now, she wondered if it all was a game, just a fling for him, only entertainment.

But it was more than that, Leslie was sure of it. "So what happened?" she whispered to herself. "Was it something I said or did? Or some secret in the past?" After the evening on the yacht he was called away for two days and when he returned he presented her with a diamond bracelet set in platinum from Tiffany's in Palm Beach and an apology. "Forgive me," he said. "My feelings are genuine, my love is true, but I can't ask you to burden yourself with my fate."

She questioned, "Why?" tears streaming from light blue eyes. But he never answered.

He promoted her and raised her salary. *He does not want me going anywhere, but he does not want me*, she thought, confused. Oh, they still dated, the typical dates of two people who cannot make up their minds; dinners, parties. Sweet, small gifts were exchanged. But there was no further talk of marriage. It was as if Robert was trying to escape, but couldn't....

* * *

"The coffee man was here, Ms. Devereaux," Kalley, Leslie's assistant announced. Kalley's voice cracked between Leslie's ears. "He delivered the order for the board meeting this afternoon." Leslie's mind raced back to her office, Robert's office. "And here is a note from the boss."

Leslie quickly read the note: "I need to see you this afternoon." She smiled.

"Brazilian blend, South African dark, Mocha, Piquet Tiger, and regular Joe, I hope," Leslie questioned in her soft and delicate South Carolina drawl, as she gently folded Robert's note between her index fingers. She was careful to crease the parchment neatly with each fold as if it was to be found on her pillow. Just like Robert always did with letters of affection.

"Exactly," replied Kalley. "And there was something else, some small packages."

"Oriental?" Of course they are, Leslie thought correcting herself. Robert makes deliveries on time, every time, if only just in time.

"Why, yes, and beautifully wrapped, too!"

There on Kalley's desk were eight delicately wrapped gifts. Each slight rectangular box was wrapped and sealed in a rice paper envelope. The hand-made paper was printed with characters of the Ming. Each delivered a different blessing or wish upon the recipient: love, honor, long life, beauty in thought, loyalty, health, adventure, and peace. Inside, each held a small secret: a ball of wool. Each a different color. Near perfection. Robert will be pleased.

"Your'e perfect," he often told her. "You always seem to know what I need and without the slightest effort, arrange it." He was always confident in her, yet never demanding. *But that was his perfection*, Leslie mused. *My Robert is a planner, a leader, and a confidant.* Leslie breathed a deep sigh. *He knows how to pick people. He knows how to motivate and lead, how to trust. How to get action and results.*

"What should I do with them?" Kalley asked in her usual bubbly voice.

"Oh, we'll place them on the Federal period antique server until Robert calls for them at the board meeting, I guess." Kalley gathered the packages up. They easily filled both of her light brown hands. "Cover them with a cloth, so they are out of sight. I'm sure that's what Robert would want. It'll add to the dramatic effect when they're presented to the members. They should be here any minute." A product of her Carolina breeding, Leslie pronounced "they" like it was floating up into the air.

"Ok," Kalley answered, grinning, and in an instant she bounded up and was gone out the secret office door directly into the boardroom.

Leslie sat down at her antique Queen Anne desk, framed by two Mizner period hand-carved table lamps, one in the shape of a monkey climbing a palm tree, and the other shaped like a pineapple. Addison Mizner had been the preeminent designer, architect and builder of Palm Beach in the 1930's. Mizner had built Robert's family home. The lamps once rested on Robert's grandfather's desk for decades, and then on his father's. "All these things are Robert's, including me." Leslie sighed.

She began to read the day's correspondence. One telegram from Hong Kong said; "It's woolly here. Stop. James," *Curious,* Leslie mused, *why use a telegram? E-mail is faster and less expensive. James, whoever that was, would be reprimanded. Robert wanted efficiency. And what could be woolly in Hong Kong?* She placed the telegram on the "most urgent" pile again. There were others, the usual reports, dailies from the partners and subsidiaries. E-mails confirming attendance at the afternoon board meeting were also stacked in the most urgent pile. Robert was the man of the moment. He wanted certainty. He expected everyone to attend the board meeting this afternoon, including her. And of course, she always did.

Yet, he grew distant, asking her in and out of his life. It was as if some dark secret, something he could not share, haunted him day and night, and he was running from its power.

So why did he send her the note? She would be there. He should know that. Her hand touched her jacket pocket where the note was kept. "I need to see you this afternoon." *What could it mean?* She sent him an e-mail, "Recommend you try the woolly Hong Kong tea for lunch. And after?" She knew he would understand. Board meeting is set. Expected packages have arrived. He would know she still loved him.

Chapter 2 The Millers

For a moment Leslie found herself staring out the office window to the street beyond. There, walking between the palm trees bordering the paving were a couple. He was tall and handsome. She was fair and slender. Occasionally, the man gestured to a sight; perhaps a building pediment or a painting displayed in a gallery window. He held her hand. She kissed his cheek. To Leslie the scene was sublime. He could have been the old Robert. She was lonely for the old Robert, the one she had grown to love.

"If only we were like before, " Leslie whispered. She wanted the days of innocent romance to return; the days when she did not care why she was with Robert, and only wanted to be in his arms. She wrapped her arms around her abdomen and imagined what their romance could be.

Why not just leave, run away to one of those places they shared in total intimacy? she wondered. *The Bahamas were not far away, an hour by plane, maybe a little more to get from the dirt runway to the beach. He could choose a beach on the East side of Abaco. One secluded behind high scrub covered dunes. A beach where gin clear water kisses the pure white sand. Water as pure as my love for him. Water as pure as his love for me. Water full of life, and all life making love and having their babies in the warm protecting swirls of wave and eddies. A beach only the natives knew about and never spoke of. One where we could be open to passion, naked and honest in our bodies.*

She imagined he would spear fish for her and roast the catch over a beach fire at sunset. His powerful nude body unconcerned, free in nature. Sun-jeweled sweat beads would glow on his dark skin and highlight every turn of muscle and bone in his broad shoulders, slender waist and hips, powerful legs. The natural motions of a man unhindered by clothing. He would take her, again and again, penetrating her very core until there was no other thought but of him. She would be his. There would be no questions to ask, no concerns, no doubts: only the total certainty of passion.

Yes, she wanted to be totally with him. But now, she constantly found herself judging, questioning the appropriateness of their affair, for there were lingering, hounding questions. Why was Robert so secretive about his past? When they first met she assumed his shyness to talk about himself was only self-consciousness. Perhaps he was insecure about some shortcoming, she had thought. But Leslie soon came to realize Robert had no shortcomings. He was a powerful man.

Kalley entered into Leslie's office, a question on her lips. Before she could speak, Leslie asked: "Are we ready?"

"As always, but, what about the packages?"

"Another mystery to entertain, involve and convince, I suppose," Leslie replied dryly.

"Ok, what's up, Leslie. Where is that glow, that spark?"

"I'm sure I'h don't know what ya'll ah talking about," Leslie replied in the teasing, Southern belle voice she sometimes used to reduce the tension of the moment. Then putting the back of her left hand gently across her forehead and drifting her gaze upwards she announced: "Why what ever do you mean. Why I'h tell you, your consternation is about to give me the vapors. Then you shall be left to entertain our'h guests alone, ma'h child."

"Miss Scarlet, Miss Scarlet, I don't know nothing about birthing no board members." Kalley's response was typical of the two friends banter. But her concern was genuine.

"Come on, come clean, Leslie. Out with it. You're not yourself again today. It just isn't like you to daydream out the window."

"I wasn't daydreaming. I was taken in the beauty of the morning. I have seen you gander out of the window for what seems like hours at a time; when a handsome man passed by."

"And I've met some interesting men that way," Kalley giggled.

"Yes, but you don't have to perch like some bird of prey, waiting for some unsuspecting male to pass under your branch and dangerously enter your personal hunting ground. Now admit it girl, you check out every man that comes into this building."

"And I haven't heard you tell me to quit giving you my experienced assessment of each and every one of them. Especially when I score their butt factor. Now, this one is a ten plus," Kalley whispered in Leslie's ear as she passed. "He's a real catch, land him Leslie."

Leslie turned to see Robert coming down the hall. His eyes caught hers and in an instant his face turned into an expression of relief and joy. Then, without explanation, his face turned somber. Robert quickly walked to Leslie's outstretched hand and in taking it drew her close to him. Their bodies touched and warmth sped through her. She could feel Robert startle with happiness at her embrace. Then just as quickly: it was gone.

Robert said in a low and intimate voice only Leslie could hear; "My dear, you are looking ravishing today. Are we ready for show time?"

"It's all a go," replied Leslie, swallowing the word "dear" and then paused as if there was a resolution of a mystery about to be coming forth from Robert's lips. But Robert said nothing and replied with a quick wink of his eye.

"Did you get my message," Leslie asked?

"I did," replied Robert with a confident smile, "and I bet you are wondering what the mystery is, huh?"

"Oh, yes, please," Leslie sighed a breath of relief. "I've wanted to scream at you for weeks, what is wrong?" she paused. Leslie misunderstood.

Leslie saw Robert's lips tremble. "I have hurt you."

"Oh, a, the boxes of wool, you know the ones wrapped in parchment bearing good wishes upon the recipients."

And then, as much to change the conversation to something less embarrassing as well as explaining what was to be done, he softly said: "This one is going to be tricky. I need to know about any requests of any information concerning those boxes outside of the board meeting. I mean anything." Then he added: "No one is immune from this. I and only I must know.

"What's wrong, what's happening?" she asked. Robert just winked. Torn between desire and anger, she wanted to scream: *"Oh who cares about some old wool? What's wrong with you? With me?"* She wanted him to take her in his arms, take her now.

"Later, love," he replied, looked around and was gone into his office. Deep in her abdomen she felt a pang.

The remainder of the morning passed without incident. The usual reports were reviewed, notated and filed. Leslie lost herself in routine. She made a concise report of morning activities for Robert. He would be pleased, she thought. At about 12:30, the board members began to arrive.

The first were Colonel and Mrs. Miller. Jeffrey and Bev were two of Robert's oldest and closest friends. Bev brought pictures of their quick little junket to Cancun for Robert to muse over. He always made a fuss over them. They had been close personal friends with Robert's parents and were the remaining link to Robert's childhood. In their late sixties, they were healthy seniors. Bev thought of herself as Robert's aunt.

And Bev always made an entrance. As one of the New People of Palm Beach, Bev knew it was imperative to make a statement. She was here. And she most certainly was "here" anywhere she went. Regaled in a pink Channel dress with Jackie Kennedy hat and bag she captured the morning sun. A neckless of thirty millimeter, matched white natural pearls hung around her neck. Her Patik Philippe Golden Eclipse wristwatch adorned her outstretched hand. Yes, Bev made certain the world knew she had arrived.

"My dear, you are ravishing as ever," Bev's voice sang out to Leslie in the stuffy office, "I hope the men around here appreciate you." Bev's announcement was obviously intended to be overheard by Robert.

"I'm glad to see you returned safely. How was your trip?"

"Excellent, my dear," Jeffrey answered, and then with a loving and teasing smile directed toward his wife, said, "but maybe a little too much shopping and not enough golf." As usual, Mr. Miller's appearance was impeccable. His pure white hair was combed back in a European style and framed his features in well-tanned skin. Sixty-nine, Leslie thought, but he could pass for sixty, very Palm Beach.

"How grown men can chase a little white ball around all day I never will understand," responded Mrs. Miller to the obvious tease. "Why their three hundred and sixty dimples still aren't as cute as my two, now are they dear?"

"Most assuredly not, love, but surely you know I couldn't ever compare you to anything in the universe. Your beauty and wit are incomparable. Golf balls can only roll, and you can dance. Golf balls are only round and you are a resplendent collage of distracting and delightful shapes all combined into..."

"And you can't bet on me, can you like you can a golf game: you old charmer. But don't ever stop, my dear." And then turning to Leslie, Bev asked, "Is his royal majesty Mr. Robinard on the throne yet? Where is he? Where's he hiding? Called him, you know from Cancun, but of course he wasn't in or by a phone or in conference, or he didn't have his phone on. Anyway, he didn't call back, the stinker."

"My dear," said Mr. Miller, "you wouldn't leave a message. How could he call?"

"Such details, always details, Jeffrey," Bev replied. He didn't call, and we had a wonderful surprise ready for the both of you," she turned to Leslie.

"Not we dear. You."

"Details, details again love. Anyway, I was thinking about you and Robert." Then in a soft voice she said to Leslie: "I thought the top of an ancient Indian pyramid would be an excellent place for a wedding." Leslie paled. She looked away. She couldn't look Bev in the eye. "I'm sorry my dear; what's wrong?"

"I don't know," replied Leslie, "I don't know what to say. It's like there's some deep dark secret keeping us apart."

Bev froze. She was without response for a moment. Then a look of understanding overcame her face. "A dark secret you say, dear? I'd say you were right. Robert needs me. Don't you worry, I'll take care of this. Come Jeffrey," she said, and they were gone into Robert's private office.

Chapter 3 The Board Meeting

Down the plush, money-green carpeted hallway came the rest of the Board of
Directors. Mr. Albert Jessup of New York led the pack. He represented certain interests
in the New York area that had a large investment. Today, as usual, he wore an off-the-
rack navy blue suit with a white shirt and a black silk tie. Brown wing-tip shoes were his
norm.

Very predictable, Leslie thought as she greeted him and grit her teeth into a smile.
As the senior executive she wanted to be certain investors were comfortable. "Good
afternoon and welcome again. The meeting is about to take place, but first, you must be
parched."

"We have prepared the usual libations for your refreshment."

"Lovely to see you my dear," replied the grinning Jessup. "You're looking as fine
as ever." He pressed his glance up and down her body. "Any chance of you showing me
the sites of Palm Beach this trip?"

"I'm sorry, time just won't permit I'm afraid. We have such a tight
schedule this week, with the board meeting and all." *You wouldn't be welcome at
any of my clubs, just not the right sort.* She wanted to shout it out. But that
wouldn't be good business.

"I'll have the usual," he told Leslie roughly, as if she were tending the bar.
"A Johnnie Walker Blue Label with spring water, if you please." He placed his
left hand on her shoulder.

"Ah-hum," Leslie grunted as she brushed his arm aside. "Right through
the doors gentlemen and I'm sure the staff will accommodate you."

Following closely to Jessup were the other two members of the board.
Tanny Knight was a rather old playboy and professional sportsman. His given
name was Theodore, but his baby brother had pronounced him Tanny decades
ago, and the name stuck. He had inherited the responsibility of managing his

family's estate. It had been considerable and cumbersome, and eight years ago an old family friend had suggested he divest himself of all other holdings and place all personal assets with Robert. It worked to his liking, though he still put together investment packages for use of other people's money (OPM) to make more of his own.

Robert Robinard Resources was known among friends as RRR or, as the business community liked to call it, Robinard's Rich Raiders. Their specialty was making money, lots of it. Robert's business plan was to provide seed money to new organizations for a large piece of the profit pie. Use of the Robinard name and its considerable influence helped get the job done. Usually an acquisition remained in the corporate portfolio about 18 months, just long enough for its franchise property to be marketed for its' potential benefits. Robert did not stay in an acquisition for the full ride, as many other entrepreneurs did. The philosophy at RRR was to make a reasonable profit in a reasonable time, or hopefully, an un-reasonably short time. RRR got there first and took a profit, but not all the profit, and moved on.

"Tanny, you only need to attend board meetings and vote with Robert to keep the profits flowing," his friend Bev Miller had once told him. She was right. Profits rolled in.

George Reit followed closely behind. A middle-aged man, George was in a mid-life crisis. He was dating women half his age. He had a great comb-over and wore a mustache. He was more than willing to take business chances having made his fortune in software before the real explosion of the PC.

Tanny tipped his Texan hat to Leslie, and George gave her a wink. Leslie smiled back in a confident, strong smile and said: "We will start in just a few moments gentlemen. Do get yourselves watered down before we begin." They passed through the double mahogany doors into the boardroom and were gone from her sight.

Leslie turned to Kalley and said: "Ok, it's time." Leslie collected a few notes and passed through the private boardroom door and made her entrance.

* * *

The boardroom was a place of power, financial power and it was decorated accordingly. The Addison Mizner slab table was thirty feet long and six feet wide, with fourteen matching, embroidery upholstered chairs. Built locally in the 1930's, it was designed to convince people it was an original antique medieval banquet hall piece. A Mizner design was the closest thing to an original Palm Beach antique one could find. Above the table hung three large 150-year-old Baccarat crystal chandeliers that had been imported from England by Robert's father forty years before. All the twelve-foot high walls were paneled in hand-rubbed mahogany and there were no windows.

"Members of the board," Leslie announced, "I trust you have refreshed yourselves. We have a single malt Scotch, Dom Perignon, and spring water. Today you will be enjoying blackened Mahi-Mahi over a bed of wild rice, seasoned the island way. Also, we have a special dessert treat for you and of course, your favorite coffees with it."

Robert entered wearing his biggest smile. "Welcome everyone," he said and proceeded to go to each seat and shake hands. Jessup stood to greet him.

"And where have you been off to these last few days?" Jessup asked.

"As usual, I have been at the proverbial grind stone. Good to see you," Robert replied with a grin, looking away from Jessup to the other members.

The board took their seats. Leslie noticed that Bev Miller had strategically positioned herself away from Robert's side and between Jessup and Tanny. Jeffrey Miller got her chair and sat at her side. Across the table from them sat George Reit, alone.

Next to be greeted was Bev and Jeffrey Miller. "Bev, you are looking fantastic as usual," he said as he extended his arm.

Jeffrey whispered in his ear: "Look out lad, she's hot about something," as Robert bent down to receive Bev's embrace.

"You didn't call me, Robert," Bev said with a faux pout. "Where've you been?"

"Really," replied Robert. "Was I supposed to call? I didn't get the message."

"You know what I mean Robert," Bev returned, scolding him like an aunt, "you are never here to get a message."

"My dear, I'm out making us money. The money here in this room we already have. I'm out and about getting us more money, you see. Why, to be after money here would be like stealing from friends." He glanced over his shoulder at Jessup.

Next, Tanny extended his hand to Robert. "What new adventure have you to share with us, Tanny?"

Without getting up Tanny pushed back his chair and grinned: "The Miami to Bimini race is next weekend and my team is in with a new boat. You should come out to see the run, Robert. We are going to destroy the competition. The victory party is going to be a blow out and you're lucky enough to know the captain of the winning team." Chuckles were heard throughout the room.

Now Robert crossed the table and extended his hand to George Reit. "George, you're looking fit as usual. How's your tennis?"

"Better than ever, care for a match?" George asked, standing. He hung onto the chair back. George always seemed to be a little out of place.

"No thanks," answered Robert, "I know when I'm bested." Robert sat down next to George to deliberately inflate George's ego. George grinned.

It was time to begin the report. Gently Leslie seated herself to the other side of George Reit, far from Jessup, and began the meeting with the announcement:

"Today marks the seventh anniversary of our before Easter meetings. It will mark the end of another fiscal year, the end of another winter season in Palm Beach. We know you will all enjoy the south of France, Newport, and Carmel this Spring. We will miss you and we are most pleased to tell you we have had an outstanding year. But first, pleasure before business." She rang the service bell and three servers entered bearing luncheon trays.

"Blackened Mahi-Mahi over wild rice and Dom Perignon to clear the taste buds," announced Robert as the caterers entered. Mr. Jessup of New York could be expected to begin a slightly cloaked assault on Robert's management of RRR at his earliest convenience, and he did not disappoint anyone.

"How much did we make the fourth quarter Robert?" Jessup asked. "We were expecting a 20% return over the year. That seems reasonable, in light of the fact that Piedmont and Blue Ridge published quarterly statements last week declaring 23%."

"They're public companies," Robert responded. "They must post anticipated earnings or better, or suffer a loss of stock value."

"Well, they certainly do post better earnings than us," replied Jessup, glaring. "I know you don't understand my proposal, but today might be a good day for us all to take a look. We are among friends, right?"

"Are you saying we should become a holding company, oh or say a mutual fund?" Robert replied, casually.

"We can create more wealth more quickly if RRR takes advantages of certain leveraged opportunities on a quarterly basis. Market movers can be an in and out of the market opportunity with little time exposure."

"That's not creating wealth, Mr. Jessup. That is simply leveraging other's misfortunes for a quick and perhaps, illusive profit. Remember, leveraged investments must be paid back with interest even if the acquisition is not profitable."

"It's the way of the future," argued Jessup, raising his voice. "Profits can be made without a long term, and therefore, a long exposure and risk to market trends."

"A point made," interjected Jeffrey Miller, "but remember my dear Mr. Jessup, if no investor had stepped up to the plate at the proper time, Mr. Edison's invention would be in the trash pile outside his workshop window and we would quite probably be sitting here enjoying our fine lunch under whale oil lamps."

"And my dear," Bev retorted, "I'm sure you would have loved to rummage through all of that junk outside Edison's window. He's a pack rat you know, Robert. He saves everything as though it was a piece of a puzzle, a map to a gold mine or something." Then added with true affection: "But I love him for it," and she pressed her hand to his.

"Friends," George Reit added, "that's why we have come together; to see what directions to take in the future and hopefully celebrate our successes. I for one I'm anxious to hear what Robert has to say."

Leslie offered: "Then let's enjoy our company and the company of the wonderful Mahi-Mahi who made the most tasty contribution to our repast this fine and warm day." Then she added: "Tell me Tanny, what can we expect out of your team? Did you create a more powerful engine? Should I call my mother and ask her to mortgage the family plantation for a wager on your boat?"

"Yes, tell us Tanny." Bev giggled, raising a glass to him: "We all know how men like to brag about their big engines," and she shot a playful glance around the room.

"One of my mechanics had an idea that just may change open-ocean racing," Tanny responded. "We've modified our engines so they can be retimed while running."

"Really," George queried. "If you know how to do that without blowing up the motor, please, tell Detroit. Or maybe Robert, and we can all make some money."

"Well, we don't blow up the engine George, we adjust the timing so it runs with less compression: blowing some gas through the exhaust valves quickly but making more rpm's and therefore more speed." Tanny explained. "You see, in calm water we do not need horsepower. We trade horsepower for rpm's, for prop turns. We make the engine run faster in the final miles of the race, where there is calm water. A faster running engine means a faster running boat. We plan to take the race in the last stretch."

"And that's what we do here at RRR, in a way," Robert interjected. "We don't try to win the race at the beginning, knowing that opportunities lay in the miles in the future. Of course, we get out before it becomes too risky."

"And how well have we done?" asked Bev. They were now talking money and Bev liked talking money.

"Let us show you," replied Robert, touching his right ear. "Please remove the lunch," he instructed the servers. All waited until the water glasses were filled and only the board plus Leslie were in the room.

Leslie began: "Our candy endeavor has matured, in my judgment. I believe it is time for us to divest ourselves. Let me show you." Leslie handed out five bound reports, one to each member.

"Remember, our window had originally been thirty months. We rescued a small after dinner mint manufacturer who was under-capitalized, Andre Dinner Mints. Originally, inventories increased and Andre was in the red."

"Until last June," Robert added. "We continued to supply Andre with lines of credit using our considerable influence and guarantees of payment. The owner was required to pledge all his personal assets: home, boat, cars, heck even his children's college fund."

"Well, now," Jeffrey interrupted, "that seems to be rather harsh."

"We made certain he was committed to the partnership," Leslie explained. "We cannot afford Andre negotiating a new profit sharing split when we have a buyer. Our investments must be in our control. Then we used our considerable influence to gain market share."

"Sounds risky," Jessup interrupted.

"Fortunately, we have a national candy company ready to purchase one hundred per cent of Andre," Leslie explained.

"And what is our selling price?" asked Jessup. "My investors want to see top dollar. They demand best return. They..."

"I believe your investors want to see a healthy profit each and every time we move, Mr. Jessup," interrupted Leslie, raising her voice. "I'm sure they understand as a seller we must offer value in our product for an intelligent buyer to be interested."

"Come on, I want profits."

"And that you'll have," replied Leslie. We're not selling land to vacationers here, though that can be profitable. A cash buyer is a smart buyer. They want to know they can make a profit with their purchase. Our profit comes from getting there first and being just a little smarter than them."

"Even better, friends," explained Robert. "Here we've a buyer that knows the potential in the product, and wants to keep it off the supermarket shelves. The buyers want to protect their product line. They're purchasing Andre to retire it and protect their own line of mints. Oh, the production line will be converted. No jobs will be lost. But there will no longer be an Andre Dinner Mint."

"And how, please tell me, can that possibly be better for my investors?" asked Jessup.

"Our sales price is private information. Terms are private. There'll be no future track record to prove or disprove our possible profitability claims. Our creditors will only know we returned their money, with interest and before the due dates." Leslie grinned.

"And the sales price will be?" asked Jessup.

"Our investment in Andre totaled one point two million dollars including acquisition of 60% of stock and and infusion in capital," Leslie tersely answered, pointing to the prospectus. "The sales price offered is six point seven million dollars and we'll all share sixty per-cent of the sales price of six point seven, or, 4 million plus to RRR. That's around a 350% profit in slightly under a year and a half. Considerably more than twenty-three per cent per annum; wouldn't you say sir? Andre's happy. He recovered his investment with a healthy profit and saved his kids college education. And it's a private transaction. There are no SEC filings. We could do it again and no competitors would be the wiser."

"Bravo, bravo my dear," Bev shouted and began to applaud. "What do you have for us next?"

"Wonderful news across the investment portfolio, as you can see," Robert announced powerfully. "And something else..." Then turning, changed the Board's attention and with a pointed finger to Leslie, he asked: "Would you get the packages for our guests?"

"Oh a surprise, how I love them if they are profitable," Bev said with a giggle.

"Oh I'm certain they will be," replied Robert and as Leslie passed his chair he pressed a note into her hand.

Leslie retrieved the Oriental packages and presented them to each member. Jessup represented four investors and he received four packages. Then before sitting, Leslie read Robert's note. It said:

Leave the room. Don't say anything. Watch for anything unusual. Your work is done here. I'll explain later,

Robert

Leslie's stomach wrenched. Suddenly, Robert did not need her. She glanced around the room, but everyone was listening to Robert. Everyone except Jessup. He grinned back. Nobody noticed when she walked out the door, none but Jessup.

Chapter 4. Land Sharks

Leslie looked out the office window to the city beyond the lagoon. On the other shore white tents were being erected. Stages were being built. Soon, thousands of couples would be enjoying the late spring evening with music, dancing and food. *Does anyone ever find true love? Is it possible? Or, just some passing hope, dream?* Leslie wondered.

She'd once believed in true love, but it seemed a long time ago. Before Robert she had thought Gerry was her true love. Her mind drifted back to an early evening in Boca.

* * *

It had been a cool Saturday in February in Boca Raton, only about 70 degrees, the sun was setting into a pool of bright red clouds. Birds filled the trees with their chirping in the park as she and her friend Kate Jenson refreshed with an early dinner on Kate's veranda. A pitcher of Kate's chilled Sangria cooler stood gaining water droplets on her table.

"Snowbirds," Kate was saying. "They're more like sharks, if you ask me."

"They are beautiful and happily full of life, Leslie answered. "Why, can't you enjoy them for their honest simplicity of song?"

"Why Leslie Devereaux, you're drifting off to that mystic place again, pay attention, girl!" Kate poured each of them another wine cooler.

"And where might that mysterious place be? I'm sitting here with you. Can't you hear the birds? They're lovely. I've always thought they were the most lovely things on earth. Why, when I was a girl on warm evenings back home, I'd lie under the big magnolia tree in our front yard at dusk and listen to them. It seemed like thousands of birds all singing their joy together at the ending of a shared day. How can you compare such simply beautiful creatures to a shark?"

"I wasn't talking about them," Kate answered rather crossly. Then pointing to the tree said: "Not them. The ones that make the trip in the winter down here looking for easy pickings, opportunities in which to take advantage of sweet young things like you. The ones that walk upright on two legs, that's who I'm talking about. And maybe one or two who have made Boca their permanent home."

"So we are again speaking about how to hate men, dear. I'm correct?"

"Not hate them, Leslie, but don't trust them with your heart either. Your heart is much too valuable an asset to be entrusted to such a bird, dear. Rather, understand their shall we say, assets; and use them accordingly."

"Why Katherine C. Jenson. Whatever are you talking about? I'm sure I don't know what you mean. A gentile lady of the South does not know of such things," Leslie answered, a giggle in her voice.

"Well dear, let me explain it to you. Men are wonderful, yes even useful. But they cannot love, not really. They think between their legs."

"Now Kate, you're not going to tell me about the land sharks and the bees, are you?"

"Sometimes I think I should. You are as trusting as a child, and men are no toy for a child. They play a different game."

"And pray tell, what you think that game would be my dearest friend?"

"Why it's simply a game of conquest. Men are only interested in conquering our emotions and getting us into the submission pose. Having their way with us."

"I know chivalry isn't dead." Leslie stated defensively. "My mother and father were truly in love. My mother ran the household finances and raised me. Dad was her devoted helper and she trusted him completely."

"Yes dear, and your mother handled all the money, right."

"Of course, what matter?"

"Well, your mom held daddy in tight purse strings, THEN trusted him dear. Remember, it was her family's money. And didn't they still divorce?"

"Mother's choice," Leslie answered, "Mother always held her own mind. One day she simply became disillusioned with him. I suppose that disease can affect anyone. They both told me it was time."

"Think again. Your dad didn't just bump into a woman fifteen years his junior. Leslie, don't you think it was just a little suspicious how he recovered from the divorce in only two weeks? Wasn't that how long it took you to find him at dinner with the soon-to-be new Mrs. Devereaux? Surely you don't think a man his age is that attractive to a woman only five years older than you?"

"You mean to say Daddy had someone on the side?"

"Yes, woman, yes!"

Leslie paused a moment, embarrassed. She looked down at her plate, then at Kate. "You must think me a fool," she whispered. "I never for a moment thought of that. But I don't think I can believe such a story." Leslie's eyes moistened.

"Or you don't want to. Dear Leslie, it is not of your doing, or your mother's. Your mom was right. It was time for them to separate. Think of it as a natural progression of events." Kate gulped her wine.

"I cannot believe infidelity is a natural progression of events."

"Oh, please, there are hundreds of books, plays, poems and movies about the activities of the rich and famous.
Shakespeare made a good living telling everyone who would listen about the infidelities of the noble class and royalty in just about every country. It's the stuff of which good movies are made."

"Okay, I may be a little naïve, I'll grant you that. But, true love is the most beautiful thing to believe in and men, as well as women, love beauty. Dear friend, I shall continue to believe in the possibility of true love."

"And have you found it? Have you found your true love?"

"Yes. Gerry may be an absent-minded boyfriend, and a little preoccupied at times."

"And more than a little self-centered Leslie," Kate interrupted, a stern look on her face. "He thinks of himself first and you second."

"That just isn't so. He's busy running his investment firm. Dozens count on him for leadership. Sometimes he just forgets, that's all."

"Well dear, what if you found that you were not number one in his life. What if you found that even when he is preoccupied you were not number two? Rather number three or four?"

"What do you mean, Kate?"

"I'm saying, dear Leslie, what if you are no longer the only woman in Gerry's life? What if he has another romantic interest?"

"Besides me? That's impossible, he actively dates me now."

"Not besides you, dear, in addition to you! Could that begin to explain what you call his absent-mindedness? When he forgets to invite you to an event or doesn't explain a hurried business trip he knows you will understand, now doesn't he?"

"And I'll always," Leslie replied, with less than total confidence in her voice. "We're in love. He knows and understands me. I understand him. He knows I require true love, and I know he needs understanding. These are the things of which true love is made."

Kate got up from her chair without saying a word. She went to the kitchen for another pitcher of chilled Sangria. When she returned she bent over Leslie and said: "Bless you, dear friend. I wish all your dreams come true."

* * *

Leslie tried to forget that sunset conversation with Kate. But, two days later the doubts of that evening were still circling through her mind. She had to admit to herself at least, that Gerry's actions sometimes defied explanation as only absent mindedness. Leslie believed true love existed. She wanted to believe. She wanted to believe men would love as completely as she imagined herself loving in return, faithfully and for life. She simply had no explanation for Gerry's behavior.

Leslie sighed a deep breath and slumped into her office chair, and remembered...

* * *

It had been a rainy Tuesday when Leslie found herself caught for a moment in a downpour. She had taken a late lunch and decided to do a little shopping at the opportunity. While standing, dripping in a shop doorway her heart fell to the floor. Across the street she saw Gerry escorting another woman into a restaurant. He held her hand and gently lifted it as he escorted her through the doorway. It most definitely apparent to Leslie this was not a business social. Leslie drew back for a moment into the store. She sank to her knees.

"May I get you a chair or some water Ma'am?" The counter clerk said as he stood over her. "May I get you something?" Leslie's mascara ran down her cheek. Perhaps the clerk thought it was because of the rain, or perhaps he guessed correctly. In any event, he only offered Leslie his hand and directed her toward the rest room. "Perhaps you would like to freshen up, Ma'am," the eighteen year old said. Leslie composed herself and went into the lady's room.

"I'm a mess," Leslie screamed into the mirror. *Just when did I stop being 'Miss' to an eighteen year old male, and became a 'Ma'am'?* She wondered to herself. "I've become a 'Ma'am,'" she said to the mirror, "A 'Ma'am!'"

Then she took stock of herself. *Hair is a mess, mascara must be reapplied, and a general drying is needed.* She opened her Louie Vuitton purse and began to plan.

Gerry Allen has more nerve than is good for him. She loved him. She had trusted him. She had trusted him with her body, love and heart. *Now it seems I'm a foolish child, just as Kate warned. It's embarrassing, even humiliating. How many of my other friends suspect Gerry. Could it be I'm the last to know?* Anger grew inside her bosom.

Leslie studied herself in the mirror as she made up. *My lips are just perceptibly thinner than when I was seventeen. Freckles on my nose are somewhat darker, but that happens to everyone in Boca. Too much tennis and boating.* "I'm not a pound over my collage graduation weight," she whispered as she turned in front of the mirror, "but it seems to have noticeably shifted; Damn and Damn again!"

Twenty strokes with the brush and then ta-duh! She was out the door with a plan. She would confront that worm Gerry with his twenty something whatever. She would catch him red handed: make him melt with embarrassment. She would walk right into that restaurant...

And then the reality surfaced. Leslie realized she had no claim to Gerry. *I am neither wife nor fiancée. I am only one of his girlfriends. A confrontation would only serve to elevate him in the eyes of all those other land sharks in the restaurant. The so-called gentlemen of Boca Raton would silently applaud Gerry for his sexual prowess, to have a woman fighting mad over him. And the young, ah, lady he was with would no doubt judge herself as the victor for having swayed him to her side. No, that would not do. I want his blood to boil with embarrassment.* She crossed the street.

In the restaurant a doubt entered her mind. *What if this was somehow only an innocent meeting. The girl could be a sister of a friend, someone he grew up with, or maybe a relative on vacation.* She decided to find out. Leslie positioned herself at the bar. She could see them at their table. Laughter drifted in the air. Both were obviously enjoying themselves.

"What will you have?" the bartender asked.

"Club soda with a twist of lemon," Leslie answered, the preferred drink of Boca ladies who are not drinking.

"Waiting for someone?" the bartender asked as he tossed a coaster across the redwood bar.

"Please just pour," Leslie responded. And she placed ten dollars from her purse on the bar.

"Let me get that for you," a tall forty or so male said as he reached across the bar and across Leslie's arm to return her bills. "A beautiful lady should be escorted around here," he said, "there are sharks in these waters."

"I bite back," Leslie replied, in an unflattering tone. She moved to the other end of the bar. Mister Wonderful did not follow.

Gerry and his guest chatted gaily, holding each other's hands. With each smile exchanged between them Leslie's heart tore just a little more. *Still, there was no proof,* Leslie thought. She sipped her drink.

Gerry and his guest talked and laughed through lunch. She nudged him in the side when he told a joke. Leslie could tell when he was telling the jokes. He always was the first to laugh. Soon, the lunch was over and Leslie could see through the etched-glass wall that separated the bar from dining area they were preparing to depart. Gerry paid the bill, got his guest's chair and then while saying good-by he pulled her elbow to him and kissed her on the lips.

Leslie's heart sank to the floor. *I've been such a fool,* she thought. She ran from the bar to the street and into her car.

"Oh, how I hate that man," she yelled. "I hate them all."

Her car sped north under the alternating flickering sunlight and deep shadow of late afternoon. Past family estates on the ocean, past private clubs and golf courses with male members standing on greens. *The sharks always seem to get their way. They can tear up any beach or waterway for their precious golf, anywhere. It is all about what they want.*

She began to form a plan. "I'll act as if nothing is wrong," she spoke softly to herself as the car coursed up Ocean Avenue. "He will not suspect a thing. I'll toss him over for another man and he can suffer the pain of humiliation. Then I'll toss away the new man like some old luggage."

When Leslie arrived at the inlet the early evening air was warm and moist. In the East the first stars could be seen. Feeling dirty and weak she ran to the end of the concrete jetty, hoping it would go on forever, and stopped just short of the surf. She crossed her arms across her chest, in a lonely caress. For a long while Leslie simply stood, salt spray wetting her eyes, hiding her tears. She seemed to be waiting for something, some meaning or event to begin her life again. But none came.

Chapter 5 Chivalry

Leslie remembered that lonely drive home. "Nothing is true, nothing, nothing," she had repeated over and over again. Her world had crumbled. Her hopes lost.

Then her dark world turned on its' heals...

* * *

It had been night when Leslie drove the convertible into the underground parking garage of her condo on the beach. The entry gate raised automatically as she approached. Inside the garage it was unusually dark. Leslie noticed half the lights were out and long shadows filled the corners. She parked, got out of the car, and pressed the remote to raise the convertible's roof. Over the sound of the convertible motor she heard a shuffle in the shadows. Suddenly, a dark shape appeared.

"Give me your purse," a dark man shouted at her, grabbed her by the shoulders and pushed her against the car. "Your purse, right now!" He smelled of sweat.

"My shoulders," Leslie shouted in anger. *If I were only strong enough to...*

Leslie tried to wiggle free, but he was strong. He pressed her harder against the car, pulled the purse out of her hand and ran out the gate and into the darkness of the city beyond.

Leslie gasped a breath of air and yelled: "Help, Help!" And fell to the concrete floor.

From outside the garage came the sounds of a scuffle, then a yell.   In a few moments a dim figure passed through the gate, not the robber, but someone else. Even in the shadows Leslie could see he was tall and built like an athlete. *He takes unusually long strides.*

"Miss," he called, "Are you all right?"

"Wh... Who are you?" Leslie called back, her voice breaking with fear. "Who is there?" Leslie's heart pounded in her chest.

"A friend, with something I think belongs to you," the figure answered as it quickly approached. "I believe I have your lost purse." There in front of her was a strikingly handsome man.

"Where did you get it?" Leslie extended her hand to the stranger's.

"I trust you weren't hurt? Any bruises?" Laughing, he explained: "This fellow ran out of the garage and almost straight into me without warning. I'm a man of fashion and could see his dress didn't compliment his purse, or maybe the other way around." A big smile passed across his face. "Anyway I could easily surmise the purse wasn't his." Then he added, "He needed some convincing to give up his newly acquired property and I'm afraid he felt it necessary to take a swing or two at me."

"Oh my, you're injured!" Leslie shouted seeing blood on his wrist.

"Not from him I assure you Miss, but I cut myself rather deeply on the fence. Fortunately for me he was only interested in getting away. But what about you?"

He cares for me. Why? Are there still such heroes in the world? "Never mind me," Leslie answered. "Let's see the cut." Leslie tenderly held the strangers arm. *"Powerful and yet gentle,* she thought. "The wound isn't much, only about three inches long but quite deep. Give me your handkerchief." she gently wrapped his injury. "You will need medical attention for that wound."

"Oh, I won't worry about it until morning. It's nothing, really." He gave her a big grin.

"Don't be foolish," Leslie said softly, "the wound could be infected by then. At least let me cleanse it for you."

"Really, it's nothing."

"Don't try to be so chivalrous or so silly. Come up to my apartment and I will bandage it properly for you. It is the least I can do. From there we can call the police." *Why am I trusting this man? Still, he did save me, or at least, my purse.*

"Well, if you are certain you want to. Though I can understand if you don't want to meet any more strangers this evening."

"Don't be so silly," Leslie answered, "you could've saved my life." And she led him to the elevator.

"Now, I certainly didn't save your life."

Leslie's face became serious. "Perhaps not tonight. But that criminal quite possibly would've returned for what he could call easy pickings if you hadn't so thoroughly ruined his evening."

"Possibly," the stranger agreed with a slight whimsy in his voice. He grinned as he looked away.

Leslie led the stranger into her apartment and to the kitchen. "Now sit here on the stool and I will wash the wound, afterwards we can make a police report."

He sat down, held out his hand and then remarked: "Do I detect a trace of South Carolina, possibly Charleston, in your voice?"

Why is he interested? Leslie wondered.

"Why yes, and where might you be from?"

"Right here. Well not here exactly, a little north, in Palm Beach."

"Born and bred?" Leslie asked as she ran water over the wound. It didn't seem to be as serious in the proper light.

"Exactly," he answered. "I'm Robert Robinard at your service fair damsel in distress," he joked and bowed. "But now it seems I'm the one in need of rescuing. How serious is the cut?"

"You'll live a long life, Mr. Robinard," Leslie smiled. *He doesn't wear a wedding ring.* "But you should certainly get a tetanus shot in the morning." She gently bandaged up the wound with gauze and then fastened it with tape. "There you are my fine knight in shining armor," she joked. "Good morning."

"And who do I have to thank for the gentle medical attention?"

Leslie added a little extra Southern Belle into her voice. "I'm Leslie Devereaux, lately of New York City but always in my heart from Charleston."

"And how can I repay you Miss Devereaux for such a lovely kindness?"

I like the way he called me 'Miss,' but I don't want another man in my life, not right now. Although, he could serve to make Gerry blushing mad and, no-matter, for this Robert is really nothing to me. Still, he is tall, handsome, successful, and sweet.

"There's no need to repay me for a simple human courtesy. After all, I'm indebted to you. You saved me from that monster."

"Still, I must properly thank you for your care of my injury," Robert insisted. "May I call on you?"

Yes so courteous and charming. He could teach Gerry a lesson. "You may repay me with a small kindness if you think its necessary. I'm an analyst with Allen and Associates, do you know it?" *He certainly should. Everyone did.*

"Why, yes I do I'm acquainted with Gerry Allen there. Do you know him?"

"Very much so," Leslie answered in a low and angry voice. *Are you another land shark?* Then she quickly looked at her guest's face to see if her tone of voice had given away any secrets. But he seemed to be unconcerned.

"Then I'll find a way to properly thank you for your kind nursing tomorrow," he promised as he walked toward the entry door. *Okay, he has what he wants...*

Then for a moment their eyes met. Leslie's heart fluttered. Leslie opened the door with a deep breath. "Again, I really am the one who owes you a debt of gratitude."

"Tomorrow then, at one," Robert said grinning over his shoulder. He walked out before Leslie could ask him: what about tomorrow? *He is nice.*

Leslie turned and went into her bedroom not caring about a police report. Somehow she now felt safe and a police report unnecessary.

Chapter 6   Romance

What can I do? Why is he so distant? Doesn't he trust me? Leslie
wondered as she sat at her desk. On the corner of her desk were a dozen long
stem roses, salmon colored. Robert's favorite she remembered a time...

* * *

The next morning, after her rescue, Leslie had reported at 8:00 am to
Allen and Associates, early as usual. Only the receivables secretary was ever
there before her. She entered through the executive elevator and crossed the open
lobby to find a bouquet of three-dozen salmon colored long stem roses reaching
toward the ceiling on the receptionist's desk.

"Oh what's happened here!" Leslie exclaimed, surprised. "Someone has
been either very, very good or very, very naughty."

"Well, it wasn't me, I suppose you don't know who has been naughty?" a
voice asked from behind the bouquet. It was Alice Goodman the receivables
secretary. She was busy pouring water into the rose vase. Alice was a woman in
her mid-fifties who worked long hours to keep her job. Though she was an
attractive woman, she no longer had the physical attraction a younger woman
might rely on to help advance her career. And she was conscious of it. Alice was
educated in Boston and had a successful career as an executive secretary on Wall
Street until her maturity caused her divorce and subsequent move to Boca. She
called her husband 'middle age crazy.' Gerry's company was several steps down
the professional ladder for her but at her age, like so many other transplants to
South Florida she was searching as much for security as a new beginning.
Alice was an excellent tennis player. At five foot seven inches, her sandy brown
hair was always up in the office and always down when relaxing. She was quite
attractive in a white tennis outfit. She had many gentlemen admirers but dated

infrequently, unable to make a commitment. She had once confided in Leslie: "I like playing the field." Alice was a brilliant woman. Leslie had hired her. She was competent in her job and indispensable to the operation of Gerry's company. But, she was insecure in the presence of younger, beautiful women like Leslie. Leslie sensed this and often extended to Alice extra recognition and courtesies. Alice was what Leslie never wanted to become.

"Why Alice Goodman is that you hiding behind that field of roses?" Leslie asked as she passed through her office door. "I can see you are breaking the heart of another beaux."

"Me? You think?" Alice had asked sarcastically, "You have a message waiting," she had replied, "and I wouldn't keep him waiting long dear." Puzzled, Leslie stepped into her office.

Leslie's eyes filled with moisture as she remembered the sight she beheld at that moment.

There were salmon colored rose bouquets everywhere; one her desk, chair, bookshelf, sofa and table. Another five dozen or more were in vases on the floor. She could not enter any further into her office. She could not see her phone or keyboard.

"Gerry," Leslie had said softly as her bottom lip began to stiffen. She felt like crying but was unsure why. *Could it be he knows I saw him and his little chippie at lunch yesterday? Is Gerry trying to make up? He could be feeling very guilty, and he should be.* Her stomach burned with anger.

"It won't be that easy," she murmured to herself. *He has lost it. I won't confess my true feelings to him. Let him think I have forgiven him. I shall twist his heart in a confusion rather than twist his neck.*

"And that's not all," Alice said to Leslie, "turn around." There standing beside the receptionist's desk was a courier with a large envelope.

"Addressed to MISS Leslie Devereaux and marked most urgent," the courier announced. "Are you the MISS in question?" He overemphasized the word 'Miss.'

"I'm Miss Devereaux. Please give it here." Leslie took the envelope from the courier's hand. The envelope was of rice paper, Leslie remembered, and most definitely was of hand made paper. "Gerry is outdoing himself this time," she said to Alice, "but I shouldn't think he understands the depth of his situation."

"Well, open it dear! Let's not be kept in ignorance. Let's see what Mr. Gerry is up to."

If it's for love, Leslie thought, *I wouldn't have a burning in my heart. But this was a only guilt gift and I hate Gerry all the more for trying to confuse my feelings for him. He assumes he can turn my feelings at his will.*

She couldn't get past all the roses to either desk to retrieve a letter opener. So, carefully Leslie had pierced the seal with her right index finger. A small droplet of blood had leaked across the seal from a paper cut. Leslie brought her finger to her lips and said; "Gerry has drawn blood again."

"Oh my, is he in trouble," Alice answered at Leslie's remark. Privately Alice hoped Leslie would give him an agonizing punishment and then drop him. She had never really like Gerry Allen as a man. He was way too presumptuous for her judgment, presumptuous and loud. "What does it say?" Alice asked Leslie.

Leslie opened the envelope and removed the message inside. It read:

My Dear Miss Devereaux,

I wish to thank you for possibly saving my life. This morning my physician removed a bit of rather nasty foreign matter from my wound.   He's told me I could've developed a blood poisoning if you hadn't washed   most of the diseased matter from my wound last night. I shall forever be   in your debt.

I trust you like salmon colored roses. If not, simply inform the messenger of your favorite color and I shall have others delivered   immediately.

Please join me at lunch today. I won't accept no for an answer. My car will call for you at 12:30. I promise you a delightful meal.

Your Humble Servant,

Robert R.

Leslie dismissed the messenger: "Thank You," she said, "everything is acceptable. Please tell my Mr. Robinard."

"Now who's been so very, very nice?" Alice asked.

Leslie had found herself without words for a moment. Confusing emotions ran through her body. The pain in her heart caused by Gerry still burned, but now it had competition from a new feeling. Leslie felt a tingling. Somehow the fire caused by Gerry was growing smaller. It was being replaced by a joy. Robert was a handsome man. She had noticed that. *He took long, confident strides when he walked. He seemed fearless. Hadn't he run after the mugger?* She thought. *And he was so very, very attractive. He had broad shoulders, a chiseled chin with a dimple in the middle, and soft yet sharp eyes.* She remembered how she couldn't help looking deeply into those eyes the evening before.

"Come on girl, tell me about last night," Alice demanded.

"It wasn't anything, really. Well, it's not what you are thinking. It was all quite innocent." It was never easy for Leslie to open up to another person about her romantic experiences; even to a woman she trusted and held in high esteem, like Alice. Leslie was a woman who was modest with her feelings and guarded them. But somehow she felt different about Robert.

"Uh, huh," Alice answered.

 "Well, I happened to meet a man, a gentleman." She paused looking into her feelings for the right words to describe Robert.

"Don't stop now. I must have all the juicy details. He swept you off your feet, didn't he? Come on..."

"It's not exactly like that. I bandaged him after he came to my rescue last evening."

"You bandaged him? He rescued you? Is he tall and handsome?"

"Yes, on all questions, Leslie had replied. "I was mugged in the parking garage and from nowhere Robert appeared. He bravely jostled the attacker to the ground and retrieved my purse. And he is handsome and brave and he is taking me to lunch this afternoon."

"And what about the bandages?"

"Oh, he was cut on the hand during the rescue of my purse. I cleaned and bandaged his wound in my kitchen. I couldn't let him go bleeding after he had so selflessly come to my rescue."

"So you got him into your apartment, or was it he got you?"

"It's not like that, Alice. He was a perfect and sincere gentleman."

She remembered how pleasant it was to feel Robert's arm resting upon her lap as she had bandaged his wound. She remembered his even, steady, and confident breathing. He had never appeared to be excited from his battle with the mugger. He was a man completely in charge of his emotions and it seemed, hers too. For a moment she had imagined the strength of his long arms as he shoved the mugger to the ground, and imagined for a moment those masculine arms around her.

"And you're going to lunch with him?" Alice responded. "What about Gerry? What should I tell him if he asks?"

I am sure Gerry won't starve." Leslie answered with a frown. "He can always find someone to feed him." *Or starve.*

"Oh, oh," Alice had said, "I think I've missed something." Then she pulled in a chair from the lobby and placed it next to the desk. "I'll just be right here dear, waiting for someone to rescue me from all these roses."

"Oh yes. We need to do something about them. I'll call maintenance. We'll share these with everybody.

"What if Gerry asks about the roses?" Alice asked.

"Tell him they were a gift from a secret admirer."

"Yours or mine?" Alice asked. Leslie didn't answer. She only smiled and walked away.

Leslie sat at her desk and remembered better times, times when she was certain of true love...

* * *

Robert's car had called for her exactly at 12:30 on the day of the roses. She left a message for "anyone interested" as she had put it: she would be out for most of the afternoon on personal business. Leslie passed Alice's office on the way out. Alice had waved and winked.

That day she wore her red silk business suit. Early that morning she had felt that was appropriate dress for the day; she was going to have it out with Gerry. But suddenly, in her life there was a knight in shinning armor rescuing her from villains. Now Leslie wished she were wearing her deep cut St. Johns white linen suit and a matching wide hat to keep the sun off her lips. As the limo traveled North on A-1-A toward the Between Ocean and Lagoon resort in Palm Beach, Leslie began to wonder about the man she was lunching with. *He is handsome, gentle, and very brave. No doubt he was wealthy and his left ring finger is uncovered.*

As the sunlight flickered through the ancient trees of family estates lining both sides of the road she tried to imagine what kind of women attracted Robert. *Did he like those women who are flamboyant and in control in any romantic encounter? Or did he like the quiet and sensitive woman who needs to be found by a gentle man?* As she looked out the window she had begun to feel a little uneasy. *What did he expect from this meeting?* She really knew nothing at all about this handsome man. Suddenly her five foot five inch frame felt small in the rear leather seat of the limo.

Leslie looked forward and found Raul, the driver studying her. She could see his eyes shaded under his cap staring at her through the rear view mirror. She sat back and crossed her arms.

"And how are you today?" Leslie asked as she looked directly into the rear view mirror.

"Just fine Miss," he answered with a smile. "Thank you for asking."

"Why did you call me that Raul?" Leslie asked.

"Call you what, Miss?" the Raul responded with a wondering look on his face.

"You called me Miss and not Ma'am," Leslie said, "Why?"

"Because you are not a Ma'am and Mr. Robinard would not date a Mrs., Miss," he answered. Then he touched the brim of his cap in a gesture of respect. Leslie smiled gently in return.

* * *

The limo turned into the Between Ocean and Lagoon drive and passed under the tiled gate. As it drove through the grounds Leslie mused on the landscaped gardens, statuary, and tower, landmarks of southern Palm Beach. The limo stopped at the club. Raul opened the car door. In a moment the doorman greeted her and Leslie was escorted to her table by a young hostess.

"Mr. Robinard will be here momentarily," the young woman told her. "He's in a quick meeting with Mr. Smith." Leslie sat down at a table for two in a little alcove in the corner of the main dining hall. Double French doors looked out into a butterfly garden of wild flowers and roses, salmon roses. The sound of a waterfall played faintly in the distance. A cool fresh breeze brought the scent of the ocean over the dune.

In a few moments, Robert came into view. Her eyes met his as he quickly walked over to their table, smiling broadly. Leslie couldn't help noticing the confidence in his walk, and the powerful sway of his hips.

"How happy I am that you could have lunch with me today, Miss Devereaux," Robert said as he held out his hand. "May I join you?" *How sweet. I have not heard such chivalrous speech from a young man since leaving Charleston.* It was pleasing to her ears and heart.

"Why Mr. Robinard, I didn't know you knew Dave Smith." Smith was someone to know, a power in investments. *The very fact that Robert chose Between Ocean and Lagoon for their luncheon means he holds Dave Smith in high esteem. This could be a business luncheon.* "Mr. Robinard," Leslie added jokingly, "I hope you don't expect this luncheon to be a social event, we have not been properly introduced."

"Why Miss Devereaux I pray last evening would have served as a proper introduction. After all, you probably saved my life with your kindness."

"Oh but it was you who came to my rescue," Leslie answered with a giggle. Leslie remembered how genuinely sincere he was and how safe she had felt in his presence. For an instant she had wished he would always be near. Then she added: "I believe you showed your mettle last evening. I am sure my proper Victorian great-grandmother would approve of you're seeing me."

"I certainly wouldn't want to disappoint her," Robert answered lightly.

"She might have wanted to ask," Leslie said, pretending concern, "what were your intentions Mr. Robinard? Are they social or business?"

"Spoken like an honest Southern lady," Robert replied. "Your great-grandmother would have been pleased. My intentions Miss Devereaux, are to steal you away from Gerry's company."

"So this is a business meeting, then?"

"Yes, most certainly and if I can win your consent, I should like to steal you away from all of Gerry's company, personally as well."

For a moment Leslie was taken aback. "You seem to me extremely well informed, Mr. Robinared," Leslie answered. *And does Robert know about my romantic involvement with Gerry?* It was a little discomforting. She moved in her chair.

"Oh, don't be displeased with me, Miss Devereaux," Robert answered tenderly, and realizing he had made her a little uneasy he extended his hand to hers with an innocent and unplanned gesture of comfort. "I simply inquired about a beautiful and intelligent lady I'd met the previous evening."

Leslie had paused not sure of her response to this handsome man. Certainly she wanted his attention. *But what kind of attention was he offering*, she remembered thinking. *He could be a shark or a friend. Still, he was appealing in either suit, and he would make Gerry furious; two plus points for him. And he was wealthy and chivalrous.* She decided to continue the conversation but was at a loss for words. At that moment the waiter had appeared.

"Good afternoon and welcome to Between Ocean and Lagoon," he said as he handed Robert and Leslie each a menu. "Today we're offering in addition to our menu a crab-cake salad, blackened and served with your choice of rice pilaf or stuffed sweet potato. I can recommend it highly. But first, may I get you something from the bar?"

"What would you recommend, Mr. Robinard?" Leslie asked. *Good not more Gerry for the moment.*

"I'm going to have my usual," Robert replied. Leslie remembered how at that moment she had felt a pang of embarrassment. She always abstained from alcohol until 6 p.m., something else her Victorian great-grandmother had taught her.

"Please, only unsweetened iced-tea for me, with a mint."

"Why my dear Miss Devereaux you don't indulge?" Robert asked, with a slight and approving grin.

"Rarely with lunch," Leslie answered somewhat self-consciously.

"Then let me reveal to you the first of my many secrets. My usual is ginger ale. With a twist it looks as though I were drinking and I don't loose my good senses. Perhaps we are compatible Miss Devereaux?"

"Perhaps," Leslie had replied as she shyly averted her eyes for a moment. Then she added: "We may be compatible, but for what purpose, Mr. Robinard?"

"Why a rewarding, that is to say profitable business relationship, almost a partnership Miss Devereaux," he replied. "And perhaps more if you permit me with time."

Leslie paused and for a moment she blushed. She was sure of it. But Robert pretended not to notice.

"I'm sure you are aware of my relationship with Gerry, Mr. Robinard. What makes you think there could be anything between us? Frankly, I'm a little taken back by your intentions."

With Leslie's remark Robert had become instantly pale. "Oh, please don't mis-understand me. Sometimes I can be rather awkward in matters of the greatest concern to me. I did not mean to suggest anything improper, or, well, ah….."

"Well what did you mean?"

"I meant to say, or offer you a position with my firm, a salaried position. You see, RRR needs an organizer, a manager, an Executive Vice-President. And I need someone who can talk directly to me; that is to say straighten me out when I need it."

"And how do you know I'm right for the position? You and I don't know each other. Really, Mr. Robinard, I think you a bit presumptuous. How could you possibly know I'd be good for your company?" Then she had paused and raised her voice: "I tend to think sir, that you have other motives for your offer. Motives that are not acceptable to me."

Robert did not react in any way Leslie expected. Instead of reddening with embarrassment he began to smile. "Exactly Miss Devereaux!" He said with conviction. "That is exactly the kind of guidance I need in my day-to-day operations. I need someone who'll tell me off when I need it."

"And I suppose that qualifies me, a short temper and a loud mouth. Really, sir, I think your proposition is short-sighted at best and sinister at worst!" She began to stand to leave.

"Please listen for a moment. I must confess, Miss Devereaux," Robert had begged. "I must tell you the truth."

"It's about time, sir." Leslie gently responded and hesitated a moment. "I've been more than patient waiting for the truth."

"I do know of your reputation." Robert confessed. "Gerry has bragged of you on several occasions. Did you know we frequently play handball? And I've inquired into your qualifications. Frankly Miss Devereaux I feel you're more than qualified for the position."

"And why should I leave Gerry's company?"

"Two reasons Miss. First, you cannot advance in your current circumstances. Secondly, I'm prepared to offer you a handsome increase in compensation." With that he removed from his coat pocket a parchment envelope and placed it upon the silk tablecloth. "Let's enjoy a fine lunch together and consider all options."

Just then the waiter had returned and asked if he could take their order. Leslie opened the envelope before ordering. The offer had been for a forty per cent increase over her current salary. Leslie blinked. Robert saw.

They ordered the crab cakes and the conversation danced around the subject of the employment offer. They briefly spoke of their reasons for living in South Florida. Leslie explained she was a transplant looking for a new beginning when she had met Gerry. Robert was old Palm Beach. That means old money. He had the good life with flair here and was not about to trade it for an apartment in Manhattan or San Francisco. Robert was careful to subtly compliment her and Leslie began to feel comfortable in his presence.

Dessert was one of Robert's favorites. "This is from one of my favorite restaurants," he had announced. "Dave was kind enough to include it on his menu. It's from Moose Point in Jackman, in the North Woods. I have a small retreat on the lake."

Leslie loved the treat. It reminded her of Charleston, her home. A delicate French pastry was wrapped around a cheesecake and deep-fried. Served hot with vanilla ice cream and a raspberry sauce, it became Leslie's favorite too. She began to think of the possibilities.

"There's one thing pressing on my mind Miss Devereaux." Robert said at the end of dessert. "If you should choose to join RRR we must be friends and confidants. We must drop this silly Mr. And Miss! How do you feel about that?"

"It sounds appropriate Robert." Leslie answered, smiled and extended her hand for a handshake.

"Wonderful Leslie, dear." Robert answered, and before she could withdraw it, bowed and took her hands. While their hands are still joined he places his other hand gently, warmly on top of both hands. A tingling sensation shot through her arms and made her heart jump. For an extended moment Robert held her hand to be certain his touch found its' way into the depths of her heart, her passions. He smiled as he lifted his eyes to hers.

"Yes, well," shebegan and could not think of what to say.

"Well what?" Robert asked trying to sound innocent.

"Well, yes we should call each other, you know, I mean the, our first names, because of the intimacy, er, I mean the close working proximity," Leslie blushed.

"Working proximity, yes of course," Robert answered. Now he could hardly hold back a smile. This new relationship held promise! "Dessert completes a meal, don't you agree?"

"Well, yes," Leslie answered not knowing what else to say.

"As with all human experiences, the sweetness must be consumed, savored. Don't you agree?" Robert smiled. This time unable to hold back a grin. Everyone in the restaurant noticed. Leslie was certain of it. Even the waiter hid a grin.

In the limo she studied this new man. He was so very, very different from Gerry. In some ways he reminded Leslie of her father. Physically tall, handsome, and viral; he was the model of a gentleman. He was powerful in business and appreciated the arts.

Leslie wanted to ask him so many questions but did not want to appear prying into his personal secrets. *It would be better if he volunteered information when he felt the time was right. I will use this as a barometer of his sincerity.*

He dropped her off at Gerry's company and the rest of the day had flown by. Now she couldn't remember if anyone had asked about her absence or the roses. It did not matter from that day on.

That evening she dreamed of Robert. She wanted his arms around her like the ocean hugs the sand.

Chapter 7 Mysteries

Kalley found Leslie in the office, lost again in her memories. *Robert had been so chivalrous when they had met in the parking garage,* Leslie thought. *That evening he'd been my knight in shinning armor, my cavalry to the rescue. Today he seems to care little for my feelings. Why has he forgotten me? Why doesn't he talk about our future any longer?*

"What is it?" Kalley whispered into Leslie's ear as she bent over her friend. "Leslie, dear, is it bad news?" She offered Leslie a tissue.

"Just a silliness on my part. I'll get over it soon enough." Leslie whispered back. "I've simply been a fool." *Is he trying to be rid of me?*

"You are no fool, girl!" Kalley responded sternly. "What's the matter with you?"

"Robert removed me from the board room. He didn't want me there. He told me to leave, why? I've done nothing wrong." *Accept maybe trust him.*

"Told you to leave? What's that you say?"

"Well, I must truthfully say that he didn't tell me to leave. He gave me a note. Rather mysterious, don't you think?" *And convenient.*

"Mysterious? Suspicious, I'd say." Kalley responded and then in a hushed tone asked: "Just what does he think he's doing, keeping secrets from you, or me?" She looked around the room and realized they were attracting some small amount of attention. "Come over here," Kalley said and pointed to a corner of the room that housed a mahogany trophy cabinet. "Let me see the note."

Leslie carefully removed the note from her right pocket as she followed Kalley to the trophy cabinet. Kalley watched Leslie painfully unfold the note, first one right fold opened then the other.

"Another mysterious love note?"

"Certainly not love," Leslie answered and handed the note to her friend. "But most certainly a mystery."

Kalley read the note in a soft whisper to herself and Leslie:

My Dear:

Please leave the room. Don't say anything. Watch for anything unusual. Your work is done here. I'll explain later.

Robert

Kalley looked confused. She stared for a moment at the parchment. *Certainly it was in Robert's hand. And the material displayed Robert's typical flare for the theatrical,* she thought to herself. *But Robert wasn't one to leave cloudy instructions. He didn't leave anything to chance.* Kalley judged Robert was, himself unsure of the possible outcomes of the situation; whatever that was.

"That man's a mystery," Kalley announced after a long moment. "Something's going on, dear friend."

"Is he tired of me?" Has he found someone else?" Leslie asked, confused.

"Hush girl, don't talk that way," Kalley answered. "He's a man, girl, and men don't know what they're doing most of the time. I think I'll talk to him right when that board meeting is over. He may be my boss but he needs a little education, a little straightening out. Why you saved his company. He couldn't have handled all the maneuverings of a certain-so-and-so without you! I'm gonna have a talk with him!"

"You'll do nothing of the sort, Kalley," Leslie warned, summoning a strong voice from deep within. "Something is wrong. Robert is strong. He needs to understand for himself. Robert will resolve this situation, whatever it is." Then, with a sob in her voice Leslie added: "Kalley, do you really think it could be another woman?" Leslie's heart pounded at the words. A sick feeling invaded her stomach. She was in love and love doesn't always give answers.

Kalley didn't have time to answer for at that moment she noticed Jessup at Leslie's desk. His hand was moving through a few papers, prying where he wasn't welcome.

"Board meeting is over," Kalley said softly and nodded in the direction of Jessup. "It's show time again." They began walking in his direction.

"Honestly, sometimes I could just strangle that man." Leslie muttered to her friend.

"I'll help you with an alibi. Just let me know when." Kalley replied with a wink of her eye. Then in a normal, if somewhat short voice she announced: "Mr. Jessup, is the board meeting over so soon? Can I help you with anything?"

"Oh, ah a match, if you have one, little lady," Jessup replied. "I need a smoke," and he produced a large cigar from his coat pocket.

Little lady, Kalley thought, *I would like to show you a 'little lady' with a hat pin through your private areas. That would 'trim his feathers' as Mother was fond of saying.* Kalley reached into the right pen drawer of her desk and retrieved a box of matches. She struck one and held it close to Jessup's face. "Inhale sir," she said coldly.

Jessup hesitated to light up a cigar in the executive offices. "Couldn't here," he replied sarcastically. "Wouldn't want to aggravate anyone's sensitive nasal passages."

"Just inhale," Leslie answered. "Inhale the smoke of the match." Then she added: "It's raspberry mint," and grinned with amusement at Jessup's surprise.

"Truly raspberry mint," Jessup whispered and then grinned. "May I have the box?" he asked. "This could be a real conversation starter."

"I see no harm in it sir," Leslie responded. "Robert was to make the acquisition announcement today, if time permitted. Be my guest."

"Well, I'll just go outside to the garden for a brief smoke." Jessup announced. "Send for me when you see Bev and Jeffrey, need to have a word with them." And with that he turned and left the room.

"Oh, I'll run with white gloves on master," Kalley announced when he was out of the earshot. "I hope he chokes on it."

"He's beyond rude. The antithesis of gentlemanly demeanor. But, what did he want from my desk?"

"Well maybe an after-dinner mint from your crystal bowl, or maybe matches for his cigar, but I don't believe it. Certainly not private correspondence or personal matters; not a gentleman like him!"

"Who knows why a snake slithers?" Bev Miller's voice came from behind them. "Fresh from the board meeting and I'm certain searching for secrets," she announced, as if answering her own question. "And feeling quite out-of-place, preferring the lower regions of the world to sneak about in."

"Why what secrets could he hope to find on my desk? If he should like to dig through the daily letters, e-mails, courier bags and memos, then let him have at it. I certainly need time away from this confusion."

"You wouldn't understand, dear Leslie," Bev responded tenderly. "One would need to have practiced and perfected their art in the gutters of Wall Street to understand his demeanor."

"Anyway," Kalley interjected, rolling her eyes: "Robert wishes us to watch for any unusual occurrences, and that Jessup is one of the most unusual occurrences I've ever witnessed."

"Robert wants what?" Bev asked, surprised.

"It's something of a secret message," Leslie explained. "He seems to think there's some mischief about but we're to keep it a secret."

"Not from me, ladies," Bev announced. "It's utterly impossible to keep any secret from my net of gossipers and spies. But this is news to my ears," she added. "So Robert thinks something's afoot does he?"

"Afoot?" Kalley asked, with a giggle in her voice: "Now what secret language is this?"

"Holmes, as in Sherlock," Bev answered and then winked and pulled her right ear. "Have to keep a little humor in espionage or you are in danger of taking it all too seriously."

"Quite right, my dear," Jeffrey agreed and raised his right hand in the air as if to throw away a distasteful thought. "I can offer no redeeming moral value to that argument. But on such a fine day wouldn't it be better to speak of value in living? Let's talk of love, romance, food, and golf! Bev, share with these fair damsels the photos of our last escapade."

"An escapade now," Leslie asked with a smile on her lips. "What've you too been doing?"

"Going dear," Bev explained. "We've been to the top of one on those damn pyramids down in Cost Rica. We planned to make mad, passionate love at the summit, but, wouldn't you know some tourists had already tried that before we got there and the authorities were sensitive to that sort of sport on the summit of one of their national treasures. There were signs posted warning of the illegality of smoking, drinking, and generally partying on their pyramids."

"As a poor substitute I drove a ball off the sacrifice table a good 260 yards before it arched to the ground below," Jeffrey bragged. "Best shot ever with a one iron." "And one not too popular with the tour guide, either." Bev added. "It's sufficient to say we won't be going back to that pyramid soon, ladies." She plopped down a pile of pictures from their foray into Costa Rica along with statements from the board meeting onto Leslie's desk. "What a romantic place it was."

A spontaneous party began with all digging through a hundred I-phone photos of Jeffery and Bev in loud straw hats, Bev hugging the tour guide, tourists climbing a stone pyramid, (shots taken from below, not the most flattering angle). And strangely, pictures of Jeffrey with a bear; or more precisely, a bear chasing Jeffrey.

"Jeffrey just had to find his ball in the rough," Bev explained. "The bear had a previous claim to that little piece of real estate."

A voice from behind interjected: "Real estate in Costa Rica, good but Australia holds a greater value if used properly." It was Robert.

"By the way," Leslie whispered to Bev, "Jessup is looking for you."

Bev gave a surprised look and then turned and said to Robert, "Hail our conquering hero, who brings us returns on our investment unequaled in capitalistic history. Robert, dear boy, take your bows."

"I owe it all to my mentors, sponsors and team." Robert modestly responded and took a small bow.

"As well as a burning desire to prove your detractors wrong," Bev answered. "And that you certainly did today."

"I'd like to think I satisfied Mr. Jessup's inquisitive nature." Robert added with a grin of conquest.

"And there are mysteries about the office, Robert," Bev announced. It seems our dear Leslie has been kept in the dark about more than one situation."

Robert face became concerned. A series of creases formed on his forehead, something Leslie saw in him only in the gravest instances. "Anything out of the ordinary?" He gently asked.

"Besides you," Bev offered, "only Jessup. But be quiet, here he comes now." Jessup approached the group with an air of mistrust, a normal mind set for him. "Solving all the problems of the world?" He asked sarcastically.

"We were just discussing our new matches, you know, the raspberry mint ones Mr. Jessup." Leslie answered, and then asked: "Do you think they will be a success?"

"Perhaps with the kiddies," Jessup answered with deep sarcasm and scanned the room.

"We have a sales contract pending under legal review," Robert explained. "It looks as though we won't have to develop a marketing plan. Some rich concerns wish to buy our scents to insure their cigarette brand's success. A short term marketing ploy to increase their international share. For RRR it means a fast and certain profit. Next month I hope to have another happy story to tell."

"Great pictures," Jessup changed the subject. "Jeffrey, a close one with the bear, huh?" Jessup had maneuvered himself over to Leslie's desk and had his hand on the pile of photos Bev had left there. As he spoke his eyes took in all they could in the brief moment of opportunity.

"Please excuse the delay, Mr. Jessup." Leslie addressed him with a sternness in her voice. "That information isn't complete and as such is not quite ready for release. You can be sure you are on the short list for all breaking news."

"Please make certain I'm on all lists," Jessup answered.

"Oh, you most certainly are on all our lists." Leslie added with a slight tone of sarcasm. She glanced about the room. Every face smiled wryly.

"Bev and Jeffrey," Jessup announced. "I have the honor to invite you to a bash this Wednesday afternoon. My New York interests are giving an all out for its' exec's and honored guests, lots of Dom Perignon and Salsa to go around. It'll be by the pool. There's a lingerie show. Everyone is invited. George and Tanny will be there." Jessup put his hands behind his back and smiled a distrustful smile.

"Sounds great, old boy," Jeffrey accepted the invitation and added, "but no talk of business. We like business meetings and we like to party, but we never mix the two."

Jessup looked around to the face of everyone in the group. It seemed he was about to say something, but thought the better of it. Leslie frowned. Kalley muttered: "Harrumph," under her breath. Robert smiled gently.

Bev broke the ice. She deemed it one of her destinies in life to break ice. With a sincere tone she asked Robert, "Jeffrey and I have a personal situation to address to you. We need to expose a mystery, dear boy. Can we sit in your office?" Then, as an afterthought she added, "Would everyone please excuse us? Mr. Jessup, we are looking forward to Wednesday."

With Bev's pronouncement, she, Jeffrey and Robert retired into Robert's private office leaving Kalley and Leslie to deal with Jessup.

"He gave you rather a cold shoulder." Jessup said to Leslie as Robert and the Millers exited. "A beautiful woman should not be ignored or they could find other interests. A gentleman should be entertaining and courteous at all times to a lady."

Kalley said: "Harrumph."

"Southern ladies don't make constant demands upon their men folk, Mr. Jessup," Leslie answered sternly. "We understand they're the weaker sex and after careful consideration, at times take them to our bosom figuratively speaking. Whenever they display a weakness in chivalrous judgment. It is a matter of Southern trust and fidelity."

"Southern trust and fidelity, it sounds like a fine thing to enjoy sometime," Jessup answered and he pressed close to Leslie, hips coming into contact.

Leslie fumed! She raised her voice as she stepped back pushing the palm of her hand into his chest: "I wish you great success in your quest for it, just someplace other than here sir!" She glared.

Jessup was visibly embarrassed and a little insulted. But as if other duties were pressing on his mind, quickly recovered. "I bid you good day then, little ladies," he answered. "We'll see you both Wednesday, right?" he asked, ignoring the social transgressions of the moment. Leslie and Kalley did not respond. Jessup frowned, put his hands in his coat pockets, and left the room.

"An odorous man," Leslie proclaimed in a loud voice, " is a blessing upon exiting. My mother, once the grand dame of societal life in Charleston would always scream that once a bore was out of earshot."

"Amen," Kalley agreed.

Chapter 8 Jason

"Can you believe, last Sunday afternoon I walked naked across the room and my husband didn't even notice?" Laura Sykes was talking to John Templar a fireman and husband of one of the office secretaries.

Jason was taken by surprise. He'd been pierced by a single remark and he was for an instant without words. Standing by his desk he blended well into the office landscape. *A security agent should blend,* he thought and smiled. From ten feet away he was invisible. *Good. John's about 40, in good shape, so maybe she is flirting with him.* But Laura's eye met Jason's for an instant and quickly winked. No, he wasn't invisible, and in some way he was relieved he was not.

Then she again turned to Templar and said: "He was watching the Dallas Cowboys game and never even saw me!"

Templar answered as any good hero type fireman would. He changed the subject. "Well, your husband walked right past me three times today and didn't say hi. So don't worry, he's done it to us all lately. He probably has some business on his mind." He grinned in a friendly and innocent way to save an embarrassing situation and then added: "You two going to the track Saturday?"

Race fans, Jason thought. *He probably thinks Laura's remark is more appropriate at the track and is trying to give Laura a hint.*

Jason analyzed everything. It was part of his job. Laura was open, friendly, about 43, and had a slightly rounded shape. "Not entirely unattractive," Jason muttered.

He'd never consciously thought of her body before. For an instant his mind raced. *She flowed. She never really walked anywhere. She lightly bounced on energetic legs. She had a way of moving all her parts in a warm wave that was flattering.*

Yes, Laura kept herself well, Jason mused. *Her makeup always looked fresh, her light brown hair articulately posed was combed back and bounced one inch off of her shoulders. Her jeans were perhaps a little too tight for a slightly ample woman, but today they shaped her attractively. They told of every gesture of her hips. She wore a loose fitting white knit pullover sweater that attempted to keep secret her round breasts. It was dress-down Friday.* Modesty was attractive to Jason.

He had never noticed before, but Laura had several beauty marks on her neck, under her right ear. *A constellation to follow to your heart,* Jason thought of a possible line. Conquest was a favorite fantasy. He imagined the scent of her perfume, her hair, and shoulders. For a moment he let himself believe she thought of him. She had smiled.

"He never seems to notice anything," Laura continued. "He works late and takes his dinner at the office most evenings. He will talk for hours on the phone to who knows, about money and plans for, I don't know what, and never shares his work with me."

This statement aroused Jason's attention. Harvey Sykes had no reason to be working late. And Jason knew he wasn't. Harvey hadn't been at the office after hours for weeks. Jason knew that first hand. Jason worked late most evenings, compiling information for Robert.

Compiling information, Jason mused to himself, *what a wonderful contrivance of words for hiding espionage.* Jason hid from the world behind veils of secrecy and misinformation. This month he was an accountant. Next month he could be a mechanic or tennis player. Whatever is needed, that's what he was for Robert. But just now he hoped to be a fly on the wall.

"This weekend, then?" John Templar was saying. *The conversation was ending,* Jason thought. *He'd missed some details!* Quick action was necessary to save the opportunity.

"That's a great style," Jason blurted out to Laura as she passed.

For a brief moment her face reddened and she appeared slightly annoyed. But then she saw Jason's face. *He is obviously self-consciously shy,* she thought. *He's trying to flirt but doesn't know how. He is boyish and charming, and very masculine, a great combination.* Laura felt safe.

"Like it, had it done yesterday," Laura answered, tossing her head back. "I didn't know you noticed such things Jason." The words came out of her mouth as if she was speaking to a ten year old. "How about my pullover? That's new too," and she pivoted on one foot.

Jason choked at the sway of her ample breasts. "Oh, ah, that's fine too," he muttered and grinned slightly. He needed to keep in conversation with her to learn more about Harvey's after hour activities but he wasn't sure he could pull it off with Laura smiling directly into his eyes. "Harvey isn't in," he blurted out. Jason pretended to innocently assume she was looking for her husband.

"Not in?" Laura asked surprised, casting a slight gloom over her expression. "Where is he? I thought I would surprise him and take him to lunch." She looked dejected.

"Sorry, don't know," Jason answered, but oh, how he would like to have known. "I haven't seen him for an hour." Jason was torn between his need to learn more information and a sudden desire to blurt out to Laura, *you've been a fool. You are so much better than him. Talk to me. We don't need him. I'll take care of you.* The emotional words seemed to ring in his ears and for a moment he looked around the room imagining someone may have heard his thoughts; they were so very powerful. Laura was staring at him. *Could she have read my mind?*

"Oh," she answered, and then to cover up her feelings said: "I've come by to pick up a phone number from him and if he wasn't too busy I'd take him to lunch."

Jason thought to himself: *the best way to get a phone number would be to call Harvey. A person could arrange a lunch date at the same time. Laura has another agenda. Stop this!* Jason shouted to himself. *Stop analyzing everything.* "Let's check his desk for the number," Jason said and led her toward Harvey's office. He entered the security code at the touch pad and the door unlocked.

He held the door for her and as she passed, his nostrils filled with the faint scent of Chanel. She asked: "Do you know all security codes?"

As a matter of fact, he did. But she was not supposed to know that. Jason had slipped. Quickly he recovered. "Codes were changed this morning, while Harvey was out," he told Laura. "The security guy gave me the new code you know, to give to Harvey."

Laura replied: "Oh." But she wasn't buying it. Laura surveyed the room as she walked to the large mahogany desk. She tossed her purse onto the desk for a moment. A gesture emphasizing the taking of full possession of the desk and its' contents. Two computer screens were on. One was displaying a spreadsheet. To that Laura said: "More boring accounting stuff." Then thinking Jason was an accountant she added: "Oh, I mean, I or, well."

Embarrassed, she turned her attention to the other computer screen. It was open to an e-mail account. "Who is Jessup?" she asked. There on the screen was a scrolled record of twenty or more e-mails to Jessup. "What is she, some exotic dancer?" Jason froze for an instant. *Worse,* he said to himself. *Harvey had no reason to be talking to Jessup.* But, right now he needed to be invisible.

"No dancer I know of," he answered Laura. "Here, check his phone log," and he pushed it across the desk and into her hand. Her hand was soft and warm.

"Well, don't pry." She thumbed through the L's to the P's and then pushed it away. "Thanks so very much," she smiled, "you're a lifesaver." Then, without looking at him she picked up her purse and began towards the door.

Jason thought he saw moisture in her eye. *She hadn't written down any information. It had all taken less than one minute.* He asked: "Anything else I can do for a damsel in distress?"

"The door, would you be so kind to release the security thing, whatever you call it, so I can leave?" Laura's voice stammered a little.

"I'm sorry, it opens automatically, the lock that is, from the inside," he answered and opened the door for her. Again the faint scent of Chanel penetrated his nostrils. He noticed several more small beauty marks as she passed and committed them to memory.

"Should I give Harvey a message when he returns?"

"Oh, tell him I was here naked on his desk waiting for him," Laura answered. She turned and headed down the hall.

Jason wanted to follow her, take her for coffee, maybe console her, smell her perfume again, but he held his foot on the office door. "Yes I will if that is what you want," he called as she left. He watched her heals as she disappeared down the hall. There was no spring in her step. He wanted to rescue her from Harvey and Jessup. He wanted her.

In a minute, Jason was back in Sykes's office. The phone log was open to Party Rentals, Veronica worldwide service, an 800 number was offered and the name Albert Jessup. Jason did not hesitate. He wrote down the number and then with a few taps on the computer keyboard sent a copy of the e-mail records to his computer and left the room as he had found it.

In a moment Jason was back at his desk, pretending to mull over some financial reports from a subsidiary when Kalley found him. She burst into his cubicle and announced: "Robert says it's Jessup, come quickly." And they were gone.

Kalley and Jason rushed into Robert's executive office. Kalley shouted as they passed through the door, a little out-of-breath: "As quick as I could get him, here he is." *What the hell did Robert want with an accountant at a time like this?* she wondered. She held her tongue and glanced at Leslie.

Leslie was standing at Robert's desk carefully arranging small stacks of papers. Unable to offer an explanation, Leslie simply raised an eyebrow and nodded in Robert's direction.

"And it definitely isn't here. The cretin must have pocketed the gift." Leslie said. "He was at my desk a moment ago. His hands were very busy moving over correspondence lying there when Kalley and I found him."

Kalley huffed. "Jessup claimed he was looking for a match to light one of those odorous leaf logs he inhales. Today, for some reason, Mr. Jessup displayed some consideration for those around him and smoked his ugly stick out in the garden."

"Pity the flowers," Leslie added.

Robert shot Jason a glance and in a suspiciously calm voice proceeded to explain. "It seems that our Mr. Jessup has pocketed a small piece of trivia belonging to Bev, a Chinese box. Now he's nowhere to be found. We may have found our mystery man. What do you make of it?"

"Confirmed, Mr. Robinard," Jason answered. "But it's two mystery men," as he glanced about the room. "It seems our Harvey Sykes is a confidant of Mr. Jessup. I only now found his e-mail account. Jessup and Styles have spoken twenty or more times in the last week. Here, I'll show you." Astonished eyes were on Jason as he moved into Robert's seat at his desk and proceeded to bring up the e-mail account he had recently copied to his computer. "I'm afraid I have to inform you we've a traitor in our midst, Robert," Jason said as he pointed to the screen. "There can be no other explanation. Styles simply has no legitimate business with Jessup"

The Millers were seated on Robert's leather couch, patiently waiting an explanation. "Two mysteries, two mysteries" Bev repeated.

"One mystery, two perpetrators, Mrs. Miller." Jason answered with authority.

"Young man, I mean you," Bev responded and demanded in a stern voice: "Just who are you?"

"Please excuse my oversight Bev." Robert explained. "In the excitement of the minute, I've overlooked introductions. Jeffrey, Bev, may I introduce Mr. Jason Palmer, my personal, er, a, investigator. Jason has my total confidence and trust." I mean to say I believe Mr. Palmer to be capable as well as trustworthy.

"Now please everyone, give me a few minutes to explain. I haven't kept anyone out of the loop, so to speak. All of you have been most assuredly been in the loop if unknowingly, until the most advantageous moment. Jason and I needed your innocent reactions to recent events concerning our Mr. Jessup. You were totally convincing. You performed your parts admirably, each and every one of you." Robert moved to the polished brass bar in the corner of his office. "Let's all enjoy some chilled mineral water while Jason and I reveal the plot to all." Robert poured water from a chilled carafe into six crystal water glasses.

"Jason has helped us, unseen, on many occasions, though until today it's been impossible for you to meet. We usually have him in some distant city arranging items for us," He added. "We rarely see him. So it is no surprise you are not familiar..."

"I recently returned from Australia, in search of wool." Jason added.

"What about Chinese wool?" Bev demanded. "Have you brought us some other gifts, from China? Or is there another mystery man in our employ?"

"None from China," Robert assured her. "Though fine parchment from a Taiwanese mail order catalogue can be arranged by Jason. It's a ploy to confuse our Mr. Jessup. We hope he'll chase the boxes of wool while we uncover his motive."

"Please excuse our ruse," Jason smiled gently. "We needed to catch a thief in the act or rather in the play and with your help we have. The packages were only bait. As it happened, they were the best bait, irresistible to Jessup. He was forced to expose his hand, to make his move."

Grinning, Robert added, "Right now, he's attempting in vain to intercept our first shipment from Hong Kong. The authorities will be waiting to capture the thieves in the act. I hear the food in the Hong Kong jails is rather unsatisfactory; neither Sichuan nor Cantonese and must be eaten with the hands. A rather pleasant thought don't you think, our Mr. Jessup crouching on the floor eating roasted rat with his bare hands!"

"But what shipment, Robert dear?" Bev asked.

"Nothing really." Robert smiled. "It's a ruse, a con, to tip his hand. Nothing can be lost. Empty boxes. Jessup has nothing to gain and everything to loose."

Jeffrey stood up and shouted "Hooray, a fine play for you my boy! And when can I get at him? He needs a good thrashing with a nine iron. I use it as a wedge, you know. It could give a good back spin to his head." He stood and demonstrated a perfect shot with an imaginary nine iron. "A clean 60 yards and a solid drop. What do you think Robert lad, can we get him within range of my nine iron?" A burst of laughter circled the room.

As everyone entertained each other by offering other tortures for consideration, Robert moved to Leslie's side. "My dear," he whispered as he gently placed his left arm around her slender waist, "can you ever forgive me for keeping secrets, if for even the best of reasons?"

In the moment Leslie's head swirled with a confusion of questions. She wanted to shout out to him, corner him, shake him and perhaps hurt him just a little. But his arm belonged around her. She slid two fingers behind the top button of his coat and gently tugged him. Their lips met. She looked into his eyes and she wanted to believe. She wanted to run away with him at that moment to a deserted beach or a penthouse. She didn't want to think. She wanted only to feel his body intwined with hers. To take his lips to hers. To take his body to hers.

"I can forgive you of a small blunder for the sake of love," Leslie answered. "But, dearest Robert, be kind when you lie, for whatever a noble reason. In your arms, my heart is fragile. Please, dear, don't keep me wondering." She stared directly into his eyes, awaiting a greater explanation. Her eyes asked what she would not dare to speak. *Why have you cooled? Is my heart a plaything to you? Do you feel only a trivial love, attraction for me? My heart tells me it is more, so much more. But why?*

In the long moment Robert's eyes were lost in Leslie's. There was moistness in his eyes. She felt the same in hers. A slight tremble passed between them.

"Leslie, I'd never deceive you, even for the most noble of reasons. As for Jessup, it's enough to say that I had security considerations. We had to make it perfectly clear to that snake you had nothing more to do with the illusion than that of the part of an innocent victim as well. He'll have no further recourse with you."

And what about you? Where do you go, why? Leslie wanted to ask. *What is so important?*

"And have his head on a stick," Bev announced. Leslie and Robert returned abruptly to the moment. They stood apart. They had a spy to catch and expose to the investors.

"Afraid that placing heads on sticks is, unfortunately, illegal now dearest." Jeffrey answered, grinning. "We may have to settle for a long jail visit for our Mr. Jessup. Harvey Sykes too."

"It appears we may add embezzlement to the list of offenses." Jason informed all. "I have been tracking a shrinking cash on hand balance for a month."

"It was the reason for calling Jason in from the field," Robert added. "Jason can uncover the most cleverly concealed material."

"And what magical powers do you employ in your duties Mr. Palmer?" Leslie asked. "Are you another secret agent, or simply another fly on the wall?"

Leslie couldn't know how her sharp remark cut him to the quick. This situation would cause beautiful Laura misery and hardship. *Laura deserves better*, he thought. For an instant he could smell Chanel again.

"Flies see and hear more than secret agents," Jason answered. "Though they do run the risk of the fly swatter," he added with a grin. "As for me I prefer the risks of the fly to that of the secret agent. Besides, I never have to shoot anyone, only listen and look." But today he did not feel victorious. He knew he might injure Laura.

"Then you are a knowledgeable person in espionage, Mr. Palmer?" Bev asked.

"More than I sometimes wish. There are always innocents who suffer. The cost of containing evil and maintaining commitment is always very high."

Leslie turned to Jason. His voice seemed familiar, if not his demeanor. She wanted to know. "Commitment?" Leslie asked.

"Good business is a commitment, Miss Leslie," Jason answered. Then he paused a moment. *Should I have addressed her as 'Miss' Leslie?* "I help to make certain RRR can keep its commitments to its stockholders as well as its customers."

Leslie's stomach tightened with Jason's word 'Miss.' "Spoken as a gentleman," She answered. "It's refreshing to meet a gentleman. Where are you from?" To Leslie he seemed all too unusual to be believed.

"Cincinnati, Miss." *I used that word again!* He wished he could disentangle himself from the conversation. *Surely Leslie had noticed*, he thought. He had learned of Leslie's dislike of the word "Ma'am" and since she was from the Deep South had found it rather amusing at the time. But this wasn't amusing. *She was digging and she mustn't dig, not yet anyway*, he thought. "After completing my Masters in Business Administration in Chicago I headed for somewhere it never snowed." Then Jason turned to Robert and added: "Robert, I think we should waste no time in informing our New York investors of the situation, as per plan."

"Yes, lets," Bev announced. "What devilish part do you want us to play?"

"Please keep your commitment to Jessup's cocktail party next week," Jason requested. "Let's see what other twist Mr. Jessup has planned. Besides, we don't want to give him any reason to suspect we're on to him. I'll handle Sykes myself."

"Then we're to be spies, wonderful!" Jeffrey added with a bright smile on his face. "I'll make the supreme sacrifice for our RRR and eat with and listen to that lump of vanity, Jessup, for an entire afternoon."

"And still in the season, too!" Bev added. "Robert, you owe us for this favor. I'll be giving up a fine afternoon with friends for that snake."

"A snake that wants to rob us and doesn't even have a gun," Kalley muttered. "At least an armed robber is honest, after a fashion, about his crime."

"Then we'll be deceptive in our defense," Robert answered with a slight smile on his face.

His expression changed to one of great concern: "Thank you all in advance for what I'm sure will be a tedious chore at best. Jason and I are going to be busy in the next few days. RRR will be on autopilot, so to speak. I'll need everyone to keep close attention to the facts as they develop. We'll need to act quickly and aggressively when required."

"We must get started immediately," Leslie interjected. "First order of business; change all bank codes. Sykes must be disconnected from our accounts. I'll inform the bankers of changes in access codes. They need to know they're to be 'out of the office' if Sykes should call. We'll keep him ignorant of developments. We will lead him to believe there's a computer glitch until he is arrested."

"Good, then we are off, Robert." Bev announced. "If you need your secret agents, phone us.

"And we'll come nine iron in hand," Jeffery added. With a wave Jeffery and Bev walked out the door.

Bev and Jeffrey's departure was the cue Robert had waited for to begin preparations. "Everyone," Robert began, as he gathered all around him with a sweeping gesture of his right arm, "we need to keep Bev and Jeffrey as far removed as is possible. I'm certain they are critical elements in Jessup's plans."

"He wants their money," Kalley interjected, "a common thief. He thinks of himself as invincible, could try anything."

"That's why our first concern is to insulate them from risk." Robert added. "I want the Millers to attend that party. They won't be suspect if they fain interest in his plans. Their attendance is critical. I'm afraid he is capable of ugly deeds if he thinks his scheme is being compromised. Caution everyone."

A moment passed in silence. All realized for the first time Jessup was dangerous. Leslie spoke first in a stern voice: "Then it's understood by all that the Millers are to be insulated from whatever comes next. Let us all agree that if we find them involved, then the plot has entered a new and dangerous arena. Prompt action will be required."

Robert began: "The goal now is to button up RRR. For the next few days we delay business decisions and tightly control the flow of information. But we must make certain to outwardly appear ignorant of the plot. Everything must appear to be business as usual.

"Kalley," Leslie took command, "we need to stay current with all correspondence. We also must create a filing and storage system for all communications, one that's easily accessed and yet totally secure. I need you to work around-the-clock, so to speak. I'm afraid your social life will have to be on hold for a while. We'll work out of the boardroom. I can use the private entrance through this office to come and go and use boxes for storage. That way it'll be easy to maintain our security. I can use cell phones for communication."

"Jessup will be watching Miss Leslie closely," Jason added. "He considers her a critical chess piece in RRR and for some reason believes she can be compromised."

"What do you mean, 'compromised?" Robert asked.

"Not sure, really," Jason answered. "But he seems to believe she can be convinced to sympathize with his cause. He would not risk flirtations at this time if they had any other purpose."

"Flirtations?" Robert turned to Leslie and asked.

"He wanted to show me a good time." Leslie responded. "I thought at the time it was out of place, even for him. The curious question now before us is why? Why would he think he could influence me? Even he must know we are cut from different cloth."

"Leslie, you and Kalley need to tie down everything in the office today, and then be hard to find. Jason and I'll be moving around a lot. Contact us through e-mail or cell phone, only." Then after a pause of reflection added: "Let me apologize in advance for not being around when you may need me in the next few days. I'm partying with Tanny Knight in the Bahamas."

With that command from Robert, all went quickly to their responsibilities. Leslie had little time to wonder about any other matters. It wasn't until late in the afternoon before she considered again the mystery Bev had said she could clear up, with a few words from Robert.

Chapter 10   Cinnamon

Leslie and Kalley spent the afternoon transforming the boardroom. It wasn't until late in the day that they had time to sit down together at the huge boardroom table and began looking over correspondence of the day.

"We can certainly hide behind all these boxes if we need to," Kalley said to Leslie as she plopped down the last carton of files. "That makes everything. Oh! Don't ask me to tote another one of those things." She grabbed her back.

"I need a bath." Leslie offered. "One with bubbles up to my ears. I'm going straight home and into the tub. No dinner and no man. Simply me and a carton of ice cream. I'll soak until I can't remember Jessup, Sykes, or whoever." She plumped down into a carved mahogany chair, put her hand on a pile of messages and groaned: "Tomorrow will be soon enough to take care of the rest of these."

"What we need is a little 'us' time," Kalley answered and she set two champagne glasses on the table. "How about a glass of Dom Perignon? Honey, we are going to need our strength tomorrow!"

"Why not? Our heads have been spinning all day. They might as well spin some more. This time with the pleasant amnesia that is brought on by alcohol. Just look at the mess waiting for us tomorrow!" Under her hand there were more than forty phone messages awaiting a return call.

Leslie kicked off her shoes and threw her feet up onto the boardroom table. "Pour," she commanded Kalley in a voice that imitated Jessup's. "Why how fortunate you are, my little lady. I'll allow you to serve my every wish. Ah, here I have this tourist map of Palm Beach. I can show you the sights. Of course, no club would allow ME inside, but I can point them out from the car."

"Why you ah too kind t' me, Masta," Kalley answered in a Butterfly McQueen voice. "I allas wants t' know what dose bright lights is." Then she added in her natural voice: "I could just stick him in the neck with a letter opener."

"Careful dearest friend. I hear that is now illegal, pity. A toast to all those men who think they can lie and deceive without recourse simply because they have an appendage hanging between their legs."

"A toast to the other sex," Kalley added. "At times they can be useful, even wonderful. But at other times well, 'mysterious' is the kindest adjective I can pin on them."

"With a rusty pin, dear, don't forget. Let's not forget to add as much misery as is possible to those villains."

"Well then we must be sure to 'pin' them in the most painful spot on their bodies." Both women giggled a loud and evil giggle.

"Pin to that of their anatomy they hold in highest acclaim, I hope you mean," Both giggled again. "Some more grape juice, dear friend," Leslie held her glass high.

Kalley poured champaign again. "They just think they can make believe, and never get caught. Lying all the time, never doing nice for you. They think they do you some kind of a favor if they call before they come over. Then if they get to stay for dinner, well, its' just because they are sooo desirable!"

"Whom are we talking about now, dear?" Leslie asked. "I'm sure it's not Jessup."

"Stewart, that lump on my sofa last night," Kalley answered. "He comes by, uninvited, and plops his behind down on my couch for the game. Never asks mind you, just barges on in and grabs the remote."

"Did you invite him? Does he have a key?"

"Girl, no man is going to barge into my apartment unless, I want him there," Kalley answered. "But that's beside the point. He gives me a peck on the cheek and expects to be fed."

"Did you?"

"Did I what?"

"Feed him, dear. If you feed them, you know, they'll never go away. Oh, they may go missing for a while, but, they'll always return to a doorway with easy pickings."

"Well, spaghetti and meatballs, some wine, and…you know," Kalley answered coyly. "Stewart smells like cinnamon after he has worked out, a cinnamon covered muscle."

"And you like cinnamon?"

"I love cinnamon. I love it on toast, on ham, and on my bed." Kalley grinned.

"And afterwards, the game, right?" Leslie asked confidently.

Kalley sighed. "Well, yes."

"That dog will always return, Kalley," Leslie stated. "He treats you like a doormat, because you act like one. How long have you been seeing him? Tell me the truth now, no fibbing. Has he even once spoken of the future? What are his plans? And how do they include you, my dear friend? I fear you are a rather convenient doormat for your Mr. Cinnamon."

"It's not exactly like that, Leslie," Kalley responded. "We are in love. He can't live without me, he says."

"Then where is he going to be tonight, dearest friend?"

"Maybe with me. Look now, it's not like he doesn't want to be. But, well, life can get complicated. He has things that need doing."

"I've heard all this before, girl. They are too busy many nights in a row. But the dogs are always somewhere, right?"

"He rooms with an old friend from college, Les," Kalley answered. "You know how hard it is getting started right out of college. John is ok, but he is a slob. I've been over there. We rather go to my place, for privacy."

"And where did you say he was going to be tonight?" Leslie asked again.

"Ok, he has a baseball game. Then he'll be going out to dinner with the boys. Every time it's the same. I won't see him, but he'll call at bedtime. He sure knows what to say to a girl. He'll sing me a lullaby over the phone."

"From where?"

"From his heart." Her voice was beginning to rise in pitch.

"Where Kalley?" Leslie sternly questioned. "Where are his toes, when he calls? Could they be perched on some other girl's couch?"

"His place, of course," Kalley said. Then she answered cautiously, "I guess."

"My point exactly dear friend. We never do know for certain where their hearts are, or toes are, do we?"

Then together they spontaneously grinned and yelled: "But he smells like cinnamon!" They roared with laughter.

Dusk was approaching as the two friends finished the last of the champagne. "There's only enough left for one more toast," Kalley announced, as she jumped up from her chair.

"Then let's make one to our big boys, of whom we want to believe anything they say," Leslie asked. "Gorgeous and childish and spoiled at times, but lovable all the same."

"Robert, childish?" Kalley asked. "Robert's a man." *Considerate, forceful when necessary, able to make important decisions certain of himself. And, of course, handsomely attractive. A hunk*, Kalley thought.

Leslie corrected: "He has his secrets. He can be selfish, and he can be forgetful. He can forget about me." Leslie sighed a gentle tear.

Kalley poured the last of the champagne into the crystal glasses and sat down. "Girl are we talking about the same man?" Kalley asked, tossing her head to one side as she often did when perplexed. "Our, er, your Robert, the modern American Renaissance man. The one with the looks, brains and money? That Robert?"

"The one that's not here, now," Leslie answered. "The Robert that is partying with Tanny in the Bahamas, of all places."

"The Robert that showers you with gifts?"

"The one that forgot to ask if I wished to accompany him," Leslie pouted. "He simply assumed I'd be happy to stand behind him, forgetting my heart has desires."

Kalley lifted Leslie's chin to speak directly into her eyes: "The Robert that is under attack girl? We have wolves at the door, or have you forgotten?"

"The one who found it absolutely necessary to fly off to an island resort filled with women in bikinis, just when we need him most, because of wolves," Leslie explained. "Haven't you ever noticed, dear friend, how he is able to leave, disappear, at all the most convenient times for him, and, of course, the most inappropriate times for the rest of us?"

"Don't you think he has a good reason to go? We have to look normal, you know, unconcerned. That bastard Jessup must not suspect anything. That's what Robert is thinking about." Kalley slumped down into her seat. "I'm sure of it," she announced loudly. She crossed her arms and stared at the wall.

"Think about it, girl. We could be catching an early dinner at the Forbidden," Leslie suggested, wiggling her foot in the air above the boardroom table. "Then a dance or two. Everyone would see us. Conversations overheard in public could convince anyone watching and listening that all was well and quiet at RRR." Leslie stared at her ankle, as if looking for some slight imperfection.

"But Tanny expects him in Bimini for the race. He's a large stockholder, he's important."

"I've a bikini. I can be packed in a half hour. Damn! I can jump on a plane. Bahamas have stores and I have a credit card. I don't need to pack. We've done that before." Leslie paused and averted her eyes. "Why not now?"

Kalley was frozen in thought. *Could Robert be using Leslie? Lying? Cheating on her? All Leslie said was true. Robert hadn't even considered her feelings. He'd simply assumed. Oh, he had voiced concern and reasons for his actions. He had apologized for any inconvenience the situation would cause. He'd been very diplomatic, but in an appropriate way.* Kalley did not like what she was thinking. "We're over reacting. I'm sure of it Les," Kalley told her friend. "It's the champagne talking."

"Inebriation? I truly hope so dear friend. But I wasn't inebriated when he disappeared for four days. And the 'little mystery' Bev said could be easily cleared up, with a conversation. Well, the conversation requires Master Robert's presence and participation. Neither of which is readily forthcoming!"

"Wait a minute, girl. What's this about a 'little mystery' with our Robert?" Leslie hesitated. She began to get up, out of the chair. Then gripped the carved arm. "Never mind. I don't own him. He can disappear for four days on the boat." She paused, pushed her face into the tapestry upholstered back of the chair and began to sob, uncontrollably. "It's all just so mysteriously horrible," she sobbed. "He says things and then he doesn't say things. And I don't say things. He should tell me. I should ask!"

Kalley dug into her purse for tissues. "Here, blow," she commanded in a soft but firm voice as she held the tissue under Leslie's nose.

"No, no, I'll be alright. A minute or two, that's all I need." She pulled away from Kalley's hand and then began to cry again. "Oh what terrible thing have I done?"

"We don't do anything that is terrible, Les." Men are just from a different planet. That's all. And we try to visit them on that planet of theirs. Trouble is, their planet is a mess."

Leslie regained part of her composure with her friend's attempts at a joke. But she was not in the mood for humor. "Another tissue, please," she asked and then added: "I appreciate your attempt at humor, but nothing is funny today." She was pale.

"It ain't no joke!" Kalley exclaimed. Then in a more somber, if considerably humorous voice added: "My mom warned me not to follow men to their planet. It is a terrible place. Sure, it looks pretty, lots of nice shapes and peaks, fertile valleys, strong, high hills. But you can't get around in it 'cause the land is really made of butterscotch pudding."

"Pudding?" Leslie asked, beginning to smile.

"Yes, that's right. Mommy taught me that nothing is really THAT good. The land of men can look stable, but you will sink into it and be lost. Can't walk in it, it's too deep. And it's too thick with sweetness to swim. If a girl goes there she's going to drown, sooner or later, in a man's sweetness. Girl, you must make them come to you!"

"Come to us?"

"Come to our terms, to our planet. We make them want us. They have to want us more than their toys, more than their friends."

"More than a baseball game?"

"More than a boat race, too." Kalley answered nodding her head.

"That's all well and fine, dear friend, but right now my planet is a very lonely place."

"Mine too. But we can't do anything for them, or TO them, if we drown." Kalley grinned and raised her eyebrows looking for approval.

Leslie stared for a moment in disbelief. She had been taught to wait for the right gentleman like a true Southern belle. The idea of reconstructing a man, manipulating him into her world, was somewhat frightening. "I dare say my mother would be shocked at such a proposal. What of my reputation, if this plan were known?"

"It's not manipulating, Les. Think of it more as setting a broken bone, or curing a terrible rash. Perhaps even returning sight to a poor, accursed man. They all need our glasses." Lesley was at a loss for words. She had never considered it her responsibility to change a man.

"Gentlemen are responsible for their actions," she told Kalley. "Don't you think we should look for the right man?

"The right man! Remember girl, all men were boys once. Remember fourth grade? They stole our lunch. How about middle school? A shove was supposed to make us notice they were masculine. Would you leave all those boys to their own devices to develop into men? A little manipulation's necessary in medicine and in matters of love."

The argument seemed to have merit to Leslie. She pondered a moment and then asked: "What would you recommend my next action be?"

"Get that Robert back here. It is time to begin molding him. We can't get results on his planet. We need him here, on ours."

"The company is under threat," Leslie reminded Kalley.

"That's all on his planet."

"He cannot, there are responsibilities to be met."

"He has a responsibility to you, to your heart, dear Les."

"He may not understand. He could become hurt and angry."

"He better understand that YOU are hurt, and angry," Kalley explained. "He had better get himself to your planet right now, before it is too late."

"Too late?" Leslie asked, becoming more frightened of loosing Robert.

"That's for him to think, Les. We both know Robert is the one for you. That you would do anything for him, right?"

"Certainly, I would die for him, if necessary."

"But, it's best for him if he doesn't know that, not just yet. Let's let him wish it was so, but fear it may not be!"

"I don't want to harm him."

"We're not going to harm him, we're going to give him glasses." Kalley answered. She looked at Leslie, studying her for some reaction, meaning, understanding.

After a moment, Leslie spoke: "We could start here, in this mess of correspondence," she said in a sarcastic voice, pointing to the pile of messages on the table with her toe. "I fear I could damage my fragile self on such a mound of duties. Perhaps we delicate ladies can find one or two requirements in this pile that are beyond our delicate powers to dispatch."

"And one or two require the immediate return of Mr. Robinard." Kalley agreed, kicking papers with her big toe.

"Here's half a pile for you and a half for me. Give no quarter."

"Give what?" Kalley asked.

"Show no mercy, give no quarter, you know, like a pirate."

"Oooh, that's evil," Kalley cooed.

"You and I are going to heal him. We are to save him from himself and get him on my planet. I shall begin." Leslie picked up a message with her toes from her pile. "Read for us dear friend," she instructed Kalley.

Chapter 11 Plans

"Marked most urgent," Kalley said and began to read. "Delayed meet next Tuesday, out on the reef, sailfish are hitting, signed Haley. Well, nothing that can't wait." Then she grinned with eyebrows raised and added: "How do you say, good citizens of Rome?"

Leslie spun in her chair in a vain attempt to thrust her toes downward. "Nay a thousand times nay I say," she shouted. But her joke failed as she fell off her chair and with a flat sound landed on the money-green carpet on her derrière. Her glass followed. "Ooh mufft. Nay I say. Off with his head," she yelled.

Kalley jumped forward and caught the glass before it crashed to the floor. "A what?" she laughingly asked. "What's a muft?"

"The sound of my feminine gentility delicately striking bottom or, er, rather my bottom striking something totally uncompromising and uncooperative....and hard!" Leslie exclaimed as she struggled to her feet and brushed herself off. She held both hands to her mouth and squeaked a sound of embarrassment. "Eek, if my cotillion instructor could see me now. I'm certain I would never come out." Then she added brushing her nose: "but it's such fun." The friends roared with laughter.

"So? What say you, Romans? Kalley asked. "Do we save them for another day?"

"To the lions, pray they do not get indigestion eating all that flesh," Leslie answered grinning. "Ok it's my turn. A McCord wants Robert to know that quarterlies are being sent by the end of the day tomorrow. He wants to make the point obvious that it is five days early. And he asks: how is the fishing? Bravo Mr. McCord. Citizens of Rome, how do you say?"

Both friends shouted: "Nay," and turned thumbs down.

Leslie continued: "Well McCord, your Emperor is indeed grateful for your sacrifices, both getting out the quarterly early as well as sacrificing yourself for the entertainment of the crowd. Too bad Master Robert will not soon learn of it." Leslie then wadded up the note into a ball and threw it across the room in the general direction of a wastebasket. "By the way McCord, have you heard the sailfish are hitting?" She added.

"Seems we're always answering Robert's personal correspondence. Les, do you ever wonder who or what the Haleys and for that matter what a McCord is? I mean man or woman?"

Leslie paused: "Why what a silly thing to wonder. Kalley dear, Robert has no reason to lie about his friends. Really, don't you think any adult would be foolish to think they must hide their relationships; whether the friend is a male or female?"

"Foolish or not people do," Kalley answered.

"Not all people," Leslie responded.

"Oh yes, all," Kalley replied. "I've never known a person to be completely open about their relationships. I would say we all hold back something about our relationships from the world."

"I don't," Leslie answered. "It isn't necessary if you are true to yourself."

"And you've told Robert everything about us, I mean the stuff I confided in you about my boyfriends, just for example?"

"Of course not. But not for some sly reason. Robert simply would find our usual banter about your boyfriends boring, if for no other reason than it's of no consequence to him."

"My point exactly," Kalley answered. "We all make decisions about our friends, family."

"Well, there's no vileness in that. It's proper conversation."

"And if one of those dates was with Mr. Jessup. One I forgot to tell Robert about. Then would my decision be proper?

"I don't think so under the present circumstances, Kalley dear. Did you?"

"So, girl, it is important, the circumstances I mean," Kalley answered. "Well, what if there are bikinis in the Bahamas? Does that mean Robert should tell you or not?"

Leslie repeated her question, in a slightly louder voice: "Did you?"

"Did I what?" Kalley asked in return.

"Did you date Jessup?" Leslie asked.

"Are you crazy, girl?" Kalley answered. "Yuck! But now you see we have a responsibility not to tell all."

"On some occasions we must," Leslie admitted.

"And not on others," Kalley added. "And if Robert is a reasonable man then it's logical that he has held back some information about the Haleys and McCords in his life."

"It's not treachery," Leslie argued.

"No Les, it isn't," Kalley responded. "But now you know he does, hold back I mean."

Leslie was silent. *Kalley was right, of course. Robert mustn't be telling me all. It's obvious. Where does he go when he disappears for days?* Leslie thought, *And why would he think he couldn't tell me?* "Oh really, Kalley," Leslie answered making light of the conversation. "If we demand all information, well there wouldn't be enough time for all information. We simply must trust those we trust."

"But, let's get those men to our planet," Kalley said. "Remember, the planet where we decide what information is necessary."

A courtship is a relationship of total trust, Leslie thought. *Courtship must be total openness, exposure, a time of disclosure when everything is shared. He isn't sharing everything in his life.* She became frightened.

"The who is our next candidate for the journey?" Leslie asked, hiding her feelings. "What say the crowd about your next candidate? Does he come to our planet? Or do we feed him to the lions?"

"Here is old news," Kalley said. "From Jason; just checking in, see you later this afternoon. Well, that sure is old news. What say the Romans?"

"To the lions, with haste," Leslie answered. "We certainly don't want him on our planet."

Kalley paused for an instant. She thought she perceived a small flinch in Leslie's eyes. "Don't trust him, huh?"

"Not totally," Leslie answered.

"Then we shall both keep an eye on him, but from far away," Kalley said and then smiled to calm her friend. "We won't let him on our planet, girl. Not yet. anyway. Thumbs down!"

"To the lions," both friends yelled and laughed.

"Here's one from Robert's mom. She called to see if he was going to visit today," Leslie read. "She's quite a lady, refined and sentimental. It pains Robert so to see her slowly fade away. I fear he will have a very bad time when she finally passes."

"Old age dementia?" Kalley asked.

"Yes," Leslie answered, "and I fear it's progressing rapidly. She now complains about the young man who tries to get her drunk on wine every evening so he can take advantage of her"

"What!" Kalley exclaimed.

"Quite so, only he's an orderly with the prescribed prune juice each evening. His job is to turn down her bed."

"I guess we've active libidos, even in the twilight of our days. That bodes well for Robert and you. If genes have anything to do with it, Robert will be loving you well into his nineties."

"I suppose so," Leslie answered, but she did not look happy.

"Girl, what are you worried about? You two have a long future together.
Everyone says so. You and Robert are the perfect match. We just need to get him
to our planet, that's all.   Now it's my turn. Here's one from an old buddy Jim, the
tennis bum. 'Be on time for a change, Robert. 2PM tomorrow.' He left a phone
number. Probably doesn't think Robert will show up, you know; just in case, you
can, call me, kind of stuff."

"This time Jim has definitely run out of luck," Leslie said. "We don't
want Robert going to that planet."

"Now you're catching on, girl," Kalley said. "How say the Romans?"

"Nay, a thousand times nay," Leslie answered and pointed her thumb
down.

"Ok it's to the lions for our tennis bum. Your turn Les. Pick one we can
really torture," Kalley said, wrenching her hands like a shrew hungry for blood.
"Give us one worthy of our wrath."

"Ah-ha!" Leslie announced. "This is the most opportune time for your
miserable bones." Leslie held up five messages all stapled together. "It seems
our bankers don't understand our communications about changing all access
codes. They want to know why we have frozen all cash and credit deposits for
four days."

"Perhaps we should answer them?" Kalley asked in a serious and
concerned voice. "We don't want any misunderstandings."

"I'll let you in on a little secret," Leslie said and lowered her voice. "The
access codes were sent. If we call and attempt a change, the bankers will believe
the first order to be false, right?"

"Yes, of course," Kalley answered.

"But you see our accounts are marked with the security directions to
freeze accounts in the event of such attempts, until personal contact is made with
Robert. In effect RRR will be shut down indefinitely if we contact them sooner

than four days from this afternoon." Then Leslie added: "Think of it as a time lock on a vault."

"What about our bank drafts, checks?"

"The bankers will employ one of their favorite tools, that of the clearance time. They will make certain no funds move for up to ten days and use the excuse of clearance-house delays. In effect they'll treat all drafts on our accounts like foreign checks, with the exception of our payroll account for the corporate offices."

"So I'll be able to cash my check?" Kalley asked, concerned.

"Yes, my dear. But our Mr. Sykes won't be able to move any money as of last night, midnight. And our bankers love it."

"Why?"

"Because, they will earn investment interest on our money. Truly our bankers would like to freeze all accounts every month. It does wonders for their day-to-day balances. So dear friend, how do the citizens of Rome rule? Do we tell Robert about these messages?"

"Off with their heads!" Kalley cried.

"Don't mix metaphors," Leslie cautioned. "A simple down turned thumb will suffice."

"To the lions with them then," Kalley said, plunging her thumb to the floor. "Though just this time I would like to cut off their money-sucking heads."

"Your turn."

Kalley rummaged through her remaining messages. "We must get Robert to return to our planet. He must come on our terms so we need the right message. The right reason."

While Kalley searched Leslie read to herself a note that appeared under the banker's messages. Not written on the usual phone message form, but rather on a sticky note. It simply said: Bobby, call me; must see you this weekend. Nora. Below the name was a phone number: 30-306-634-5789. 30 is the direct dial code for the south coast of France. Leslie's heart sank to her knees. A knot formed in her throat. *Could she be the reason Robert slips away at times?* Leslie wondered. She looked at her friend. No, Kalley had not noticed. Leslie swallowed hard. Carefully she slipped the note into her pocket.

"How about this one? A Mr. Z-something wants Robert to know he has a contract in hand for an offer on heavy scents. 'Now is the time,' he ends it. No phone number. What say the Romans?"

"No phone number?" Leslie asked. "That means we must contact Robert. We cannot handle the important matter. We will need the powerful Mr. Robinard. I give him a thumbs up!" Leslie exclaimed and stood with both thumbs in the air.

"A gracious crowd spares the life of the Mr. Z," Kalley cheered. "This should be an easy one to watch. We shall see just how much honesty Robert has stored in his head."

"It'll be your first chore in the morning, dear friend. You'll call Tanny. He must get in touch with Robert immediately. Make certain Tanny believes it's almost a life and death message from Mr. Z. But don't give him the contents of the message. We'll see exactly how long it will take for Robert to return the call."

"A good measure of his whereabouts," Kalley agreed. "But what if Robert calls Mr. Z directly?"

"Good question," Leslie answered. "We should make the message urgent but completely ambiguous."

"Let's dumb it up a bit. I'll say an urgent message was received about a pending contract, but I cannot divulge the name or contents, for security reasons. How does that sound?"

"We certainly are dedicated, if inept females," Leslie smiled. "That shall require a phone call from the great Master Robert."

"Now it's your turn. Let's find a juicy one, something with romantic espionage written into it."

Leslie flinched. Kalley was intuitive. *Could she possibly have seen me reading the note from the mysterious Nora?* "Let's see what else we have," Leslie announced as she spread the remaining messages across the table. "One from the florist?"

"Boring, to the lions," Kalley answered.

"How about prices on shipping boxes from Hong Kong?" Leslie suggested.

"Way obsolete, considering we have exposed Jessup."

"Lions?" asked Leslie.

"Lions again," Kalley responded, thumbs down.

"Ooh, this one could make a fine play," Leslie giggled. "It seems my Robert has priced a holiday in Argentina, apparently a snow ski week. I don't ski. He's an avid skier and it's apparent from the quote he's priced a week of lessons."

"Les, don't think that way," Kalley warned. "I know the lessons are for you."

"So do I, good friend," Leslie answered. "The note states: '14 lessons for Miss Devereaux,' but we can pretend, can't we, that the caller omitted that weighty bit of information?"

"Ooh, how perfectly evil, Les. Robert will have to return to our planet if he wants to save the romance. We've got him on this one. His royal majesty won't trust anyone else to this task. All others simply aren't up to the most important things in his life. We'll have to teach him the rules of OUR world," Kalley reminded Leslie.

"He may have to learn as he lives, so to speak. I shall be so very upset, devastated. He shall be shown no mercy. It's time he learns the ways of our world. The game is a-foot." Leslie pulled her ear lobe and winked. "Then how do the citizens of Rome say?"

"Spare him," Kalley cried. "Thumbs up!"

"Thumbs up indeed." Leslie agreed, but secretly she wondered what she would learn when she spoke to the mysterious Nora. "We have our play, dear friend. Now let us see if we can catch the conscience of the king."

The remainder of the afternoon was spent in laughter about how they would twist the great Robert Robinard into knots of confusion. The friends planned little treacheries to gain control of his heart. They would bring him to their planet, heart in hand.

By six o'clock it was time to secure the offices. Evening watchmen were coming on duty. Leslie made certain they knew that neither Jessup nor Sykes could gain access. "If they ask why, tell them to ask for me in the morning." She planned not to be available for snakes like them.

Before leaving, Leslie surprised Kalley by warning her she might not be in early: "I might make myself scarce, if I'm not here, please call Robert about the mysterious Mr. Z. Draw the blade lightly across his neck at first," she told Kalley. "There's plenty of time for selective incisions. Let's wait until we have learned a few secrets."

Puzzled, Kalley answered: "Ok." But deep in her heart she realized for the first time that her friend was genuinely, deeply frightened about losing Robert.

They parted company with a laugh and a hug. On their drives home, Kalley whistled, Leslie fumed.

Chapter 12   Phone Call

It was completely dark when Leslie arrived home. As she turned into the underground parking lot of the condo, she caught sight of Charles, the new evening doorman, lightly tipping his hat in her direction. He flipped a switch to open the titanium gate and scanned the parking entrance as Leslie drove through. Charles watched everything through the guard room plate glass window. Leslie found that reassuring. *That's worth the move to Palm Beach,* Leslie thought as she drove through. She wanted no more evening surprises waiting for her in a parking garage. She imagined the silhouette of the mugger she had encountered the day Robert came to her rescue around every corner.

Her Mercedes dipped down into the subterranean level garage. Well-lit and with bright white stucco walls, Leslie had no need of her headlights. She reached to the center console and flicked the switch. Her nails tapped the car's hand rubbed maple wood trim for an instant. *Ok, let's,* Leslie thought as she tapped the shift lever out of the drive position and took manual command of the gears.

"Once around the block," she said to herself. Down into first gear; the transmission responded. Leslie liked to drive fast. Like her father, she liked European sport car rally races. A quick spin around the underground lot was the closest thing to a rally course to be found on the island. Not that the maze of small, narrow, and well landscaped streets and lanes that marked the northern most reaches of the island could not entertain a rally driver, they certainly could. But the Palm Beach police frowned on such behavior. The police had an informal way of meeting every sport driver on the island. In a presuming manner, they are known to introduce themselves without a social reference, but rather a ticket. They could make the introductions rather expensive.

The Mercedes spun around the underground lot. Sliding on the newly painted concrete floor, it dug for a hold. But this only added to the fun. At each turn the rear wheels lost the traction and the car slid almost colliding with a parked BMW, then a Lexus, Bentley and Rolls. For the finale Leslie accelerated down the rows and licked the brakes as she cut hard left. As the Mercedes' rear wheels lost traction and slid sideways she stepped down on the accelerator and then braked. Her car spun hard left and then lurched to a halt in her parking space. *Record time*, she thought. Leslie liked to go fast. She left the top down.

"A good evening, Miss," Charles announced as he held the door for her. "Any packages this evening Miss?" he asked, ready to retrieve them from the car and deliver them to the service entrance of her home. *He looked somewhat like a reverse penguin,* Leslie thought, *in his white coat and slacks with black tie and shirt.* Charles's coiffure was always impeccable. Well over 60, Charles looked like a retired athlete turned banker. About five foot-ten, he showed no signs of a stomach and was always well manicured.

"None, but please schedule a detailing and cleaning for the Mercedes in the early morning," Leslie told Charles. She wanted the car clean and fresh before returning to work tomorrow.

Charles's expression momentarily changed to one of slight confusion, but then he regained control of himself and displayed the usual mild smile with eyes slightly averted. "Will that be necessary before 7 a.m. Miss?" he asked. Leslie nodded. Charles would see to it. *Civilized comfort.* Leslie gave Charles an approving smile.

"Very good, Miss," Charles answered, "and a good evening to you."

"And to you too, Charles," Leslie replied. "And what are you watching this evening on TV?" Charles was always monitoring the closed circuit system for intruders.

"Hallways and gates this evening, Miss," he answered, "and the occasional wave spray over the retaining wall. The sea is running south this evening, Miss. It looks as if the wind is strengthening."

Leslie quickly looked over the doorman's station to see a bank of closed circuit TV monitors. One was trained on the sea wall. As she watched she could see wave spray make it over the wall; starting at the north boundary and crawling along the wall dropping spray and water over the wall as it went south and out of the picture. "The sea is running high for this time of year," she observed. "What do you think?"

"It's either a late spring rain or an early summer storm, Miss," Charles replied. "Only time will tell."

"And your bet?" Leslie asked.

"An early summer, Miss," Charles answered politely. "We could be in for an early storm. The sea could be a heavy spring sea, but I fear it will be a long summer." Then he momentarily looked uncomfortable as he wondered if he had overstepped his bounds.

Leslie knew what he meant. South Florida can expect heavy seas during the winter and spring, but in summer the ocean can be like a lake for weeks at a time, unless there was a storm out beyond the horizon. "I suspect the same," Leslie told him. "In Charlestown we live with the sea also. I feel there is too much cloud activity for a late spring. Don't you agree?"

"There is certainly lots of energy in the sky for May, Miss," Charles answered cautiously. "We usually don't see rain and cloud build up like today until August or September."

"So, you are guessing an early hurricane?" Leslie asked.

Charles looked concerned. It was not good service to talk of unpleasant things with those you served. "Not to worry Miss," he answered after a moment's hesitation, "we don't have hurricanes in Palm Beach."

"Oh, of course not, nor in Charleston," Leslie replied with a wink and headed for the elevator. Charles smiled. Leslie liked Charles. *He is courteous, extremely efficient, and called me 'Miss' nine times.* Leslie smiled.

Leslie walked to the elevator door and it opened automatically. Once inside she announced: "Devereaux, Twelve B." The elevator door closed automatically and she began to rise. *A voice-activated control is a genuine convenience when my hands are filled with bags* Leslie thought, *but more than a little ostentatious now.* Still, the luxury of not pushing buttons was enjoyable. The system also aided security. It recorded all vocal instructions with day and time notations. As she rose Leslie apprehensively examined herself in the full wall mirrors. A feeling of relief came over her. The elevator was bathed in a soft, subdued instrumental version of a 60's rock song and Leslie wondered if the elevator had been programmed with a sense of humor. The slight scent of gardenia filled the little rising room. Presently the upward movement slowed with a slight shake and then stopped. "Twelve-B" a computer generated female voice announced. "Have a good evening." The private rear door of the elevator opened to Leslie's foyer.

The foyer was bathed in gentle light descending from hiding places in the ceiling. It spread across the green marble floor like a wave. A still life watercolor of the sea in a storm hung quietly on the beige wall, only slightly visible in the dim glow.

Suddenly Leslie realized she was alone, truly alone for the first time that day. There were no more board members to be suspicious of. There would be no Robert calling on her this evening.

Leslie stood motionless for a moment in the foyer. She tried to remember how she felt when she left that morning. She concentrated, trying to discern sensation somewhere from her skin, something to remind her of her own self-existence. She felt only the numbness of an intolerable day. She was alone. Presently, Leslie heard the faint thump-thump of her heart in her ear. Then she could feel the beating in her neck. With a flash of that unnamed emotion that validates credibility, Leslie again accepted the fact that she was alive. *But only just alive. I'm a definition, a thought, but only a thought. Others have somewhere else, and someone else. Oh, where is Robert?*

Habitually, mechanically, Leslie entered the security code. Inside she retrieved the mail of the day. Caroline, the maid had left it out for her on the key table. Leslie casually looked through the letters, studying the return addresses. There were the usual bills, and a card envelope postmarked Charleston. Leslie turned it over to see the return address. "3100 North Santee Drive," she read aloud to herself. *Who could possibly?* She silently questioned. Leslie placed it in her pocket. The bills she threw on the table with her purse.

In the kitchen she noticed her phone demanded attention. Leslie picked up a pen and listened. "Les, dear, so sorry for not calling sooner. I just realized your invitation didn't get mailed until yesterday. Bad me. You know how forgetful I can be. Anyways, I must have you at my wedding," the falsely perky voice called out. "Really, really, really," it continued. "Day after tomorrow, and you'll hoot at the guy. It's not a joke, Les, really. Can you come, please?" The message ended with a: "Les, come, please," of several female voices and then laughing. It was obvious there had been a party in Charleston.

"Sandra," Leslie addressed the answering machine. "Is it the third or fourth husband? I can never keep count." Sandra Cox was a life long friend in the loosest meaning of the word. Leslie had learned long ago to detest her, but she was of society, and as such could not be ignored. Though it would be so very easy to misplace the invitation, a phone call as well sealed the deal. Leslie would be going to Charleston. *Besides, Sandra might just want me to be absent. It is after all too easy to forget to mail your own wedding invitation until the last moment.*

Leslie glanced around the kitchen, considering eating. A note posted on the microwave read:

Kalley was again taking care of Leslie. *Gentle friend, thank you.* Leslie decided not to eat and threw the dinner in the refrigerator. She took a glass of cranberry juice and proceeded into the bedroom.

The evening was dark and only the ocean breakers could be seen through Leslie's sliding glass doors. Ocean buildings were equipped with roof flood lights that illuminated the surf. There was always a view to behold. Leslie left the room lights off and undressed in the dark. She retrieved the day's notes from her pocket. Then she walked into the bathroom beside the tub. There, she found six rose scented candles already lit, glowing between mirrored wall and glass window. The Jacuzzi was already circulating hot water in the tub. Leslie tossed two towels down beside the bath, placed a CD of Mozart's sonatas in the player, and put her big toe in the water. The digital Jacuzzi control read 94 degrees. *Perfect.*

With the care of an almost religious ceremony, Leslie gently slid into the water; first one leg, then another and then she slipped in up to her shoulders. She placed a towel under her neck. For the moment she was lost in the scene out the window. Below in the distance, endless rolls of unceasing waves passed over the reef and crashed into the sea wall. It seemed all too impossible. Leslie breathed a sigh of relief. At first, she could feel the warm water between her toes. Then it softened her calves. Soon it was caressing her tummy and breasts. She put her hands over two water outlets and felt the soothing massage of flowing liquid over her fingers. The scent of rose oil filled the air. Candles flicked the walls with intermittent sprays of light; their random intersecting patterns were mesmerizing. Leslie pressed the sponge over her body in a ritual washing.

Leslie almost forgot about the day. But there on the floor were the messages from her pocket. Like ghosts they haunted her consciousness demanding to be noticed; their existence needing verification. They would not be ignored. After a few minutes Leslie knew she had to accept their message. She picked up the first one, carefully unfolded it, and read; "I need to see you this afternoon…"

"Well, Master Robert," Leslie spoke to the parchment, holding it high above the water, " you have again had your way with me." A tear came to her eye. "Why do I always do your bidding?" She wondered just how it happened that Robert was away in the Bahamas and she was alone, again. There was a good reason, but there were always good reasons for his disappearances. "Will I ever tell you no?" she asked the paper. Then she set it on fire in one of the candles. It glowed brightly for a moment and then was gone. Leslie wondered if Robert's passion for her was like the parchment; a brief explosion of ignited furry that quickly turned black and cold.

Silence returned to the bathroom. Leslie felt small, alone and almost lost in the water. She felt small enough to hide from everything in the world. She closed her eyes and tried to look only at the back of her eyelids. Darkness descended at first. It was pleasantly surprising, as if all emotions had been erased. Then slowly, almost imperceptibly she began to notice color. At first it was only a random swirling of purple and yellow, rather like clouds in fast-forward. Leslie sensed time passing rapidly. Presently the yellow clouds began to swirl in a faster and ever increasingly aggressive mix of light and dark. It was much the same as the sensation of confusion that had permeated the day.

Colors changed to the shade of green pine and cypress forest mingled with Robert's eyes. The dream descended upon her, wrapped her in the memory of the warmth of a long forgotten day as the water pulsed against her soft skin. She had never felt so safe that day, so surrounded, so protected, so loved. They had played softball in the park. Later they followed a nature trail deep into verdant woods. Silence had fallen from the trees and surrounded them. Private and yet intimate with nature they made love in the flickering shade of a late afternoon. Robert had smelled of sweet perspiration. He had devoured her.

Suddenly all sense of pattern was lost as the scene became filled with a shadow of red. Leslie was becoming angry. A point of light appeared that Leslie tried to ignore. But she couldn't. In a moment the point of light flickered and Leslie was transported back into reality. A candle glowed in her eye. *I've progressed from disbelief, through denial to anger; all in one soaking bath. I'm a little liked a fool!* She became filled with a feeling of strength as she accepted the events of the day. She began to think clearly.

Leslie picked up the card envelope and squeezed it in her hands for a moment. As she had done as a child, Leslie brought it to her lips and held it firmly between her teeth as she smelled and tasted it as if wanting to experience even the smallest piece of the message carried within. She paused. *Lilac and parchment, and raised print. Definitely an invitation. Let us see what Sandra has been up to this time. I would like to bite Sandra.* As a child she had. Without knowing details, Leslie's intuition told her this would be an appropriate time for such action if they were together again as girls. "Time has rescued you, Sandra," Leslie announced to the empty room as she inserted her nail into the seal and broke it open.

It was a wedding invitation. Without removing it from the envelope she could see that. Raised gold leaf forming a ribbon tying two gold bells together were illuminated in the candle glow. If the announcement were not Sandra's, Leslie would have believed it heralded true love. Love to Sandra was simply an efficient tool to get what she wanted and Sandra always wanted something. She had conveniently forgotten Leslie from the guest list of her last wedding, one to a tennis pro. *Perhaps it was a marriage of too obvious a convenience. Or perhaps he couldn't demand the necessary envy of me*. Sandra liked to marry for power; and envy was a formidable power. In any event, those who were not invited feigned rejection while harboring gratitude for not having to attend, while those friends in attendance mimicked celebration while wondering just how long sex would sustain the marriage.

At thirty-love it was over. Sandra had won an early concession.

Leslie removed the announcement from the envelope and read:

Mr. And Mrs. Eugene Allen Mahoney

Happily Announce the Marriage of

Their Daughter

Sandra Anne

To

Mark Gardner, M.D.

Of

Charleston

Wedding Services to be Held...

And so on , with an accompanying reception invitation. Leslie was included in the inner circle this time. "Ah-ha," Leslie shouted with a laugh in her voice, "So now you think I will hopefully be just a little bit jealous." Mark had been one of Leslie's boyfriends in high school. He had taken her to the junior prom. They had left the dance floor early and Leslie had never explained to her friends why. Rumors had abounded about a love affair that night, but the truth was that Mark could not hold his liquor. A secretive pint of Jack Daniels had been shared by a few jocks and Mark had succumbed to that one illness that no self-respecting football jock would ever admit. The drunken heaves. After all, football heroes in the South were supposed to be masters of sour mash whiskey. She had taken him out of the ball. He had threatened to vomit on the dance floor, holding his stomach and moaning. Leslie had rescued him from a fate worse than death for a jock. Outside he had relieved his aching digestion in a flower box. Leslie decided then and there the date was over and drove him to her home. He had been in no position to argue. Rather, he frequently had begged to stop the car for further relief on the way home. She had sent him on his way and never offered a reason for her early return to her parents. They simply had assumed that their girl had made the right choices and left it at that.

Her friends had expected the couple at an after-the-ball party at Sandra's house, in the boathouse to be precise. When Mark and Leslie failed to appear, rumors started. Leslie never explained Mark's affliction to her friends, simply opting to turn a shoulder to their questioning. Mark had chosen to be quiet about the evening, another fate worse than death for a jock.

Now Mark was marrying Sandra, *A hopeless match.* If Sandra was hoping to inflict a pang of jealousy into Leslie's heart she couldn't be more wrong. Pity was more like it, pity for Mark. Sandra was the most un-nurturing female Leslie knew and Mark needed nurturing, an excessive amount of it. *Perhaps that's why I never found him attractive*, Leslie mused. Leslie always fell for the strong and not so silent types. "Their daughter Sandra Anne," Leslie read aloud, "so convenient a way to avoid the subject of other past husbands." The name Cox had been conveniently omitted from the announcement.

The day after tomorrow, just enough time to get things in order. Away one day by plane and Robert can wonder where I went. Kalley would have to manage the affairs of the office. What she could not handle could share a corner of her desk with other "To Be Ignored for the Time Being" files.

The Jaccuzi timer beeped. It was 10 pm and it wanted to turn off. Leslie reset the heater for an additional half hour. There was still another message to be considered, the one from the mysterious Nora. It was 4 am in the south of France, much too early to call. Leslie picked up the telephone message on the sticky note. *Who would dare call Robert Bobby?* she wondered. Such familiarity was never used, not even with his closest of friends. Robert hated nicknames. Only his mother was allowed to call him "Bobby" and she most definitely was not on the South coast of France.

Leslie pondered the note. It was yellow, with lines and had a sticky patch on the back. It was definitely not written on the approved RRR telephone message form. That meant there was no copy, mysterious. Leslie did not recognize the handwriting; "Bobby: call me; must see you this weekend. Nora 30-306-634-5789."

The hand was bold, almost flamboyant and yet feminine. Leslie decided she would wait no longer. She reached for the phone and began to enter the code for Europe, 30. A pang went through her heart. *What shall I find?* She asked herself. *It is only 4AM should I be calling?* Her hand trembled and hesitated. *Kate would tell me to go on.* Leslie continued to enter the number, 306, to the Costa de Soliel, 634, outside of Tolouse, 5789 to the unknown Nora's phone. A few beeps and chirps later and the familiar buzz of European phones could be heard. Six, seven, eight. *Perhaps I can hang up now.* Nine, ten, and there was a click and a muffled sound.

"Who the hell is calling me at 4 in the morning?" the voice shouted in the earpiece, "someone better be dead!" It was a female's voice, but not feminine, rather drunk or hung over. "Who the hell is this?" the voice demanded.

"An international call for Miss Nora," Leslie spoke to the obnoxious voice across the Atlantic. The great distance was not enough comfort. "Returning a call from Mr. Robinard, may I help you?" Leslie stated coldly. She wanted to give up no more information than was necessary.

"You can't help me but he can," the voice demanded. "He can get his butt on a plane and see me this afternoon. I have what he wants."

"And what might that be?" Leslie asked.

"What are you, dear," the voice demanded, "some driftwood Bobby has picked up in the islands?"

Leslie froze. She did not want to think about Robert in the islands, especially not with Tanny. "His personal secretary, Ma'am," she answered. "What message can I give him?"

"I told you," the voice answered. " He needs to get his butt over here!"

"And who should I say wants to see him in France?" Leslie asked.

"Its none of your business," the voice said. "Its family business. Tell him his wife Nora wants to see him, pronto!"

Leslie simply hung up the phone and sank under the water.

Chapter 13   Nora

The North side of Bimini was blustery. "That's the best that can be said about it, blustery and to hell with it!" Tanny exclaimed as he stood in front of the piano bar's glass doors and watched as the harbor water battered his boat about. It was 10 PM over on the mainland but early in Bimini. Tanny slammed his drink down on the sofa table: "Damn blustery!" He winced as the boat's chine struck against the bumpers with every wave.

"Why don't we run out there and tighten the ropes, hold it off the dock?" one of the guests offered; a dumb though obvious solution to the untrained eye.

"That would do the trick, if it were a rising tide," Robert interjected. "But the ocean is running out of the harbor and seas are dropping, look." Through the drizzle they could just make out the jetty and swirls of salty bubbles coursing through the pilings and out to the open ocean. "She'll need all her line at low tide."

Tanny's 46 foot racer was moored between four green wood pilings connected by catwalks. Each one held the boat with a line. "As it is we'll need to lengthen the shock line." Robert pointed to a rope from a front piling to a cleat on the rear of the boat. "Watch," he ordered, "the next swell will pull the stern first, but the shock line will flex and hold the hull from swaying with the sea roll. It stops excessive sway and helps all mooring lines share equally in the stress." Dutifully, the ocean obeyed.

"Even the seas obey Master Robinard," a slinky young woman quipped as she smoothly walked over to his side. She pressed her hips against Robert's while smiling through dark mauve lips. Robert thought the lips looked bubonic. He pulled tactfully away as he reached for his drink on the sofa table. Robert was not at all interested in the false affections a perfect tropical island evening filled with music and alcohol, can stir in a woman far away from home. He no longer allowed alcohol to cloud his thoughts.

But for Tanny, ladies were a necessity to this business trip. They attracted the businessmen. "It was easy, really," as Tanny explained. He had only to invite twice or three times as many young, un-attached females as males. Coming from local West Palm Beach companies, these were secretaries, accountants, minor department heads, professional types. The offer of an all-expenses-paid vacation to an exotic location was attractive. So there was always lots of female companionship available. And Tanny's parties had a reputation for fun. As long as the ladies were under 35, it worked. The businessmen always accepted the invitation and Tanny had a captive audience for his newest business propositions. "It's easy, really," Tanny told Robert. "They all get to tell their wives it's a business trip. After all, it can be argued that a personal investigation is prudent; prior to loaning money or investing in a limited partnership.

Robert did not care for Tanny's method for doing business, but he tried his best to hide his opinion. "What if the ladies don't find your 50 and over businessmen attractive?" Robert asked.

"At odds of three to one, any balding, pot-bellied Romeo can score. So why should I care!" Tanny laughed. "No one is coerced."

"And if the ladies don't choose to share their favors with one of your guests?"

"No problem, I just won't invite them on the next vacation." Tanny responded confidently. "The same with the gentlemen. If we don't consummate a business agreement sometime after they return home, I simply won't invite them again."

Robert hid his annoyance at Tanny's methods. "So these ladies are willing?"

"I let nature take its course, no pressure. A beautiful tropical moon, lots of booze, no friends around to talk; well there are always enough ladies who decide to let their hair down. In a way it's every woman's fantasy," Tanny grinned.

"And the gentlemen, are they quick to share information about the success of their amorous advances?"

"Men like to boast," Tanny answered with another grin and winked.

Now Robert found himself in circumstances he did not care for, not in the least. Locked into playing the part of a playboy to delude Jessup, he could not leave and his conscience refused to let him stay. Worse, he needed to stay very close to Tanny. RRR could not afford to lose Tanny to Jessup. Not now. Votes would soon be needed.

Time was passing. More of Tanny's guests began to fill the piano bar. The bar was reserved that week for Tanny's private party. Guests who appeared there could be certain to enjoy food, drink, music, and the companionship of the opposite sex, all without charge. *Not bad work, not really*, Robert tried to convince himself as he checked his topcoat button. *If you must work in the evening, this is ok.* Dressed in a cashmere sports jacket, he need only mingle with a drink in his hand and avoid the ladies.

But he was unsuccessful in deceiving himself. In a room filling with people, he was alone without Leslie.

"Come on buddy, loosen up," Tanny chided. "Where is your head anyway? You have got to learn to smell the roses." He put his arm around Robert's neck and whispered in his ear: "And smell the ladies, too. They're sooo.., delicious," and let out a laugh. Robert grinned slightly to appease Tanny. He moved over to a corner by the plate glass window and studied the rain striking the glass.

Robert missed Leslie with a passion. Though the bar was filling with other perfumes, he did not notice. Yet he felt guilty. He had been deliberately distant the last few weeks, trying to avoid an explanation for his reluctance to offer his hand in marriage, to continue that natural progression of love. But he couldn't not now, and perhaps he never could. He worried about what she might be thinking. *If I could only summon the courage to lay it all on the line, to tell her the complete and awful truth about myself,* he thought. But then a fear grabbed his heart. *Would she ever accept him if she knew the truth?* He felt unworthy of her love. *Or destined to lose her?*

Memories began to fill Robert's conscious thoughts. "That night had been like this one," he said to himself, looking out into the black, rainy darkness.

Suddenly he remembered the note. He placed his right hand into his pant's pocket. It was still there. He retrieved it. It was hand written on a small yellow notepad and for that he was grateful, for there should be no copy in the office. Again he studied the note. All day he had avoided the certainty that he would have to call. The note only disclosed the name of the caller, Nora, and an international phone number. He crushed the note in his trembling hand.

Looking back, he never understood why Nora had married him. After the twins were born she had lost all interest in Robert and his business affairs, and the drinking had become worse. Now he did not understand why she insisted on remaining married. But his sense of guilt prevented him from divorcing Nora without her consent. After the accident there was nothing but guilt to hold him to the marriage.

* * *

It had been two years ago when Robert's life had come to a crashing end. He had been out to a cocktail party hosted by Jeffrey and Bev Miller. They always noted Nora's absence and Robert explained it to Nora as a necessary, if not mandatory business party. But Nora hadn't believed him. She had been drinking more than usual that week and so she heaped more than the usual amount of abuse upon Robert when he told her of his evening plans. He had hurriedly escaped Nora's alcohol and pill delirium and left his four-year-old twins in the good care of the nanny. But in his haste to escape he neglected to hide the car keys.

Nora was once a beautiful woman. She had been tall and graceful. Robert met her at the club. He watched from a distance as she dove off the high board. She appeared as delicate as a ballerina dancing across the stage when she swam underwater the length of the club's pool. He watched her legs kick and push against the water. They made her hips flow as if in a dance. When she surfaced, he had offered a towel.

They dated and after six months it seemed the normal to talk about marriage. She had been married before, up North. Robert never thought about her alcohol dependency then. It only made dates more interesting. Nora could do the unexpected when she was drinking. Her green eyes danced more wildly with alcohol. She was fun to be with and Robert had been lonely. They both were of the right social circles. But they never made plans for children.

The girls were born on a Sunday, early in the morning. Twins had been a complete surprise until the fifth month of the pregnancy, when a Sonogram clearly showed that Nora was pregnant with not one but two girls. Robert's friends had again announced that he lived a charmed life. "Two children for one pregnancy; definitely the Robinard way," Tanny declared. But Nora was bedridden for the last trimester. The drinking weakened her and their marriage had already begun to come apart. The girls were born three weeks premature. None of his friends really noticed. Then, after the accident, Robert's charmed life was no more.

That awful night Nora found the car keys and dismissed the nanny for the evening. The girls, not knowing why Nora awakened them, were hustled into the car. While they rubbed sleep from their eyes she told them they were going to find daddy.

The report said Nora's blood-alcohol level had been 1.7, clearly over the legal limit to drive. She hadn't been able to control the Mercedes and plowed into a tree. Nora was wearing a seat belt, but the girls were not so lucky. In her drunken state Nora had dropped them into their car seats. Their seat belts were never fastened and upon impact they were ejected from the car and were killed instantly. Robert blamed himself.

* * *

Now Nora wanted to talk, Robert thought to himself as he watched droplets of rain streak down the glass, *after all this time she has decided to surface again.* Robert knew she must want something, probably money. He knew that he would give her anything she wanted, he had to. Robert signaled the waitress for another drink. He held two fingers against his bourbon glass and said, " The usual." After another moment of staring at the rain the waitress brought Robert his usual, ginger ale on ice with a twist of lemon and stir-stick. Robert never drank alcohol. He slipped the waitress a ten-dollar bill and she smiled.

Chapter 14 Alone

The bedroom was filled with filtered moon light streaming through the white cotton gauze drapes when Leslie entered. The dim light cast a pale yellow-green glow on the room's contents and like an ethereal leach drained the red spectrum from Leslie's world.

Robert's picture stared at her from the woven rattan nightstand. Together they had chosen the silver frame at an antique shop on Worth Avenue. It was a relic of the Gilded Age of Palm Beach. Patterns of grape and vine encircled his likeness. Robert stood there in her room every night still clutching a champagne glass, naked to the waist and shinning with a light sweat from a sun that had long since disappeared.

Leslie found her bed, but sleep did not find her. Lying alone on cotton sheets, she slowly melted into the creases. She was beyond crying. Leslie was again alone. She lay motionless, staring at Robert's framed face for what seemed an eternity.

Smaller and smaller she became as she thought about her life. At first, the shrinking promised some shelter from her thoughts. As though the painful memories would not be able find her heart if she could only hide. But, memories intent on breaking that gentle heart, the memories of incomplete wishes and desires crept into her mind.

Mysterious to Leslie, an image appeared in her memory. Her second grade Easter vacation picnic revealed itself onto the inside of Leslie's eyelids. Stunned, a pang of short but intense pain had shot through Leslie's chest and stomach as she saw Jimmy Cook kiss a girl for no reason while in line for ice cream. Leslie had been behind him in line and he hadn't even noticed her. In her mind, Leslie again ran away and sat under the willows; but now the pain was familiar.

Ken had been her beau early on in high school, her steady. Leslie trusted Ken. But one evening at a freshman dance Ken had favored the company of a girl named Genie, "from up North somewhere," as Leslie's mother had stated with that slightly lowered growling voice that meant the basest of insults from a true Southern lady. Worse, he made an improper advance on Leslie, touched her right breast during a slow waltz. She had pulled back, astonished, but he simply grinned and kept dancing. When the music ended Leslie walked away, not knowing what to do. But she had felt betrayed. Later that evening, Leslie noticed Genie did not complain when Ken touched her right breast. On the ride home Leslie's father asked her, "Is there something wrong?" She had only shrugged her shoulders. Now Leslie smiles when she thinks of his adolescent passion, but down deep the betrayal still hurt.

But Gerry was different. Not that Leslie was now any more surprised to learn of his infidelity than any other man from her past, but she was rather surprised how quickly she accepted the truth of her situation and had recovered. *Rather matter-of-factly,* Leslie thought. Although she knew to trust in love only so far, she still was always surprised to learn of the finite nature of other's affections; for she believed in the possibility of a life long true affection for another. When she discovered Gerry's infidelity she had known what to do in short order.

In truth, Leslie was greatly relieved to be rid of the responsibility of reconstructing her life after Gerry. Revenge was never really sweet and besides, Robert was handsome, considerate, and gentle. At great personal risk Robert had come to her rescue in the parking lot and returned her purse. Robert was her most recent knight in shining armor. Or so she thought.

Leslie didn't want to think about Robert. She didn't want to plan revenge or even a confrontation. She hoped to herself that some mysterious turn of events would wash the situation from her life.

"Be sensible, be sensible," she whispered to herself as she buried her head into a pillow. "He must have a reason, some noble purpose for keeping secrets." *Hadn't he alluded to some problem too large for even himself? Perhaps he was only sheltering me from the truth. Or perhaps he felt he could not trust me to believe him.*

Robert is not a philanderer, but more a sad victim. I know it, I simply know it. She sat up in bed and turned in embarrassment to see if anyone could be in the room and have overheard her. No, she was talking to herself and she was still alone.

The moon glazed the objects in the room with gentleness, sensuousness. Her bed was half empty without Robert; and it seemed strangely inappropriate. *What use of a bed,* Leslie thought to herself. *Without Robert I shall never sleep again.* Leslie rolled over on to her back and bent her head down and stared at her abdomen. *I am certain of my love for him,* she mused, *and of his love for me, but...* The voice from the South of France rang again in her memory. *His wife! But Robert couldn't be married. It just wasn't his way!* She pressed her palms into her abdomen and asked: "Oh, whatever is wrong with me?"

Leslie reached for Robert's picture, lifted it off the nightstand and placed it upon her breast. She drifted into a twilight sleep and began to dream.

It had been late in the day, late in a wonderful, perfect day of boating with close friends, when the silver framed picture had been taken. *You are my dream come true,* Robert's voice repeated in her memory over and over again. *You are my dream come true.*

Leslie and Robert had just finished saying goodbye to the last couple to leave the yacht. Bare to the waist, Robert firmly grabbed Leslie by the hips and with both hands lifted her effortlessly off the deck. Before her surprised body could resist he spun her around and pulled her tightly to his body, suspending her in air. She had slowly slid down his gleaming chest and tighter into his arms. Her string Bikini bottoms slid tightly up against his jeans. Her triangle top had momentarily caught on his chest hair and floated upward, revealing her nipples to the fading sun.

"Eek!' Leslie had exclaimed and pushed Robert back. He had released his hold with a laugh. Leslie had stepped back, a little embarrassed, and a little excited: "How could you, you?" she laughed; and then exclaimed: "Why anyone could have seen us, seen me! You dreadful, randy man!" She had said with a smile and quickly pulled her top down and into its proper position.

But Robert stood there on the rear deck: "You are my dream come true." Leslie stared for a moment at this tanned six foot, two inch dark and handsome athlete. His black hair grew thickly out of his head. A light "five o'clock shadow" began where his hair ended and continued down the middle of his chest, framing powerful muscles. From there it had continued, forming a line down his abdomen until it disappeared in a powerful velvet mass behind his fly.

Leslie had reached for the camera. Robert had simply winked, grinned, and picked up his glass of champagne. "You are an absolute cad, sir," Leslie accused him in jest. "Why take such liberties with a lady.?" It's then that Leslie snapped the picture and said with a grin: "Now let's do it again." Robert had then grabbed her up and whisked her away into the yacht's salon, and behind closed drapes.

Leslie slept.

Chapter 15 The Stream

In Palm Beach Leslie rolled over in bed and awoke. She felt pain on her side. Robert's portrait, framed in silver, was again pressing into her. *The Bible has it all backwards,* she thought, *he is like a proverbial 'Eve's rib; the painful act of God that created a spouse in the Garden of Eden, she mused. Men are the beautiful curse of women kind. Here I am, anguishing while he parties with Tanny and who knows with what else!* The thought of all the Bikini clad gold diggers hanging on Robert's every word pained her stomach. Leslie stared at the ceiling. *This is so totally unfair. I have been nothing if not true and honest with Robert, as with any man I have loved. But they always seem to think I am only a plaything, someone to have around for a convenience, an accommodation, only a steady and reliable assumption.* Leslie fumed. It was 1:30 in the morning, but she could not sleep.

* * *

On the island of Bimini, in the middle of an ocean, Robert was idly staring at the rain droplets pelting the sliding glass door. It was 1:30 in the morning when a spike of reality, thrust into his mind. *If Nora called me she most certainly called the office. A personal message was certain to be forwarded to Leslie!* A pain gripped his stomach. *I should have explained things to her. I should have listened to Bev!*

Robert reached in his pocket and removed his cell phone. His hands shook as he entered her home number. It rang 15 times before the computer-generated voice announced the party was not answering the call and requested he try again later. He called again, but the results were the same.

Robert stared in horror at the little device in his hands. *So much for being in charge,* he thought as he stared into the glow of the illuminated screen. He was helpless. He was more than that. He was the servant of the little computer god behind the keyboard. He called the international operator. But the results were the same, no answer. Leslie would not answer her phone. She knew.

* * *

While Leslie packed the phone rang again and again. She threw a pillow over it. *I do not wish to ever know who that is.* Only a few bare essentials were hastily thrown into an overnight bag on her bed; medicines, 2 changes of underwear, cosmetics and sundry items, two pair of shoes, one pair were black flats, and another canvass tennis. She would travel in leather sandals. *Whatever else I need I am sure the stores in Charleston shall supply. I only need to get out of here!* She threw a light tennis sweater over her shoulder, grabbed her purse and overnight bag and proceeded out the apartment door.

The doorman was surprised to see her. His expression begged an explanation, but she offered none. Leslie only said; "Good evening," and "I shall be gone a few days to Charleston," and left the building. Charles tipped his hat, wished her an enjoyable trip and cancelled her car detailing for later that morning. Leslie quickly drove to the bank to make a deposit. In a few moments Leslie had crossed the central bridge to the mainland and was flying low, north on I-95. Leslie did not look back.

* * *

Furiously Robert banged his fist on Tanny's door. Tanny didn't come to the door for a few minutes and when Robert saw his eyes Robert knew why. "You look like crap," Robert told him. "How are you going to race tomorrow?"

"I'm not," was Tanny's reply. "Ralphy is running the course. I own the boat and the ideas. I console the fair maidens and stroke the investors. Is that the burning question that brings you to my door at 2:00 am?"

"We need to move quickly," Robert began. "I must get to the mainland and," he paused and gasped: "whew, your breath smells worse than a skunk!"

"Not surprising," Tanny rebutted. "But, you look awful yourself, what's wrong?"

"Nothing, you're just looking at me through blood shot eyes," Robert answered and added "you're drunk."

"Ho, not enough," Tanny replied grinning. "After all, I answered the door, didn't I?" Then he added: "Ok, what do you want?"

"I've got to get to the mainland, to Palm Beach fast. The charter service won't be open until 6:00 am and I need to be there by then."

"Is that all?" Tanny exclaimed sarcastically, "just wait a minute while I pull a magic carpet out of my ass! Really, Robert old boy, don't hold back now, you're among friends. How about giving me a minute to rub my magic lamp? The genie will be pissed being woken up at this early hour, though. We'd better let my fine young companion of the evening do the rubbing. She shows talent in such matters."

"Cut the crap, Tanny," Robert ordered. "You owe me." Robert's voice pitched higher as he thrust his left index finger at Tanny's nose.

Tanny's back stiffened. His face became red with anger. He was not a man to take orders. The button of his robe loosened as his chest filled with air. He was about to explode in anger. For a long moment Tanny stared into Robert's eyes, assessing, judging, questioning if he had himself had misjudged Robert's character.

Presently Tanny's expression softened. "Calm down Robert," Tanny ordered in a somewhat soft, if stern voice, "I'll get you to the mainland if you need." Then he stepped forward and flung his muscular right arm around Robert's shoulder and pulled him into the room. "Put that thing down, though," Tanny ordered Robert in a friendly tone as he nodded to Robert's still outstretched left index finger. "You could frighten someone with that thing!"

Robert blinked, suddenly he realizing how "assuming" he had been with his friend. Robert was fond of telling his employees he spelled "assuming" A-S-S. He felt like one now.

"You are a sight, Tanny," Robert replied, smiling, "and a friend in need." Then he added: "And you better put that thing away though," gesturing with a nod to Tanny's crotch, "before you scare the help off."

"Like you said," Tanny replied shortly, "cut the crap. So why should I get you to the mainland before morning? Is someone after you?"

"Trust me on this one," Robert answered. "It's an absolute necessity, an old problem. One that perhaps I should have resolved long ago. Anyway, it is back to haunt me."

"Damn it, Robert old boy," Tanny added. "No need for a panic. If you really must get there tonight I'm your boy. Ralphy can handle the preparations himself. With a little luck I can drop you at the old north end pier in three hours and be back here in six, just in time for Bloody Marys by the pool and no one will be the wiser."

Robert's face began to relax: "What about customs?"

"I'll run in the inlet, drop you without shutting down the motors and spin out of the inlet again before anyone gets a clue. We won't even go into the Intracoastal. We won't get close to the Peanut Island Coast Guard station. I'll be out of and back into international waters in ten minutes. If they want me they can chase me. It won't be the first time. You can call someone to pick you up at the pier. But tell them not to be late. Sure as hell the Palm Beach police will be called if they pick us up on radar."

Robert thought about this idea for a long moment. As a boy he had regularly fished at the island's north end pier. Back then the pier had also housed a bait shop as well as a fueling station. As a boy he had spent many an hour trying to hook a sheepshead while chugging a Coke. The pier was located in the cut channel that was the inlet. Because boats incoming could refuel, disembark or take on passengers and supplies all without checking in first with customs, it was closed. Today, you could still fish, but the police removed anyone but locals found there. The pier still thrusts into the cut channel at the North end of North Ocean Road, lonely and forgotten. *It could work,* Robert thought.

Robert looked at his old friend. Tanny was a sight. Hung-over from fine bottled in bond Scotch whiskey and smelling faintly of female perfumes, he didn't have the ordinary deportment of a hero and savior. Robert frowned and thought *He'll have to do.* Robert nodded a yes. "Ok, let's do it," he told Tanny.

"A, one if by land and two if by sea sort of thing?" Tanny inquired sarcastically and after a moment of hesitation asked: "Who are we hiding from, certainly not the Red Coats? What other evil force could be settling down on us from the Continent?" Tanny plopped down upon the couch, reached for a bottle of Johnny Walker Black, and began to freshen his drink. "My drink after I am drunk," he announced.

Robert stepped forward and pulled the bottle away. "We need to move," he said. "Come on buddy, we need to move, now! Get me to the mainland."

"So what is the danger, good buddy?" Tanny asked cautiously. He thought he would have a little fun with his friend. "Could it be revenuers? No, that's not your style. How about a gambling debt, nope, Robert only bets on a sure thing. Women? Well now, there is a possibility. But what woman could shake you so, I wonder?"

"Tanny old buddy, let's go." Robert said with a slightly frantic twist in his voice. His unusual composure tipped the secret to Tanny.

"Ah, a woman it is. But what woman could drive you so? You look frightened." Tanny paused a moment, looked directly into Robert's eyes and soon began to smile. "Nora!" he announced. "Its' Nora isn't it? She's back!"

"Fraid so, and worse," Robert answered in a low voice, staring at the floor. "Leslie doesn't know."

Tanny's eyes opened wide. He pulled his robe closed as he stood up. "You mean to say you didn't tell her? Robert, you're in deep shit! We better get started. We'll take Boomer. She's in dock beside the racer. If the seas stay we can make landfall in 3 hours off of Fort Lauderdale and then run north to the Palm Beach inlet. We'll radio the Coast Guard as soon as we cross the Stream and tell them we're checking in at Peanut Island station. They won't ever notice you jump off at the old dock. Then I'll be out before they turn their heads."

"It's a plan," Robert announced confidently. While Tanny rushed into his bedroom to put on some clothes, Robert phoned home. His car would be waiting at the North end of the island in exactly four hours. The police would accommodate a favor for a favor and not ticket, but rather stand watch.

* * *

On I-95 the weather worsened. Rain began to beat hard against Leslie's windshield. She turned on the radio to 90.7 public radio. The prediction was for increased rain and wind from Cayo Romano on the Eastern shore of Cuba to the Jupiter inlet. An early tropical low was inching its' way up the hurricane slot to the north of Puerto Rico. Nothing for land based interests to be concerned with, the announcer read from his printout from the National Weather Service, but sea going interests should expect three to six foot seas on both sides of the Gulf Stream and increased rain as the day progresses. The announcement added that the low was not expected to strengthen and should pass well south of Miami. He ended his report by suggesting that any interested parties should keep informed about the storm's progress. Though further strengthening was not expected, in this season it was possible.

Leslie smiled. *Good, I hope all those Bikini clad gold-diggers have a fine time vomiting over the side. It should be a perfectly awful time at sea tomorrow.* She grinned faintly as she sped north.

* * *

At the pier Robert and Tanny were busy untying Boomer's moorings. The Boomer was a 32 foot Cigarette racer that had been outfitted for pleasure. Its' pop-up cabin was air conditioned and appointed in plush padded furniture accented with hand-rubbed teak. It had a small stateroom forward and a full wet bar topside. With twin Caterpillar engines it could make 45 knots in a two-foot sea. Boomer was the boat for speeding to a party or bringing the party with you.

The rain began beating hard against Boomer's deck as Tanny opened the engine compartment hatch to freshen the air before turning over the motors. Tanny opened a locker under the captain's seat and produced two rain slickers. "Throw this on," he told Robert. I'm an old salt, don't trust electric ventilators, besides this way is faster." With the hatches open Tanny started up the two power plants. A whiff of diesel fuel momentarily passed Robert's nostrils and was washed away by the rain. Quickly, Tanny closed the hatches and pushed the Boomer free of the dock with the heel of his shoe.

"What about fuel?" Robert questioned. Robert was no newcomer to the sea, especially the Gulf Stream crossing between Bimini and Ft. Lauderdale, and he knew the force of the Stream. It was always prudent to take extra precautions.

"A boat is like a gun," Tanny replied. "A weapon is no good if it is unloaded and a boat is useless without fuel. I always keep both topped off. There are weapons stowed in the locker behind the wheel if we need them."

Robert looked down at the illuminated instrument panel through the driving rain. "The port tank reads less than half," he shook his head.

"Not to worry old buddy," Tanny assured him. Ralphy had her out yesterday. Probably just forgot to fill her up. No time, you know, with the partying and all. Besides, we have another tank on the starboard side."

Boomer cleared the harbor and throttled up as it passed the last light. Customs would pay no interest in one boat leaving a little early in the morning to get a good spot from which to watch the race. Bimini was always accommodating to the guests that could afford what it had to offer. Boomer roared ahead, dead west and into the darkness.

* * *

On I-95 Leslie was making good time in spite of the weather. She again turned on the car radio for company. The local country classic station was playing a classic hit. Leslie listened in the darkness:

"I've been cheated like an old hound dog..."

But it gave her no comfort to hear a lament from the 50s. She turned off the radio. In her purse her cell phone rang, but she did not answer. Leslie sped north into the night.

* * *

Robert held on to his chair in the pounding sea as he listened again to his cell phone ringing. With every wave a wall of sea spray flew over the bow and into the cockpit, thoroughly drenching both men. The sea had continually built as the Boomer headed into the Stream. Two foot seas had turned into six foot seas and then eight. By now the boat had crossed the northbound current and was fast approaching the Florida coast. In those waters the sailor's unwritten rule promises whatever conditions you find on one side of the Stream will be reversed on the other; unless you are heading into a tropical storm. Tropical cyclones are thought to be the exception to any rule of the sea. Robert had heard them called a hole in the atmosphere. *Hurricanes do behave like holes,* Robert thought. *They suck in and drain away everything in their path.* He called Leslie again, but Leslie was not answering.

"No luck?" Tanny asked, shouting over the sound of the storm. Beyond the bow of the Boomer and just beyond the horizon the lights of Ft. Lauderdale began to illuminate the sky. Even on such a dark and rainy night the lights of the huge city could not be ignored. "We're in range of the signal, of that I'm certain. Only about eight miles out," Tanny said.

Tanny was becoming concerned with the weather, but refused to show it. He was relieved when the roofs of the office buildings on Broward Avenue in downtown Fort lauderdale came into view. Tanny pulled back on the throttles and Boomer responded, slowing to about 10 knots. The seas were now running over ten feet and though Boomer was not designed for such conditions, he knew they would make landfall. They were close, so very close. Still, entering an inlet in these seas he knew would be another matter. "Looks like you will keep your date old buddy," Tanny yelled with a confident grin to Robert over the roar of the wind, wave, and engines.

At that moment the port diesel sputtered. Tanny looked at the fuel gauge. The port tank's gauge read below empty. He nudged Robert and pointed to the gauge. "Prime the starboard tank," he ordered Robert. "We'll need it in a minute."

Robert switched on the starboard fuel tank pump. The starboard tank's gauge should have come alive, but it didn't. Robert tapped the gauge with his knuckle, but nothing happened. He motioned to Tanny who had been watching. Tanny looked worried.

"Only thing we can do is shut her down," he yelled to Robert. "But it's going to be one hell of a ride." Without power if only for a minute, Boomer was in for a thrashing at the mercy of wind and wave. "We'll have to manually switch over and prime the pump. It's going to be a mess in these seas."

The plan was simple. Tanny assumed a vapor lock kept the pump from moving fuel. There was a bleeder bulb on each line. Squeezing the bulb would move fuel into and prime the pump. If that didn't work they would open the lines between the tanks. Fuel would then flow by gravity from the starboard to the port tank where the pump could move it into the engines. But it meant someone had to crawl down and into the engine compartment below decks. Robert was nominated.

Robert twisted his six-foot, two-inch frame and squeezed into the engine compartment as Tanny cut off the engines. Mother Ocean began her merciless beating upon Boomer. Robert squeezed the priming bulb, but he could not feel any resistance; the sign of flowing fuel. He signaled to Tanny above and turned and opened the valve between the tanks. Tanny watched the port fuel gauge, but it did not change. Tanny turned pale. He jumped down into the engine compartment next to Robert and pounded the starboard fuel tank with his fist. It made a dull, hollow sound. "No fuel," Tanny shouted to Robert through the wind's fury, "we're screwed."

Slowly the land passed as they crashed against the bulkheads in the terrible seas. Together they huddled in the cabin for shelter from the storm. Tanny called the Coast Guard for a tow. Now all they could do was wait to be found. Every ten minutes or so, Tanny sent another message to help rescuers fix their position. In a while the land lights fell away. "That tells me we are north of Jupiter," he yelled to Robert above the noise of the storm, "the coast is falling away. We're not heading east but the land is heading west."

"So we've drifted north of Palm Beach?" Robert asked.

Tanny nodded a yes.

Chapter 16 Father

The world sped past Leslie's car window in the dark. Except for the few
intermittent and brief moments of harsh light from a roadside sign that beckoned
the traveler to buy gas, donuts, ice cream, cigarettes, and the odd pecan log roll;
Leslie was alone. She was in a universe of secretive shadows that disappeared in
an instant in the car's rear view mirror. Charleston was in the deep distance
ahead.

Presently, it began to rain. The first few drops fell and smashed out their
brief life onto her windshield; small, random thuds alone and lost in the night.

"Small comfort. A few lost droplets who hurl themselves into oblivion,"
Leslie whispered, then muttered lines from an almost forgotten verse by Shelley
to the doomed pellets of water:

>"The fitful alternations of the rain,
>
>When the chill wind, languid as with pain
>
>Of its own heavy moisture, here and there
>
>Drives through the grey and beamless atmosphere"

Soon the droplets had exhausted their energies in brief attacks upon the
windshield. They deformed into blobs of limp liquid and searched for the easiest
path of escape. A few blobs slid down into her car's windshield wipers; others
vanished into the air stream in a vain attempt to reunite with their own kind. Each
began again their search for Mother River.

Leslie was alone again on a lonely highway. She reached over and into
the glove compartment to retrieve a CD. Her hand found an old audio cassette
buried under tissues. By the glove compartment light, the label read: "Golf and
Steak." It was from Leslie's father. Before his death he frequently sent her
cassettes telling Leslie of his "exploits of the gray and impotent," as her mother

had once called them. Now that he had passed, each cassette became a treasured artifact. But this evening she was alone and without a cassette player. Leslie tossed the audiocassette on the leather seat beside her and frowned.

"You're my dad and you loved me, of that I am certain," she whispered to the cassette. "But why oh why did you leave mother? Now what do you have to say for yourself," she scolded.

"*It just wasn't like that.*" Leslie imagined her father answering. In Leslie's mind he appeared in his golf shoes. Sitting in the leather seat next to her. He smiled. His dark eyes beamed love for his child. *"Not like any of that, that crap. You know your mother's friends are so very certain of themselves when they put on their Southern airs in conversation. It's as if they could summon from the heavens needed credibility. They will lower their voices and avert their eyes as they pronounce a person to be: 'Someone from up North."*

"*Not that I don't like those persuasive voices,*" her father continued. "*They are sexy, very sexy. Every one of them. I mean an eighty-year-old woman can sound sexy using that most persuasive Southern drawl found around those parts. It just happened one day that I was fed up with it. You know, the constant assessing, measuring those unfortunate visitors against the hard, made-by-the-hands-of-slaves of the Old South, brick wall of judgment. You know, the kind that you can find at most any street corner, and behind it there is always a summer's tea party floating in mint juleps.*"

"Let's hear your reasoning, father dear," Leslie whispered and she glanced at the empty seat beside her. "Though I'm certain I shall not be amused."

"*I began to find excuses to be late and leave early,*" her father spoke in her head. "*One day, and I cannot remember when because it was just so very innocent, but your mother decided to stay at one of THOSE gatherings. I left one of those damn parties early and thought I'd enjoy the privacy of a quiet walk out to the Old Slave Market. Edith found a way home with friends and I found myself downtown at eleven in the evening, innocently, mind you. But, you know, well, it just felt good, fine, smooth. I meandered around a flowered veranda room. I didn't have to remember your mother's instructions on who to snub, who to engage in polite conversation, or who to "develop," as she used to say. Not that Edith Devereaux needed to develop anyone; they came to her, heart and lineage in hand. I have to give her credit. In her day Edith ruled the highest social circles of Charleston. I wasn't checking my collar."*

"And what was wrong with your collar?" Leslie asked, squeezing a faint smile.

"Leslie, you know what I mean. At those damn parties I had to even be wary of my posture. Your mother made me watch the angle, or level, or damn; well the line of my collar as a way of checking on my posture"

"Edith used to say: 'It is a river, flowing down the valley at a certain pace and we in Charleston are never in a hurried frenzy, nor are we reluctant to engage in a gentle conversation. George, we do not bound up from the table like some Philadelphia attorney lunging at his quarry. Rather, we here in Charleston take a pace of gentility, sensitivity.' Damn it, she would actually catch me and count the times my collar was not at the correct angle. She said I moved in an ungentlemanly and ungraceful manner! Damn, but that collar would give me such a pain in the neck."

"And downtown?" Leslie raised an eyebrow in his imaginary direction.
"Where downtown?"

"Not where, who?" Leslie asked out loud to the empty seat beside her.
"Who?"

"You! What happened there?" Leslie demanded out loud glancing over to the empty seat.

"Well, what do you think? You're a big girl now. Temptation at first only one though, and only a temptation. It wasn't an act of commission, but, well, rather an act of omission."

"Did you confess this in time?" Leslie asked.

"Oh, you mean before my departing, demise, passing... er, well no. But have no fear dear, I am in good company!"

Leslie fumed. Dad was again getting the best of her. *What do you mean, an act of omission?* She thought sternly frowning at the empty seat.

"I didn't do anything and that's the all of it. You know a painted lady is again at times hard to refuse, but even harder to stay away from."

"Again," Leslie gasped out loud.

"Not at all. It is relatively easier to refuse an offer of accompaniment from a 'lady of the evening' than it is to force yourself to leave those neighborhoods frequented by them and never return. I easily told myself that I was in 'those places of dark reputation,' as your mother would say, for the music and fine liquor and not the flattery of a pass from some sweet young thing."

So that's how it starts, Leslie thought, picturing her father nodding in agreement. It occurred to her that Robert was perhaps in one of those neighborhoods.

"Not that your mother is to blame. But she could have given me some grief. She could have questioned me on many occasions. But that first evening, well, I guess I decided I was no longer quite as important to her as I once was. Yes, that first evening I would have liked a thorough tongue lashing a-la Edith."

"Kind of like a parent's love expressed in punishment of a child?" Leslie asked.

"Exactly," her father replied. *"But then, well, I'm not nor is Edith a child. Don't you think two romantic adults should have an infinite union and communication? I mean to say, it should not be a matter of right and wrong but rather what each partner in the union wants. Dear child of mine, remember both partners should have all their wants and needs fulfilled. Never make an accommodation. Insist on completeness in your relationship, for your partner as well as yourself."*

"Mother would say that could make for awkward moments," Leslie answered.

"There was a time, my dear daughter, a time when I could get anything from your mother, anything, and with a passion! But I worked too much, and she had personal goals she could reach without my input. We slowly grew apart. Accommodations only made the gradual separation easier to bear. One day, she did not notice I had not gone home with her. I was assumed to be coming home later for whatever reason. I had become a fixture in her life, a steady and reliable assumption. And, she had become the same in mine..."

Leslie envisioned her father's figure slowly fading into the leather seat and disappearing.

Leslie shouted out: "And are all loves doomed to eventually fade and disappear? To be crashed against an imperfect life as the rain drops crashed against my windshield?" *Are we all simply a factor of nature, not really capable of choosing our fate? Is true love only a fleeting hope before our destruction? Is the world simply too big, too powerful, too determined, and will have its' way with us?*

It could have been perfect. It once was. She had once been certain of Robert's undying love and she wanted it back into her life. She would have waited for his return. She would have listened to Robert's explanation dutifully and just as dutifully would have believed. She would have accepted Robert's passion within her own. They would have folded together their emotions, each sensing the other's needs, each passion fulfilling the other.

It can never be, she thought. *Robert is not really special, but like all men. Being certain of my true love, he fabricates one brief romance after another. Women are supposed to understand, accept the nature of things while Robert joins the masses to be dashed into oblivion like the rain droplets, their love exhausted. We are to accept, and dash our hopes with them.*

Still, she missed Robert's smile, the scent of his warm body, his firm touch. She ached. Robert was far away, and she was now so very, totally alone.

Chapter 17 Jax

Rain came down in light horizontal sheets across I-95 as Leslie flew north. The continuous subdivisions and shopping centers had long since given up to an earlier Florida; one of deep fields of pines that would some day be newspapers and packaging for the population of those subdivisions. In the night the road had descended into darkness. The road became a place of secrets: a place where reality was hidden in the deformations of reflections on the pavement. The occasional roadside light bounced along the wet pavement, glistening, turning, and twisting reality into a dull and fragmented glow. But to Leslie the alternating darkness and twisted light seemed a comfort. It was a dark place, a place to hide. And Leslie was alone, so very alone. The cell phone in her purse had rung continuously for the last hour, but she had not answered. Leslie wanted to be alone. She was alone again and running toward home.

A dull yellow-orange glow began to grow on the horizon. Road signs announced: Jacksonville 42 miles, then 35 and then 20. Jacksonville had grown into a metropolis in the last 30 years, complete with its beltway, or rather, a half-beltway; the Atlantic Ocean was a considerable barrier to urban expansion on the East. *Should I drive through the center of town on I-95 or take the loop around town on I-295? At 5:30 there should be no traffic, not even in Jax.* At that hour of the morning she could retain her numbness to the world on either road. There would be nothing to detract from her mission. *The shortcut through downtown.*

Presently the skyline of Jacksonville appeared and began to grow in the distance as the sun rose in the East. Pine trees faded away and the water of the St. John's arose along side the road. Ahead lay a silver metal bridge and, to Leslie's dismay, a long line of red brake lights appeared. *Damn construction*, Leslie thought.

As Leslie's car rose slightly as she approached the bridge over the St. John's. Surprisingly, the traffic had now grown to something one could expect to find in the center of a large metropolis. The early dawn hour was not a favorite travel time. Roads were filled with legions of clerks, filers, form handlers, adjusters, accountants, and middle managers that kept the Jacksonville skyline populated. As the last exit passed before the span she contemplated swerving through traffic and darting to a side road to escape. But then, just in time, the line of traffic began to move.

Ahead of her stood a blond Adonis, bare to the waist, directing the cars to move forward. He held a sign on a pole, the red side said stop and the green side go and just as Leslie's car was about to pass him and leave him behind, he turned his sign. Now it said: "STOP."

The Mercedes responded instantly and Leslie was stuck again. Now she could easily see the way to freedom across the river, for she was first in line. Now the bare-chested gatekeeper with his little sign could stare directly at her. Only inches from her window, she could watch his chest as it rose and fell gently with each breath. There he stood barring her way; sign in hand. *Quite taken with himself,* she thought. *I am certain he deliberately pulls his pants down that far to display what he thinks no woman can possibly do without.*

The young man was physically fit. About twenty-five, he worked out and for a few moments Leslie was his captive. He smiled at her. She starred back trying not to show any emotion. But he was an eyeful; a "hunk" Kalley would have called him. His blond hair was pulled back, stuffed under a white hard hat and tied into a tail that brushed his tanned back. Bright blue eyes stared into her car and he grinned. Leslie could not help noticing the slight beads of perspiration that had formed across his chest. They glistened like jewels in the early morning light. His knuckled hand tightly gripped the signpost as if to squeeze compliance to his wishes out of its core. His other hand was tucked deeply into the front of his pants.

* * *

He stood in his black boots, leaning more on his back leg and stared into her car, into her eyes...

For a moment Leslie enjoyed his attention. She found it flattering. *In another time* she thought, *I could certainly have found you interesting.* As though he heard her thoughts, the blond Adonis winked then took a deep breath and held it in a confident pose. Leslie's heart beat rapidly. She blushed with embarrassment. *Yes, you are quite taken by yourself. But you are not the only fish in the sea. And I am not interested in swimming in your little pond.* As delicious as he was to look at, Leslie was tired of men who were in love with themselves. *You are not welcome on my planet and I have grown too wise to visit yours.* Leslie stared in disbelief as she watched his lips move. First he moistened them and then she was certain he had said ,"Cinnamon." She couldn't have heard his voice, but there was no mistaking the form of his lips; "cinnamon."

The Mercedes responded quickly to Leslie's commands. Jumping over the curb, she turned around and sped back down the causeway, from where she had come. The Adonis jumped back into a stack of forms covered in concrete and grease. Leslie sped away. In the rear view mirror, she could see the Adonis mount and start his motorcycle but she didn't care. She would wait no longer in line to entertain any man.

In a moment, Leslie turned right into a treed parking lot along the river. A few fishermen could be seen in the distance, working cast nets out in the flats. Spanish moss in the trees held each beam of the early morning sunlight glistening off of the flowing river water framing them into a thousand twinkling pictures. The fresh smell of early morning greeted her nostrils as she put down the convertible top and turned off the engine. It had stopped raining. The air had the freshness of a bathed baby. Leslie was alone again and she tried to convince herself she liked it that way. *Better,* she thought. She stepped out of her car, closed the door, leaned against the Mercedes, and took another deep breath. *I could have been here once before.*

Before Leslie realized, the Adonis on his chromed-out Harley pulled along side her Mercedes. Inches from her feet, he kicked down the stand and removed his helmet. Golden hair showered down and across his shoulders. He raised his arms to push it out of his eyes and revealed rippling muscles. He smelled like cinnamon and Leslie was frozen in time. He threw his leg over the chopper and faced her, face to face and inches away, but Leslie did not resist. For the moment she did not care. He pressed against her, his sweat against her chest. She breathed with his rhythm. His arms spread across her back and pulled her up and into him. Her breasts pressed tightly to his.

She felt a pressure from his jeans. Leslie sunk into his arms.

Leslie threw her head back, looked up into his steel blue eyes and whispered: "Tell me what to do, I need a truth to believe in, even if it is only the truth of passionate lust. I must have honesty: passion and satisfaction, certainly, but always honesty. Make no false promises and neither shall I."

His face hardened slightly and for a moment Leslie was frightened. He knew he had her. She knew she was his. Then he smiled gently and lowered his mouth to hers. Thrusting into her with his tongue he caressed and searched her every corner. Firmly he held her off the ground. His hand passed down her back and pulled her hips to his. Leslie said: "yes..."

* * *

The Adonis replied: "Green." *Green,* Leslie thought a moment, *your chest is not green.*

"What?" She asked, escaping his hold, pulling back into reality.

"Look Ma'am," the Adonis replied, pointing to the green sign that read GO. "It doesn't get any greener than that!"

Leslie thawed. She found herself in her Mercedes, in traffic, waiting to cross the St. John's. The Adonis was again standing outside her car window.

"Let's go Lady," the Adonis said as he waived her to proceed on. "There are lots of people behind you, let's go!"

Embarrassed, Leslie looked down and stopped making eye contact with his steel blue gaze. She floored the gas pedal. The Mercedes responded with a lunge forward that made the Adonis jump back. In a few minutes she was over the bridge and heading toward Georgia. *Next time,* she thought, *I shall take the beltway.* Soon Jax was a distant, and rapidly fading memory.

Chapter 18 The Wager

Adrift in the Stream gave Robert time to think. In the storm battered boat, soaked with salt water, cold and hungry, he dreamt of Leslie, of the day he had found her...

* * *

Business before pleasure, Robert had thought as he raced up the stairway to his dressing room, *too many parties, too many with the same hungry people. But, that's what makes it profitable and business is for the profit-hungry people.* Tonight they would be hungry for vindication of their lives, like they always are, his mother taught him. As he passed through the mahogany doors to the bedroom suite and turned for the formal clothes closet across the room, he again prepared for the night asking the questions mother had told him to ask of himself. It was as if she were in the room.

What do your friends of this coming evening want in asking you to cocktails? What business do they need? What do they wish you to put into their lives tonight? Are they bored, greedy, lonely, anxious, envious, depressed, what? His mother taught him to think of the feelings of other people before his feelings. Her voice resonated in his head. But she had taught him this somewhat charitable lesson in a business context.

Robert's mother had been known as the paramount party hostess. Tonight he would again be asked how she was, "coming along?" He would avoid phrases like "senile dementia," or simple, "old age" because it pained him so to place those words in a thought about his mother.

An Armani black tux with matching cufflinks and belt buckle, standard black shoes and a white silk shirt. This was another required business party, he had told himself, trying not to be disappointed.

It was only a few minutes' drive over the Northern Bridge and south on Flagler Drive to the Senator's Club at Hut's Point. There had been no reason to put the top down on the Jag. There was no reason for a date to accompany him. He planned to stay only about 45 minutes; just long enough to find out what the Millers were doing that summer. And Bev Miller was the last emotional tie he had with his childhood. It had been just like Bev to have a cocktail party in the middle of the week. She never wanted to miss any weekend affairs with her own party.

As he passed over the bridge a thought struck him. *Perhaps Bev was again playing his Cupid. She could have a thirty-something divorcee waiting innocently for him at the club.* He considered turning north but then continued. His loyalty to Jeffrey and Bev Miller was total.

The carhop took his keys at the entry to the pink stucco landmark. Soon he was rising to the fourteenth floor on the express elevator. On the way up, he quickly combed his hair, checked his nails, viewed his teeth in the wall mirror, and adjusted his belt. As the door opened into the Senator's Club he whispered: "Show time."

The lobby had been full of people. In the lounge beyond a pianist was playing "Misty." Robert remembered wondering why so many people like to pretend. He had expected this night to be like so many others; *filled with idle chitchat from the ladies and grossly exaggerated sexual conquest claims by the men. As time wore on, the claims would become bolder; no doubt embellished by the fine liquors served.*

He was pleased when he passed unnoticed through the columns and to the full wall of windows in the lounge. There, for a moment he looked out over the Lake Worth Lagoon and to Palm Beach beyond. He always loved looking at The Island from a distance. *Beautiful rows of homes filled with beautiful people.* Robert truly loved Palm Beach. He belonged to Palm Beach.

A waiter brought a mixed drink to Robert on a silver tray without being asked. "Your usual, Mr. Robinard," he had said as he presented the drink to Robert.

"Thanks, Mike," Robert replied.

"Quite something to see?" A voice said from behind. "Quite something, wouldn't you say?"

Robert turned to greet an elderly gentleman dressed in a dark blue silk Tux. "What would that be?" Robert asked in reply.

"Why The Island.?"

"It can be exciting. It can be soothing."

"Oh," the elderly man asked, "how can it be soothing?"

"The values, the values of my youth are preserved and alive there. I can see them twinkle in the evening sky."

"You don't look old enough to be Old Palm Beach, young man," the elderly gentleman said, "have you been here long?"

"My whole life," Robert had answered, "several lifetimes. My family is Old People. I'm Robert Robinard," and he extended his right hand.

"Of the Robinard Raiders fame?" asked the elderly gentleman.

"Exactly."

"I am very pleased to at last make your acquaintance. Bev has been trying to get us together for quite a while. Do you suppose you know what she wants? She is a dear, but she can be devious. What do you suppose is her plan for us?"

"Well," Robert replied, "she is always trying to play matchmaker, but I think we can rule that out."

"Well, that's quite all right," the elderly gentleman said jokingly, "you certainly are not the type for me. But let's have some fun with Bev."

"Okay, what do you have in mind?" Robert asked, happy to have some innocent fun at Bev's expense.

"Let's say we are overheard discussing our latest conquests in the field of love. Let's make sure Bev hears of it.

"You mean, make her think we may find lovers without her help?"

"Yes, and more than that," the elderly gentleman answered. "Let's get her busy trying to end a relationship she could never approve of. Here she comes now. Turn your back to her and I'll begin."

Bev was sweeping down upon them from the bar. She obviously had a message for Robert.

"I quite see your point," the elderly gentleman began to say. "Women can be quite ignorant in the war of the sexes. But I cannot take you up on that bet sir; propriety forbids it."

"Forbids what?" Bev demanded, a look of disapproval on her face. She was ready to give someone a thorough tongue-lashing.

"Now you've done me in," exclaimed Robert. "I'm finished."

"Certainly, if you deserve to be." Bev responded. "About what?"

"Well, dear hostess, I have caught this young gallant ready to take my money and the bloom of some fair and unsuspecting young lady," the elderly gentleman reported to Bev. "It seems he is willing to bed the next female to enter through those doors, and wager with me he can."

"Robert I will not have you becoming the kind of scoundrel your drinking partner here is," Bev warned. "Desi was notorious!"

"Is, my dear," the elderly gentleman, Desi stated. "Is, not was."

Bev stepped forward and whispered into Desi's ear loud enough so Robert could also hear: "Your eyes are sometimes bigger than your 'you know what,' down boy!" Robert chuckled. Bev turned to him and winked.

At that moment Gerry Allen entered the club with a beautiful blonde on his arm. "How do you feel about blondes as opposed to brunettes or redheads, young man?" Desi asked. "As long as cuffs and collar match?"

A stunning woman was on Gerry's arm. She was about thirty, five foot five inches tall, and her light blonde hair glowed under the crystal chandeliers. Dressed impeccably in a soft pink gown that emphasized her hips, she had seemed to float across the room. Curiously, as they entered the room Gerry seemed to lose interest in her. As Gerry moved toward Bev his date slowly drifted to another group of party goers.

"Here you are dear," Gerry greeted Bev, "I see anyone who is anyone, or wants to be, is here tonight. How are you my dear?" He gave Bev a peck on the cheek.

"In my prime," Bev answered. Then she nodded toward his date and said: "You seem to be losing someone. Such a stunning woman should not be left unattended in this pool of sharks." Again she winked at Robert.

"Sharks, dear?" Gerry replied. "We all look more like penguins. How is it Bev, that the ladies dress in all colors and we males are installed into black straitjackets at the beginning of the season; not to be rescued until Easter?" He then glanced toward his date. She had migrated to the far side of the lounge. He was perhaps a little relieved at her departure from his arm.

Robert spoke to him: "Ger, old man, how is it that you have only one lady on your arm?"

"The night is young, Bobby Boy." Gerry was way beyond his limit of Black Russians. Robert hated being called Bobby, especially Bobby Boy. He motioned to Mike and nodded toward Gerry. Soon Mike brought another "usual" for Robert and a Black Russian for Gerry.

"Then, perhaps your friend would be interested in the wager, Robert?" Desi asked.

"A wager?" Gerry answered.

"Not a gentleman's wager, certainly." Bev frowned and added flippantly and she moved off to another group of guests.

"Desi wishes to bet me," Robert explained. "Though I feel the wager would be more interesting between the two of you. As for myself, it would be a foolish bet. Better I give Desi my money now and save the pain of embarrassment. You on the other hand, Gerry, you could relieve Desi of his money."

Gerry looked at Robert with a dry poker face. Untrustingly, he tried to size up the situation. Fortunately, the black Russians were having their effect on Gerry and he wandered from the thought. "And what is the wager?" Gerry asked.

"I wished to bet Robert that he could not leave with any young lady he wanted." Desi explained. "Any young lady?"

"And the amount?" Gerry asked.

"Name it." Desi replied. He knew when he had a fish on the line.

"The contents of your pocket in cash." Gerry responded, and removed a stuffed money clip briefly from his right pocket to show his capabilities in rude and foolish betting. Robert grinned. Gerry was known to be a braggart and would always carry too much cash. Robert knew he was hooked.

"Done," Desi replied confidently and gave Robert a wink..

"Then where would you like me to begin?" Gerry asked.

"How about that lovely one in the red sequined gown beside the fountain, not too much for you, I hope?" Desi teased.

"Not much of a challenge there," Gerry answered, "she must be forty. I'll need little effort with her. How about that brunette with the large, or let me put it more tactfully, small bodice over ample bosom?"

"Why not both, if you're so accomplished in love?" Desi challenged.

"Yes Ger," Robert added, "show us how to woo two women at once." *He wouldn't know what to do with the romantic attentions of two women. Gerry will make a perfect fool of himself.* Robert glanced in the direction of Gerry's date. She was pleasantly talking with several people near the fountain. As she sipped

her drink she glanced over at Gerry. She sent Gerry a slight frown. *She is hurt.*
He obviously wants nothing from her. What a cad!

"Watch the pro," Gerry said and strolled over to the fountain. His date smiled for a moment as she watched him approach. Gerry ignored his date and went directly for the forty year old in the red gown.

"I'm Gerry Allen," he said to the woman in the red dress. "A long time friend of Bev and Jeffrey and I can't believe my misfortune not to have met you at one of their bashes before." As predicted by Gerry, the forty year old was very receptive. He was within earshot of Desi and Robert. As he spoke to the woman in red, Robert thought he saw a tear form in his date's eye. Gerry joked with the woman in red for several minutes and stole a hug. Next he moved to another target. His date's eyes watched him as he romanced several women at the party, never speaking with her.

What coarseness. What had begun as harmless party chatter was
beginning to turn into an embarrassing soap opera for Gerry's date. Gerry
planned to abandon her at the party and leave with one of his victims. Robert asked Bev: "Do you know the lady Gerry came with? She seems to be in need of a friend."

"Gerry is up to his old tricks again." Bev responded. "She is Leslie Devereaux, from a long established family of Charleston, South Carolina. The dear now works for Gerry's company and I'm afraid she's going to be hurt. Such things shouldn't happen to that sweet woman, Robert."

"Gerry certainly does not consider her," Desi added.

"I wish someone would teach that cad a lesson." Bev responded, then turned to Robert and said: "Nothing too serious, mind you. Perhaps just trim his tail feathers a bit."

Robert gulped down the last of his drink and signaled to Mike for another. In a moment Mike was at his side. "Mrs. Miller expects Mr. Allen to experience a learning moment this evening. How is our friend Micky?" Robert could command the loyalty of the help. He was always the one who thanked and congratulated the chef after an outstanding meal with a visit to the kitchen and a handshake stuffed with a hundred dollar bill. His admiration for the wait staff was also well known and well rewarded. The next black Russian served to Gerry would have a little something extra added.

Robert then picked up a pad of paper from the bar and wrote a quick message to his driver Raul and gave it to Mike to deliver. Next he headed for Gerry.

Robert found Gerry back with the forty something year old in the red gown beside the fountain. Gerry's next drink found him there also. Mike made certain he was standing by with a towel when Gerry turned a slight shade of blue and deposited the contents of his stomach into the flowing fountain. As the crowd gasped Robert took Gerry by the elbow to steady him. "Good god old man," Robert shouted. "Can't seem to hold your liquor tonight. Here, let's get you cleaned up."

They led Gerry by the elbows to the kitchen where they held his head under the sink faucet. "Try to take shallow breaths, old man," Robert instructed him. "Breathe slowly."

As Gerry regained his composure, Robert sat him on a chair and rested his head on the sink. "You're looking better now, Mr. Allen," Mike added after a few moments. "Soon you'll be fine and ready for our boiled squid hors d'oeuvres." He grinned at Robert as Gerry moaned and resumed his activities with the sink.

"We better call it a night, Ger," Robert offered. I'll say your good-byes and make arrangements. Rest your head." Gerry mumbled some inaudible approval and Robert left him in the care of Mike.

Robert went directly to Bev with an innocent explanation who winked approval. Next Bev approached the charming Miss Devereaux, Gerry's date of the evening. Even with the unbearable treatment she had received she was genuinely concerned for Gerry. "Will he be all right?" Leslie asked Bev. From a distance Robert thought her voice was perhaps the gentlest voice he had ever heard.

"Certainly, he only needs rest now." Bev answered faking concern, and then added: "I've taken the liberty of calling a car. Raul will take you home dear. I'll stay here and tend to Gerry." Leslie's eyes were moist. As she turned and left, Robert could not help noticing the soft freckles on her left shoulder and the way her gown swayed with her walk. Her Southern accent stuck in Robert's ear the rest of the evening...

* * *

Robert woke from his nap to find Tanny shaking his arm. "Here, put this rag between your ear and the bulkhead, otherwise you'll pound your brains silly in this sea. It's going to be a long wait."

Chapter 19 Puzzle

Jason was up early that day, even for him. Predawn greeted his eyes as they opened. The smell of early morning in the suburbs filled his nostrils; moisture, green trees and car oil, had successfully found their way into Jason's open window. He always slept with a window open. Fresh air helped him sleep and an open window could give an early hint of any changes coming his way.

Usually, he ran two miles before breakfast, something left over from his Marine Corps experience. But today for some reason he felt compelled to get to the office early. A shave, shower and shirt, and out of the apartment and down to the parking lot below.

Jason flipped on the car radio. A reporter was saying: "A strong storm last evening, leaving many of us soaking and floating. Some western communities got out their boats after receiving up to 11 inches of rain in 4 hours. And it looks like more is coming."

Jason turned up the volume.

"A tropical front off of Puerto Rico shows signs of circulation. The National Weather Service has dispatched a hurricane hunter plane out of that island to investigate. If the front develops into a storm, it will be number one of the season and the earliest on record. And let's not even think of this visitor becoming a hurricane, but if it does, it will be named Agnes."

As if on cue a sheet of rain crossed the road and momentarily blocked Jason's view. *All too familiar,* Jason thought. *With Robert down in Bimini and Jessup up to his old tricks the last thing I need is a hurricane to mix things up.*

He had survived hurricane Andrew as a child in Homestead. He had lain under his bed as the roof lifted off. The storm planted a new red Ford pickup from a dealer's lot three blocks away in the family's living room. Jason had asked his dad if he could keep the pickup truck. Fortunately no one was hurt and for the twelve-year-old boy living in a tent in the back yard for two weeks it was an adventure.

Only there were no trees, none anyway with branches or leaves remaining. No green bushes either. Across the street a neighbor's citrus grove had lost all of its' leaves and bark. Debris propelled for hours by 200mph winds had stripped them clean. The trees stood barren and white in the daylight. In the fields no animal that was smaller than a horse or cow survived. A surreal landscape had appeared overnight.

Now as an adult, he worried about the power of a hurricane let loose on the Island. *Crap, the flying glass shards from thousands of windows alone*, he thought to himself, *better to not talk about it at the office. We'll be busy enough with Jessup and don't need Agnes to worry about.*

He arrived at RRR in time to greet the janitorial staff hurriedly exiting the building. "It's a great morning, isn't it?" He asked Ramon with a friendly smile. Ramon gently smiled back but didn't respond. Instead he slightly averted his eyes as he passed but Jason could feel Ramon's shy gaze study him as he entered the building. A recent escapee from Castro's Cuba, Ramon was still uncomfortable speaking English.

The security scan recognized him, chimed and automatically released the glass door. The system recorded the time of day he entered and saved his picture. Anyone entering had to be recognized. It made Jason's job easier. The offices of RRR were not open to the public.

Today Jason would be occupying Robert's private office. From behind closed doors he would monitor the day's business activities. He passed accounting, assessment and security mini-suites as he headed for the executive suite. There was no door into the executive suite, only two five foot tall Chinese ceramic statues of lions to pass between. The pink marble floor transformed into a deep pile money green carpet that muffled all sounds, giving a degree of privacy to each work station and private office. At the end of the walk were the double doors to the boardroom. Jason turned right and through Leslie's office to Robert's inner sanctum. The door to Robert's office was rather common when compared to the rest of the offices of RRR. It was stained a light oak, *rather open and friendly,* Jason mused to himself. It opened freely on polished brass hinges. Robert's office was a mix of social and business trophies. But none got in the way of business. In the center of the room was a conversation area framed by two immense, upholstered cranberry leather couches opposing each other and separated by a hand carved square coffee table. Robert's massive mahogany desk was unobtrusively set in the far corner, surrounded by four matching chairs. Jason had spent many days there in "power it out meetings,' as Robert liked to call them. And he had slept on a couch more than once when critical communications were likely to be needed. He imagined he might be spending the night there again, soon. Jason headed for the desk.

He slumped down into Robert's blood red crushed velvet executive armchair. He sunk into its soft contoured padding. He spun around and leaned back. The chair responded to his orders as if he were Robert and presented to Jason a panoramic view of the office suite. The west wall was open glass looking into a tropical garden. There were no seams in the glass and no framing visible. The effect was one of no boundaries, limits, or exclusions. A viewer had the distinct impression of being in the garden, not in an office. In the evening, landscaping illumination continued the impression in muted, alternating tones of green and shadow.

The north and south walls were constructed of simple stucco, painted a cool, pastel salmon and sea foam green respectively. Everywhere, and in an apparent random order, hung reminders of past accomplishments. The mounted head of an Indian water buffalo, a set of carved and painted wooden Easter eggs, trophies for swimming and tennis, black and white photos of unrecognizable people apparently having a wonderful time water skiing on a freshwater lake in central Florida from the 50's, a straw hat with the word "Bahamas" stitched with straw, and watercolor landscapes of the Keys from the 40's in muted tones, hung as if evidence.

Jason had heard Robert explain some of his treasures. But Robert changed the stories each time in telling. One day the eggs would be a gift from an old friend of his father's from the South Pacific. The next they would be objects he bought in a blind auction for a ridiculous amount of money, but for a worthy cause. It seemed to Jason, Robert wanted to keep his precious memories near to him and also very private.

The eastern wall was pure, here and now, Robert Robinard, Jason thought, *always watching the money.* It was solid glass again, but unlike the garden wall it looked into the offices of RRR. It was a double wall of glass. With the click of a switch Robert could electrically charge the ionized gasses trapped between the glasses and reduce the transparent qualities of the wall to almost zero. *More powerful than simply closing a drape,* Jason thought to himself.

The next order of daily business waited. Jason removed his phone from his pocket, called up his e-mail and viewed his messages. There were the usual; some from friends, some junk, and one, curiously, from King Kong. Jason smiled. No doubt this was the confirmation of Jessup's capture. He opened it and read:

Hey Jase:
Got no clouds in the sky today, great weather for a visit, but we are still waiting for our friends to arrive. Could there be some engine trouble? Anyway, the champagne is chilled and waiting. I have the presents ready. It is going to be a great party. So, what's the hold up? Waiting to hear.

King Kong

Jason frowned. *Where the hell is that bastard? Jessup hasn't taken the bait. He was not in Hong Kong looking for the wool supplier, making his side deals, exposing himself as the bastard he was. "Got no clouds," that meant there were no glitches, problems to get in the way. "The champagne is chilling," everything is ready, "have presents ready," the police were ready to make arrests. "Waiting to ear,"* concerned Jason. The obscured reference to an ear meant that King Kong was considering the possibility of a breach of security, you cannot believe all you hear; the hustle is on. *But who's hustle?* Jason wondered.

He hit the reply button and wrote:

Kingy:

Got no answers for you right now. I just got up. After my run I'll make some calls. Keep your ear to the e-mail. Ciao

Jase

He reviewed his message before sending. *Right now will let King Kong know I'm concerned by the delay. Jessup should be there right now. I just got up, and after my run, will tell them to wait patiently, I'm busy. Keep your ear to the e-mail, will be easy. Something definitely is not right, watch for the hustle.* Jason sent the message. Both considered there was a possibility of breach of security in e-mail communications. Both would now multiple route any further communications through multiple servers automatically.

Jason returned to his e-mail list page. A new one had appeared from Robert. He struck refresh and it appeared again. He stuck refresh again and it appeared 30 more times. *Multiple routing to the rescue,* he thought. Jason scrolled down to about the middle of the pile and opened the message. It read:

Jason:

Just now got within reach of cell phone tower to send this message. Tanny and I out in the stream in Boomer, engines dead, out of fuel, but CG and Sea Tow are expected soon, fuel stolen in Bimini. Can't reach Leslie. Keep ears open.

Robert

Just to be certain, Jason opened three more e-mails at random. All were the same. There had been no compromise, no manipulations of the message. Multiple routing saw to that. Using a certain e-mail address Robert had sent his message including a virus that accessed several dozen other e-mail addresses within the host memory. The message was sent to those machines with a new virus, one that would scan for patterns, variations in patterns, and compare with the computers in the e-mail loop. Each computer had a different virus scan and security search program in its memory. Each machine would share the results with Robert's computer at RRR. And all this was done without the user of the machines ever knowing they had been a part of a security routine. If a hacker gained access to one or even two or three computers he would still have no way of knowing of the others.

Jason sat back in Robert's chair and took a long breath. Suddenly he felt older and a little worn. He knew it was going to be a long day. He needed Leslie. Jessup was loose and Robert was adrift in the Atlantic. Someone had sabotaged Boomer, or at least stolen fuel. But he could not rule out sabotage, not with the other circumstances surrounding the event.

Jason decided he could not wait. He called Leslie's home. There was no answer. He tried several more times and her cell phone also with no success. *Either she's not answering the phone or worse*, he thought. He did not want to consider anything worse. *Sometimes I hate it when I'm always right,* he thought to himself. *I knew it was a good idea to get to the office early.*

He smiled to himself and began to analyze. He took a pad of paper out of Robert's desk and started making observations, one per piece of the puzzle and arranging them in an assumed chronological order. When he wrote, "no contact with Leslie," he pushed the note up to the top of Robert's desk to begin another column. It happened to come to rest in front of something new on the desk: a gold-framed picture of two little three-year-old girls with green eyes. They were sitting on their proud father's lap, staring, smiling into the camera. Robert was beaming with pride.

"Crap, not again!' Jason exclaimed to the empty office, worried about Leslie. His voice echoed through the building, unanswered. *It's going to be a long day.*

Chapter 20 Charleston

The sun was high above the pines when Leslie's car sped over Rantowles

Creek. On either side of the Savannah Highway sunbeams glistened like a million

small sparkling jewels off the stiff tall grass of the tidal waters. A familiar aroma

greeted her, fresh mud unveiled at low tide released smells of sea life, welcoming

her home.

Leslie looked out her window at the passing tidal basin and estuary as if

for the first time. During her long absence she had come to expect beaches and

rocks clearly defining the boundary between land and water. But here in the low

country, the land slowly, reluctantly, gave up its presence to the salty ocean.

Creeks meandered for miles, muddy and briny, with no clear boundary to show

where land ends and water begins. Imaginary banks are hidden in tall grass.

Rivers change with the rain and tides. And all is covered with endless grass.

Leslie took a deep breath and smiled. She was home.

"The sea's nursery," her father called it. The salty wet grasslands were the

breeding ground and nursery for the abundance of fish and shellfish in the low

country. As a little girl, she had frequently accompanied her father on

backcountry fishing trips. Her father had taught her to fly cast like a pro. "With

confidence, Les," he would prompt and wink. In the tall grass up to her knees

standing in rubber, leg length boots, the seven-year-old would twist and snap her

whole body around to send a fly lure out over the still water. Frequently there

would be an explosion of activity from beneath as a fish struck wildly, answering

a primeval instinct to devour a moving object of particular combinations of

colors.

"The secret's in the feathers, Les," he taught. "The fish know what tastes

good. We just watch what they strike, maybe a red bug with a long green tail, and we make one. Sure, the fish knows it's not a bug, not the right noise and hey, it flies real strange for a tasty bug, but then, fish are not smart, not really. There are still so many left in the grass waters because most fishermen are even more stupid. So you see, the fish are hungry and they see the colors and, well they stop thinking. They strike and as soon as they feel that hook, they wake up real fast, but it's too late for them. Remember to count to three and then pull two quick yanks to set the hook. After that it's just a matter of working the fish until it tires and just gives up."

Leslie wasn't always sure that fish weren't smart. More often than not, they returned from a fishing trip by way of the fisherman's wharf at Stono Marina. Nicely cleaned and dressed fish and shrimp all wrapped in white butcher's paper would be presented as the trophy of the day to her mother. They never returned from a fishing trip empty handed. "We are real fishermen," her father used to say. "We come in when we have made our catch," and would wink his eye.

Leslie crossed the Ashley River Bridge. In the distance, lay her childhood neighborhood. Soon she knew she would be driving up oak and palmetto palm lined narrow roads. Each home guarded, enclosed, by wrought iron fencing. Impeccable verdant green landscaping partially hid each home from view of the road.

Her mother's house was on the corner. A large, white columned second story porch sheltered an arched atrium below and turned the corner with the house until it ended into a three story wooden minaret which Mother had turned into the music room. "Now all of Charleston can listen to you practice," she used to say as Leslie sat one hour each day in front of the bent glass windows, watching the hummingbirds outside, striking the keys with a deliberate force as to inflict pain in the ear of all who were foolish enough to stop and listen. But mother always had her way.

Leslie hesitated a moment at the front gate. Not that she was afraid to enter, not any more. She and mother had it out four years ago when she left for New York. Mother had not wanted her "tramping round that town populated by nothing more than jayhawkers and carpetbaggers." But when father passed, Leslie returned rather victorious from the Big Apple. She had not "succumbed to the temptations and villainy" of New York, but prospered, though she admitted to her Mom it was time for a change. After the funeral she moved to Boca.

Leslie wanted her mother's comfort. She wanted to be held, cuddled in her mother's lap like a child whose playmate has hurt her feelings. She wanted to hear her mother say: "There, there, my child, it will all be all be right tomorrow. That so-and-so is not of our quality. He and his kind are something we all must bear gracefully, so wipe away your tears and smile at the world." But Leslie did not want mother to say: "I'h told you so. There is nothing in Palm Beach that we don't have right here. And if I'h must say, we do it better!"

Sandra's wedding. What a perfect excuse to return, if not victoriously, at least conveniently.

* * *

Leslie decided to forgo a grand entry into the front yard and instead turned the Mercedes into the service alley behind the house. In a moment the car was crawling down a shell rock path and turning into an unpaved parking space usually reserved only for the gardener or pool service boy. Cele, mother's housemaid would never park in the back. "Rear parking is ok for some folks," she would proclaim to anyone who raised the question, "but any soul that keeps up with that woman has the right to park like a veteran!" Leslie's mother was known for her short patience at times. Cele would park out front with the other honored quests if Leslie's mother did not want to clean her own toilets. She pondered a moment before she turned off the engine. Mother could not see the parking space. It was sheltered from view of the main house by the gardener's shed and tall bushes. *Mother did not ever want to admit that her kind of people ever had need of the common things in life like cleaning, fertilizing, and maintenance. Edith,* Leslie thought as she looked through the windshield, *are you to be kind or victorious today?*

Leslie shut off the engine and got out of the car. Quickly, she passed around the deep green bushes and found herself in the garden. The distance seemed shorter to Leslie, and before she could react there was mother, on her knees, bending over some flowers, instructing them in a demanding voice: "Don't listen to the sun. It never knows what day it makes. We need to bloom this weekend, not now."

She was dressed appropriately for a weekday morning in Charleston, if one was intending to stay home and the only callers were unexpected. Her white linen sleeveless top with a Nehru collar and green gardening pants were protected from the errant dirt and dust by a cotton floral salmon cobbler's apron. A large and wide brimmed straw sunbonnet with a pink silk scarf that wrapped the bowl of the hat, traveled around her chin, emerging on the other side adorned the outfit. *To keep away freckles.* Leslie remembered the freckle examinations she had to bear at the end of a day of play. "Did you keep on your bonnet, young miss?" Looks not," she frequently heard from mother. *Robert said my skin was like milk.*

Leslie hesitated. For a woman in her seventies her mother still had no freckles. *Inhuman,* Leslie thought, *possibly in league with the devil.* "Surprise," Leslie announced as she strode to her mother.

"Leslie my dear," Edith exclaimed and still on her knees, she smiled and threw her hands out toward Leslie. Then her expression turned to one of false concern. "You are a little late. Had engine trouble?"

Leslie was immediately taken back. "Late?" she asked, confused. The greeting froze her.

"Why you were expected last month, or maybe next fall, but I knew you were coming," her mother replied as she stood up. "Besides that charming

Kalley from your office called this morning looking for you. She sounds to be a reliable assistant. Am I not right?" Already digging for information?

"Why mother, I decided last evening it was too long since we have spent time together on the porch, and besides Sandra is getting married, again. I shouldn't want to miss this performance." Leslie paused and gave her mother a hug. "My, mother, don't you look younger every day. I am truly hopeful I will be as young as you when I meet my golden years." They exchanged deep hugs in the flower garden, two women who had been separated far too long.

"If only that were possible, dear daughter. However I am afraid you must share my genes with those of your father and for all his charms he was not one who held up well. There is a possibility some of those bad Yankee habits he taught you have ruined your complexion." Leslie thought a moment about her freckles, the ones Robert found so very attractive. "But come on girl, let's get out of the sun." With that Edith grabbed Leslie's arm and walked her to the rear porch.

"Cele, come see who has come for a visit," Edith shouted out as they climbed the four steps to he wooden porch. " Can you get us some iced tea, and make it with a mint leaf ?"

From inside came a voice, loud, low, and stern: "Get it yourself if you in such a rush! I'h'm busy cleaning!"

"Cele, I said, iced tea," Edith yelled back, frowning more with each second that passed. She stamped her foot on the wooden porch and it reverberated like a drum across the rear of the house.

"Hold your water," came the voice from inside, "I 'll fix it right soon."

"I should fire that woman," Edith grumbled as she sat down on the white wicker rocking chair. "She does not know how to show a lady the proper respect."

"I hear that," came the voice from within. "You be lucky to get anybody to put up with your ranting" With that remark the screen door opened and out came a black lady of about three hundred pounds wearing a cotton dress large enough for three Leslies and looking as if she was ready for a battle. Cele plopped down the serving tray she was carrying on the wicker table. On it was a chilled, wet pitcher of tea with a sprig of mint floating on top, surrounded by three tall glasses, sugar bowl and four long silver tea spoons. "It be fresh and sweet," Cele announced as if to warn that she would take no criticism of her preparation. Then she sat down next to Edith in a wicker chair. "Whew," Cele said, "it be getting warmer ever day." She began to fan herself with a newspaper and turned to Leslie: "Been waiting on you, child."

Leslie bent over and gave Cele a peck on the cheek. "Missed you too, dearest Cele," she said gently in Cele's ear. "I've been away far too long."

"Child we is your home," Cele whispered back, "we is always here for you." Cele leaned back in her chair and looked hard into Leslie's eyes. "Is ev'rything' right with you?" she asked suspiciously.

"Sandra, is getting married and I thought..." Leslie tried to answer, but Cele interrupted.

"Sandra, phew, you not coming all the way for her, child. Who you think you fooling?" Cele replied as she pulled back her head and surveyed Leslie with suspicious eyes. Both women waited for an answer.

"Let us say it was time for a time out," Leslie reached for a glass. The other women looked at each other with knowing expressions, but decided not to press the matter, not yet anyway.

"Charleston is the perfect place for a break, dear," Edith offered, to put her daughter at ease, "and we have everything the big cities have dear. Why don't you stay and enjoy?"

"You mean for a while, don't you?" Leslie asked coyly. "Mother I have duties, relationships..."

But she could not finish. To hide her eyes from direct view of the women she raised her glass to her face. The women looked knowingly at each other again.

"Well, Spoleto is here again. Your visit could not be more timely arranged dear. We are to parties or concerts every evening. The club is buzzing with affairs. It is the most wonderful time for Charleston. Do you remember, dear?"

"We is?" Cele asked accusingly. "I seem to remember I go shopping and such and you get out only."

"Poor black folk!' Edith exclaimed. "Why woman you hold some of the first shares of ATT which my daddy gave you for your birthday. They must have split six times since then."

"Eight," Cele replied, smiled a pleased smile and looked out into the distant garden, ignoring Edith's obvious aggravated frown.

"I suspect I'll be with Sandra first, it is after all her wedding," Leslie answered. She hoped to derail any attempt by her mother to organize something or fix her up with some eligible bachelor. "I'm certain we will be busy the next two days. I'll need to call her immediately." Leslie desperately wanted to keep her mother out of her business.

"Oh, dear me, I believe there will be no need of that call," her mother answered and pointed with her glass of iced tea to the figure emerging from the hedges. "It's Taylor, Leslie. I suspected she would be over as soon as you returned, but this is record time even for her." Taylor Morgan had grown up next door to Leslie and had been somewhat of a younger sister to her. At 28 she was still living at home, unmarried. Taylor was dressed in a skimpy pastel pinstripe tube top darted in the back and white low-rise hipsters with a split leg and white tennis shoes. She dressed as if she was 17.

As Taylor crossed the back yard, she let out a squeal as she threw out her arms, "Eeek, Leslie dear, I'h can't believe it's you." She waved and crossed the yard in record time and bounded up the porch steps, bubbling over with enthusiasm.

Leslie said nothing but beamed a huge welcoming smile and opened her arms for the embrace. Taylor crashed into her with a bear hug. "I just can't believe it, I mean we are all together again, like old times, and we'll all be together tonight. Eek! It is just so perfect!" Leslie thought she smelled bourbon and momentarily pulled back to look into Taylor's eyes. *She's drunk at 10:30 in the morning!* Leslie thought. *Does anyone know?*

"My sweet little adopted sister. Why you haven't changed in years," she exclaimed in a warm greeting designed to mask what she was thinking. "Quickly, sit down and tell me all about it, I mean everything. How is everyone? What new beau do you have wrapped around your little finger?"

"You got our message! Sandra is getting married, and to Mark. Can you believe it? Isn't it just too dreamy? I mean, like, they are the perfect match! They look just like those tiny little statues they put on top of wedding cakes. Can you believe?" Taylor answered as she sat down. Leslie sat next to her and wondered if her face could disguise her disbelief. Leslie glanced at Cele and Edith to see if they were as confused by Taylor's remarks. But both just looked at each other with a raised eyebrow. Leslie realized they were not surprised by Taylor's behavior. "And what of you?' Taylor asked in Leslie's direction.

Leslie swallowed and summoned all her southern charm to avoid telling the circle of women the truth about Robert. He was a philanderer, but she did not want him to become the topic of one of Sandra's performances. Sandra could represent herself as definitive authority in matters of the heart. *She is after all far more experienced with men than I,* Leslie thought sarcastically.

"Robinard Resources keeps me busy. We are making money and isn't that what it's all supposed to be about?" Leslie replied with a gentle smile and soft voice. "And my beau is a dream."

Taylor reached forward and pointed to the tennis bracelet on Leslie's left wrist. She had forgotten to take it off at home last evening. Eight carats of flawless diamonds mounted in platinum from Robert spoke volumes about his love for her and his business skills. But to Leslie's mind, the diamonds were a screen; a method of hiding the truth.

Taylor stared a moment, speechless, at the bracelet as if it were a trophy, and then grinned. "And does he have big hands?" she asked Leslie, as she shyly grinned and looked about the circle of women for an approving reaction and hopefully agreeing countenances. Taylor began touching the bracelet with her index finger covetously, if subconsciously.

But she was met with mildly disapproving stares from the two senior members of the circle. "Really, child, Edith scolded, a little under her breath. "Your proposition is a little too invasive for a Southern lady to speak, at least this early in the day." Edith looked for Cele to approve of her chiding remark and received an approving nod.

"Miss Edith, I only meant he must be a powerful…"

"Robert is a dream come true," Leslie interjected. "He is tall, handsome, powerful, gentle, and quite wealthy. He is a true Southern gentleman. And I make certain he adores me," she added with a knowing smile.

"Then you are here, my sweet sister, for doubly intriguing purposes," Taylor announced as she bounded up from her chair. "We shall have a fine wedding and an opportunity to further test Master Robert's fidelity and devotion," she declared as she circled the group of seated friends. "Tell me Leslie, how much information and direction did you leave unsaid in your rapid departure for Charleston? Do we expect a telegram, pleading phone calls, or perhaps a wonderful personal visit from your Master Robert? Can I help tease and torture the man?" Taylor paused, raised her left hand above Leslie's head and snapped her fingers. "Let's test his mettle," she declared.

For a moment, all eyes were on Leslie. Edith's face slowly changed from an expression of mild confusion at Taylor's suggestion to one of a mild and approving grin. Cele's lower lip thrust slightly forward and over her upper lip, as it always did when she was beginning to figure out some child's weak excuse for bad behavior.

Taylor raised both arms up and down and bounced crying: "What a perfectly evil plan, why Leslie, we can have such devilish fun with your beau. I should be making arrangements. Sarah and Debbie must know of this right off. Oh, we're going to have such a wonderful time, a wedding and all."

"Well, get to it girl," Cele ordered, again wearing her poker face.

Edith looked at Cele in momentary disbelief and then added with enthusiasm: "Why yes, yes, get going girl. You don't have much time. Only about four hours!"

Leslie froze in disbelief. *What a preposterous idea!. I'll have no part in it.* But then she noticed her mother's wink of an eye and thought caution the better part of valor. She paused, regained her composure and asked: "And what about four hours from now?"

"Why Sandra's already reserved a table for just us girls at the club, 3:45, for drinks and plan-making." Taylor replied. "Oh, I forgot to tell you, well we are going to have a wonderful time. Isn't it just wonderful, all together again. I better get going. See you at the club, and bring your best steamy stories about Robert."

Leslie watched in disbelief as Taylor hopped down the four wooden steps and skipped of to her house turning every few steps to wave good-by.

Edith broke the silence: "Only middle morning and she has the scent of bourbon on her lips. Leslie, it seems you are going to rival Sandra as the center of attention. Better get some rest child, you are going to need it."

Chapter 21 Changes

"Watch that step," Cele cautioned as she and Leslie ascended the staircase. Her heart ached for Robert, for the old Robert. Her Robert. Knots formed in her stomach. Tears invaded her eyes and she brushed them away. Leslie missed a step.

"Carful now," Cele warned. "This one been loose for two years. Can't get your mom to hire no carpenter, she says they's too dirty. Won't let 'em in the house."

"Cele," Leslie asked, knowing her old friend would be truthful, if blunt, "I truly hate to ask this question, but, well, how long has dear Taylor had a problem with liquor?"

Cele turned to look back at Leslie. Her burden of fresh linens hung over the stair rail and threatened to fall to the hall below before a big brown arm wrestled them into submission. She was the woman who could always handle a situation even when her own natural mother could not. "You know she's been gettin that way for years," Cele whispered.

"But she is so, well..." Leslie answered, not knowing how to put into words the concern she felt.

"You finding her embarrassin, I bet," was Cele's sharp response. "You'll be more embarrassed later, I reckon. It seem to always be ok if a man gets so drunk they makes a fool of themselves, but a woman right long beside them, well, people say she must be some floozie. That's what people always think. Same drink, mind you, but different prisons each. Oh, Lord." Cele shook her head.

Leslie decided to change the subject. "I have missed this house," Leslie sighed.

"I be staying here weekdays now," Cele announced at the top of the stairs. "None home at my house till Friday," Cele explained and then added: "and Miss Edith needs me."

Together in silence they remade Leslie's bed with fresh linens, neither knowing what to say although each felt an exploding need to explain things. Cele walked out of the room and threw the old linens down the stairway with one big arm. Upon returning she began.

"Child, you sit down right here, I need to educate you." Leslie knew that tone of voice. She sat on the edge of the bed and folded her hands, waiting for her chastisement as much out of curiosity as respect.

A whiff of jasmine passed into the room from the garden below. Cele sat down beside her and placed her right hand on Leslie's, as so many 'educational sessions,' as Edith liked to call them, began.

"Child," Cele began in a low and somber voice, looking deep into Leslie's eyes, "men and women are different. The world thinks it can just add a woman to the world and they be just like men. And it ain't never be different for a woman. Work or at home, it's that way always. They never seems to care about our needs. Look at poor Taylor she don't want to go drunk, it just happens, like with anybody."

"Why doesn't she get some help?" Leslie asked. "There are programs to help."

"Why a lady ain't going to stand up in front of no room full of strangers and say: Oh... I ain't no good, an I don't think about who I hurt. She just ain't! A lady needs friends, real ones, an hugs, an understanding. If they don get it they just go from bad to worse. Chronic they is called."

"My dear Cele, have you adopted another lost soul?" Leslie smiled.

"We have," Cele answered. "Miss Edith and me. Someone got to do it and Lord knows that family of hers ain't no help. Changes must come, they gotta be made."

Leslie now knew why Cele had moved in. For years her mother had consumed too much alcohol and always at the most inappropriate times. Now it seemed Edith was getting the Cele cure. And it apparently was working. The bottle of Chablis that had been a fixture in the kitchen all of Leslie's childhood was notably missing.

Leslie smiled, leaned over Cele's forehead and kissed her. "Dearest Cele, you are an angel, our knight in shining armor, here to save us all," she said.

"What saving do you need?" Her eyes piercing Leslie's. "Why is you really here, girl?" She turned to face Leslie and grabbed Leslie's chin with her strong, firm hand. "Don lie to me now! What's drivin you?"

"Why haven't you gotten to sleep yet, dear?" It was Edith at the top of the stairs.

"We is just getting to the bottom of things," Cele answered in her commanding voice. "Miss Leslie got something goin' on with her."

"Oh," Edith gasped and sat down on the bed. "Now dear," she began, "tell. What's up."

"Nothing, really," Leslie answered. "I just felt it was time for a brief change, a hiatus from the normal. That's all."

"It is what we all want one time or another," Leslie's mother replied. "I think the question is why. Why, dear, why do you want a change? Oh, I suppose you now think we are just two old nosy women with nothing better to do with our time. But, dear, we can help. Just tell us the awful story."

Leslie thought a moment. *How can I tell my mother and Cele I have fallen in love with a married man, even if he has not been truthful with me?* "It's only the smallest of situations," she replied, her heart beat between the words. "I returned to Charleston for a little time out, a change of pace, that is all." Leslie swallowed hard. "Really, I don't want to talk about it." She stared at the floor.

Edith stood, folded her hands, smiled, and said: "Dearest daughter, we in Charleston have all the benefits of humanity found anywhere else: love, divorce, thieves, friendships, business. We like to think we live through them better, with a certain flare, Better than anywhere else. That is all. Perhaps we can offer you some of our Charleston savior-faire to fit needs as they surface from those evil depths of discouragement. We party with friends to re-enlist fond memories and bury the ugly ones. You know dear; cultural denial. Changes however, may be something else indeed."

Leslie paled.

"Well, child, it now time to get some sleep. You been up and driving all night and you don't make much sense with what you are saying," Cele announced, winking at Edith. "We be down in the kitchen when you wake up." With that, the two old ladies left the room. Leslie breathed a sigh of relief.

Leslie showered before getting in bed. She found the hand soap in the wall tray, just where she left it years before. The towels hadn't changed, nor the bath mat. Her room was just the way she left it. Nothing had changed. Nothing but her. *What a curiosity*, she thought as she slid beneath the linen sheets. *I have come to a place that never changes... to find change.*

Chapter 22 True Love Waits

Leslie buried her nose into the pillow. The familiar smell of home entered her nostrils and for a moment she was transformed into the girl who once slept in that bed so very long ago. It was an easy journey back in time. By order of her mother, who said she always knew Leslie would return someday to Charleston, nothing had been changed in that bedroom belonging to her once distant child. But it was that smell that sent Leslie spinning into the past.

Her bed smelled of the flowers and the earth of the backyard garden. Of freshly turned soil and pollen, of herbs drying on hooks from the ceiling of the rear porch, of bread dough rising and pies cooling. And of faint salty breezes from the ocean on bright Southern days. Most importantly for good dreams, it smelled faintly of those loved ones who labored to make everything be the way it should and would and must be. Like a baby chick knows its nest, Leslie knew she was home. It smelled like home.

Slowly Leslie spun down into a dream world and she did not resist. Everything was right in her world as she softly lost consciousness. All her desires would be fulfilled in this never-ending land. It was a place without questions or answers; only satisfactions. And she welcomed the transformation of her existence as her world darkened behind her eyelids.

Leslie dreamt...

* * *

She felt soft, warm sand between her toes. A fading burgundy light cast out the yellow tones of the surf rocks. Robert appeared. He was in his white swimsuit, the one he had worn on their weekend trip to Bimini. Suddenly he held her by the arms. Strongly he pressed her to his chest. Leslie's foot slipped. She realized the waves were beneath her, lapping the hot sand. Leslie fell into

Robert's strong grasp and let him carry her to a cove in the rocks. They fell together to a powdery bed. Nestled and unseen at the water's edge they were alone in the world. Robert threw himself over her and began to unbutton her bodice with kisses.

Momentarily overpowered by Robert, Leslie tensed. "No, not here, not yet," she whispered to him. But she did not look into his eyes, for she knew he would discover the truth in them. She wanted him, yet she pushed against him. He forced her to kiss and she felt the power in his hips. They took a deep breath together.

* * *

A strange sound came from the darkness beyond her dream and Leslie turned to see. In that moment, Robert was gone. In her dream she was alone as a cold wave passed over her stomach. Startled, Leslie got to her feet and called Robert's name. Then she saw him. He was standing by a large rock, dressed in a black tuxedo, speaking into a cell phone, unaware of her. She turned and ran into the burgundy sunset, into the ocean.

Suddenly, Leslie was 14 again. Father was waiting for her downstairs. Cele was yelling, getting her ready for the cotillion, her first.

"Don't wiggle child, hold still. I've been doin it long time….an thats why they come good," she announced as she pulled and teased Leslie's hair.

Cotillion was being held in the Huguenot Hall that evening. "The steps up from the street," she remembered her father had told her as he took her arm, "are the steps of her passing from childhood into young womanhood." Inside all the women were dressed in white and Leslie wondered how Robert would ever find her. Dizziness overcame her as she spun around looking for him.

In an instant, Robert magically took her hand for the first dance. The opening waltz spun dresses around the room, into and out of young men's arms. Leslie was at last fulfilled. Robert smiled into her eyes and just before he spoke darkness descended. As if unwilling, but compelled, Robert stepped back, out of her arms and into the darkness.

Leslie dreamed about the special treat offered that night, a musical carousel. All couples were running toward it as it appeared in the center of the dance floor. They called to each other and to Leslie, but alone, she hesitated. The carousel's music began. It started to revolve. Leslie jumped on and landed bottom first on the white-planked deck. A laugh, loud and demeaning came from the girl on the black horse. It was Sandra, bobbing up and down and pointing to Leslie.

Robert reappeared, his arm reached down to aid her. Leslie was pulled up into his arms. He sat her on a white horse and caught her as she slipped reaching for the brass ring. She slid into his arms. He danced her over to the white swan seat as the carousel turned to the music of a Viennese waltz. Robert held her in his arms and began to speak: "Leslie dear I have not been honest with you." As he spoke the music increased in tempo and the carousel increased speed until he was pulled from her arms, his arms stretched out. Leslie reached for him, but he was gone again into the darkness outside the carousel. Leslie followed and emerged back on the cotillion dance floor. Robert was not in sight...

* * *

"Leslie, its time," a voice said from the darkness.

"Not, yet, not without Robert," she answered from her sleep.

"Leslie, wake up dear, you're going to be late for the girls," her mother's voice said.

For an instant Leslie wondered why her mother was on the cotillion dance floor. Her eyes opened. "Oh, did you have to wake me up?" She asked.

"What have you done to your bed?" Her mother asked looking at the pillows and blanket thrown across the floor.

"Just a dream, it was just a dream."

"And what of Robert?" "Her mother asked. "Is he your trouble, dear?"

"Me to," Cele's voice declared from the top of the stairs. "I wants to know what's troubling you too. You don't keep no secrets from me, I wants to know!"

Now both women were seated on Leslie's bed. There was no escaping the coming conversation. "Robert has a secret he has chosen to keep from me. He has deceived me, I'm afraid."

"How?" mother asked.

"Miss Edith, don't you know, I says you can guess," Cele announced, "her beau has got someone else. Thats how men are, you can't trust them. Ain't that true dear?"

"Hush, you silly old woman," Leslie's mother ordered, "my daughter would not stand for such behavior."

"Mother, it is not like that," Leslie began to explain.

"Oh God, he a two-timer, a scalawag. He married, ain't he?" Cele asked. Leslie could not answer.

"The bastard," Miss Edith announced, "I know my daughter would not stand for it if she knew. He is a cad of the worst order, and a liar. He has deceived you. If I get my hands on him!"

"It isn't like that," Leslie explained. "He was so very truthful to me. I just know in my heart there is something, something so very terrible that keeps him from telling me."

"You means he didn't tell you?" Cele asked. "How you know girl?"

"A call from his wife," Leslie explained, "but he is unaware of it."

"Oh! Begin at the beginning," Edith ordered. Miss Edith was a woman to take command in a time of troubles, and so was Cele.

"Give us the facts, they tell the truth about this Robert," Cele demanded as she placed her strong brown arm around Leslie's shoulders.

"I got a call from someone who said she was his wife, demanding to talk to him immediately," Leslie began. "The woman called from the French Riviera.

Robert never spoke of her, I don't know what to say to him. He loves me, I know, but he stays apart, distant. Oh, his friends told me of some dark secret he keeps hidden. Something he and only he can tell me, but…."

"We should make him the gelding!" Cele exclaimed.

"We will help Leslie find out what she wants," Edith announced. "Leslie dear, do you love him?"

"I thought so. I dream about spending my whole life with him, having children. I know he feels the same. He is caring and attendant. He is gentle with my heart. He protects and nurtures. He is never selfish. He is totally honest in his emotions excepting that one mystery he keeps from me. This I know with my whole heart."

"Is it true love, dear?" Leslie's mother asked

"I thought so," Leslie answered as she rested her head into her mother's bosom. "But now I don't know what it all is."

"True love is all devouring my dear," Edith began to explain in a gentle voice. "It is your beginning of the day, and your end, and everything in between. Those lovers who have something else, are only waiting for true love. Or worse are satisfied pretending. Some people don't even try or believe. They just go through life not ever looking for true love and offer as proof of its non-existence the fact that they do not possess it."

"But it hurts to have it and hurts to not have it," Leslie answered.

"Child, you got it, always have," Cele answered sternly.

"True love is in you dear," her mother explained. "But you can lose it if you are not careful. You see; true love waits. Do you understand, dear?"

"And just how long does mister cupid expect me to wait?" Leslie sobbed.

"You don't wait," Cele explained, "True love waits in you! People sometimes have it all bottled up in them all their lives, like the prophets of old. Sometimes it waits til you is old and grey likes me and you thinking there's no man for you. But if you kept that true love a waiting inside your soul he finds it; if he's the kind lookin for a true love for his."

"True love waits within you, my dear," Leslie's mother concluded. "I can offer as proof of its' existence in you the dream you have so recently completed.

"But waiting don't mean you sits around a moping," Cele scolded, "If you love this man go out an get him. And don't take no for no answer."

"I think Cele means," Lelsie's mother corrected, "you should not hesitate to show him the depth of your love, to say it in the kindest of terms."

"Hit him over the head if the need be," Cele instructed. "He needs to know about his consequences, fiddling around with your feelins. If you don't, he may start to think your love is not that deep."

"Wait child, but with some vigor," her mother added. "Go and find the love to share and remember he's looking too, if he's the right kind of man. Go and find a love to share."

"I was certain he loved me," Leslie announced. "Now it seems he is married."

"You don't know that!" Cele exclaimed. "Not as fact."

"Cele means, if he is important to you don't let anything stand in your way," her mother added. "Don't stop until you are certain, one way or the other." Then, with a puzzled face her mother added: "Leslie dear, have you run away from this into our hands? We're not the answer, dear. Go and get him, or toss him away if you don't like what you find. But, go dear, and do something. True love can wait only so long."

Leslie nodded a "yes" to the old ladies. Cele tossed her a box of tissues and Leslie used them liberally to clear her face of tears. "The girls await my appearance at the club," she announced as she rose from the bed. Leslie hugged each of her mentors and promised to, "wait for true love." But this afternoon she had a circle to visit.

Chapter 23   Circle of Friends

In ten minutes Leslie was out of the shower and standing at her closet looking in. Years had passed since she had placed anything new into it, anything. *Oh why did I ever agree to this afternoon,* she thought to herself. *It is bound to be a disaster. I have nothing to wear!* She thought of canceling, or simply not going, *but that was certain to start tongues a-waggling, and Sandra would feel victoriou*s. She settled on a silk paisley okra cocktail dress with a cowled neck and flare-rolled hem. A beige, linen and polyester sweater, tied over the shoulders, and diamond stud earrings completed her attire. She laid them out on the bed for review. *A standard in any season, now or in the past,* she thought to herself, *defensible in any situation.* For shoes she had to settle on brown pumps, the only thing in her closet.

Leslie decided on light makeup. Not sure exactly why she had accepted the invitation, she convinced herself she was not interested in meeting anyone interesting, renewing old ties, or leaving lasting impressions. *I most certainly am not interested in doing battle for attention with Sandra. She may have the day. After all, it's Sandra's wedding.* Still, Leslie made certain to wear her tennis bracelet.

* * *

The afternoon was overcast, cooler and dry. Rain was not threatening, so Leslie decided to leave the Mercedes at her mother's home and walk the four short city blocks to the club. As an extra precaution, however, she grabbed her mother's pansy print umbrella at the front door. It was the best time of the day for Leslie. As a girl, she had spent many a late afternoon once school let out roaming. She walked past bright pastel single houses of the below Broad Street quarter; one at a time recalling their history. *History is something as dear as life itself*, she remembered her father telling her. *People of Charleston love their history so much they never sell.* It was true. Most houses in the quarter were owned by members of the same family for hundreds of years. *People did not buy a home*, she thought, *they simply maintained ownership for their descendants.*

In colonial Charleston, built on a peninsular jutting into the harbor, land and roads were at a premium and so most houses were built only a single room wide, and sometimes with a large two-story porch opening into a garden on the side. For this reason they were called 'single' houses.

But they opened into rear alleys which could be run through to the next block by a little girl. Leslie recalled how she had climbed the wrought iron fences of many to get into the side gardens and beyond. A behavior something her father had found thrilling, and her mother horrifying in its' telling.

Leslie took a short detour to Rainbow Row. She loved the old ballast stone paving stones that surfaced the street and the slate slabs that finished the sidewalk. Gas lit streetlights and planters of lavender crepe wax myrtle alternated with white oak along the curb, just as in colonial times. Tight row houses displayed their original colors, and in many homes, original doors and windows. The French influence was evident in wrought iron second story balconies that seemed to float unsupported, in mid air above the sidewalk.

As a child Leslie had imagined colonial times. The street would be lined with men and women in their Sunday best. Women in the latest Paris fashion, trying in vain to keep their layers of hemmed petticoats out of the mess left by horse-drawn carriages on the colonial street. They would be chivalrously escorted on the arm of some handsome beau as they paraded. Men were at all times perfect gentlemen. *How I wish it were true today. In times past, friendships whatever gender, were respected, valued, trusted.*

Soon Leslie found herself at the club gates. The club was not how she remembered. In her childhood the club had been the one place of modernism, and activity from and about the world outside of Charleston. Music and topics for a lively conversation were gathered from radio, television, and newspapers and turned over again and again at the club as if in an old butter churn, until they were homogenized with the Charleston air sufficiently for consumption. To the child Leslie, the club had been like Mount Olympus of old. Not a building, but rather, a place of wisdom, style, knowledge, and free thinking surrounded by the commonness of mortal day-to-day needs. When entering the club, the child Leslie had been transported back to a time of excellence.

Nothing has changed, she lied to herself, *and I suppose that is what I wanted.* But the club seemed to have lost some of its' charm. Now Leslie could see the cracks in the wall, pavement, and old windows.

Leslie passed through the six white Doric columns, up the thirteen white marble steps, "one for every state in the Southern Confederacy," her father had taught her, and to the Mahogany doors. On her dresser still stood a picture of her in her first evening dress at these doors and Leslie hesitated a moment as memories flooded her mind. Her first kiss happened behind those doors, her first drink, her first pass from a man.

* * *

She waited. Presently, the door opened to reveal a doorman, dressed impeccably in white from head to toe in a white tux, excepting for an oversized black top hat. His dark brown skin contrasted his dress dramatically and for the first time in her life Leslie found something comically demeaning about the doorman's traditional attire.

"Why where's Moses?" she asked the doorman.

"Tired, mah lady," was the reply, "tired and retired. I am Joseph. Will you be dining with us this evening?"

"It is so good to meet you, Joseph," Leslie replied with a broad smile and a trained pleased voice, as she entered. Her mother had tried to teach her the proper manners when speaking with people of color at an early age.

Remember to let them know you approve, but from a proper distance, She thought her mother would say. *Our colored folks are never a problem because we treat them, and they treat us, with proper respect. We will give them approval in our certain way. One that lets them know we honor our respective positions in life.*

Wonder what Cele would say, she thought. *Are times here still kind to such arrangements?*

"I am to dine with Sandra Cox and friends. Have they arrived?" she asked.

"Miss Taylor is taking refreshments at the bar," Joseph answered, smiled a broad smile and tipped his hat.

A slight confusion momentarily overcame Leslie as she passed Joseph and walked toward the bar. She had never gone to the bar unescorted before. It fact, she had never gone to the bar before dinner. *But today I am meeting a friend at the bar, like a gentleman would, perhaps*, she thought to herself. *Still, gentlemen should meet a lady in the dining room and order drinks, if wanted.*

The atrium of the club gently widened and opened into the main dining room. On the right Leslie passed alternating floor to ceiling mirrors and open areas interspaced with high relief columns, service rooms, a tobacconist shop, coat and hatcheck, restrooms for ladies. On the left the bar was screened from view by columns and open plantings of tropical vegetation common to Charleston. Before descending the four steps to the dining room Leslie turned into the bar. Five small tables with two or three chairs each, pressed against the columns that separated the atrium and bar. *These are new*, Leslie thought, surprised. *In the past only seats at the bar were available. And only men spent time there. But now there are women seated at tables, and at one table, women seated without benefit of a gentleman chaperone.*

"Leslie!" a female voice shouted her name from the rear of the bar, "Leslie dear, over here." From a small group of admirers Taylor called out. Taylor was seated at the bar, in the back, near the cigarette vending machine and was obviously enjoying the company of three gentlemen. For a moment Leslie hesitated. *A lady did not approach a gentleman at the bar with whom she was not closely acquainted. But this was Taylor.*

"Leslie dear, meet some of my friends," Taylor announced as Leslie drew near. "The very best of eligible young men." She stepped forward, slid by a tall, balding and bearded man, and gave Leslie a hug and kiss on the cheek. "Look, let me introduce you. This is Kit, Harold and George," Taylor said and gave George an arm hug, at which he blushed. Leslie thought the blush was a little to easily made and decided Taylor's George was drunk. He wore a wedding ring.

The three men stood and each offered their hand. *At least common courtesy has not been forgotten.* She would be courteous and reserved, so as to avoid becoming the subject of wagging tongues. She returned their handshake in order.

"I am George Partner," The first announced as he limply touched Leslie's hand. "Have you known Taylor long?"

"Yes indeed," Leslie answered with a firm and yet gentle grip. "I've known her since her birth. We grew up together, living beside one another. Taylor is like a sister to me."

"Then we are graced with the company of two angels," the second man, answered. He made a slight bow. "I am Harold Connors and am honored to make your acquaintance."

"Pleased to make yours, kind sir." Harold gave Leslie a firm hand, one of a confident man.

"And this is my Kit." Taylor announced and took Leslie's hand and placed it into her friend's.

"My deepest pleasure." Kit replied, as he took Leslie's hand. "Will you be staying with us for awhile? There is much to do in Charleston and I'h would be happy to show you around." As he withdrew his hand Leslie thought he may have deliberately traced his index finger across her palm.

"We would, if there were new attractions to show her," Taylor interrupted and threw her arm around his waist, pulling them together. "Leslie is of old Charleston blood, not like you new scallawags." Taylor pushed a playful finger into George's chest, and he again blushed.

"And how about another drink, my dear?" Kit asked Taylor. "We still have time. The girls have not yet arrived."

Yet two ladies had indeed already arrived and this conversation could as easily been held at a dining room table. "None for us, kind sirs," Leslie announced to a groan of disapproval from each man. "You must excuse us. We've lots of girl talk to do, lots to ketch up on. Taylor dear, does your nose need powdering?" Leslie took Taylor gently by the elbow and began walking out of the bar toward the ladies room on the other side of the atrium.

"Please, please, ladies don't go," George pleaded, "without you we will only have our poor, miserable selves to entertain and delight us; a sorry matter at best. Stay only a little while longer, take mercy on us, poor miserable men that we are." He stepped into Leslie's path.

"At times a lady must repose herself." George stepped back, politely, but Leslie felt his hand pass down her back.

In the atrium Leslie firmly held Taylor's elbow. "Taylor, don't you think that is a little too forward, I having drinks with men unescorted by another lady. It's just not done, not in descent circles. Really, I don't know what you were thinking."

"Why don't be such a prude. Really Les, it is after all just harmless play. Nothing is to be made of it. You're being very silly," she responded with a growing impatience about her friend's concerns. "I swear, your gallivanting all over New York and Boca means nothing to you. But if I happen to have a few drinks with close friends, well, there's hell to pay." She stumbled as they walked into the ladies' salon.

Leslie realized that her friend was more than a little drunk. "Should I have thanked that Mr. George Partner for dragging his paw across my back? The beast practically fondled my rear! Really Taylor, how do you find such friends as these?" By now they were in front of mirrors. Leslie composed herself as she saw the reflection of her anger. "Anyway, I'm rid of them."

"Oh, now we can't all be the perfect one. After all, there is room in Charleston for only one Leslie Devereaux." Taylor quickly retrieved a hairbrush from her purse and tidied-up her coiffure. "There," she announced as she decided all was in order on her head. "I shall forgive your remark about good George. You must not be jealous, dear Leslie. After all, you have been away a long time. Charleston can't wait for your convenience. Life goes on, you know," defending the assault on her friends, her life.

Leslie thought to let the comment pass unharmed into the ladies' room walls, as many a prudent feminine social politician had done in just the same circumstances. But, like her father, she despised those who take advantage of others weaknesses. And like her mother, she found disgust in those weak individuals who allow sharks to take advantage of their faults. Leslie decided to speak her mind.

"Your so-called good friend George is a bore of the worst kind," Leslie began. "His drunken attempt at fondling by behind was an embarrassment more to him than me. Taylor, he wears a wedding ring! How can you stand him!" Leslie realized she was clutching Taylor's purse as if to squeeze truth out of it.

"George is a good friend. So, his marriage is experiencing a rocky time, but I will not abandon him." Taylor answered.

"He appears to be the one who has abandoned, his marriage, and where is his wife this afternoon?" Leslie asked.

"I'm sure he has a perfectly innocent reason," Taylor hesitated and then added: "He is my mentor. He helps me with my problem. Come on now, dearest friend. I'm sure your mother wasted no time telling you of my great and looming fault."

"You mean the drinking? Mother and Cele are both quite concerned. But, tell me, how does this miraculous George aid you with a drink in his hand?"

"Dear jealous friend," Taylor answered shortly, "He gets me back on track and to meetings if I waver or falter."

"With a drink in his hand!" Leslie answered. "Is that one of his steps?" Taylor did not answer. She only bit her lower lip and stared. She was at a loss for words.

Her friend was crumbling from within. She wrapped Taylor in a giant hug. "Forgive me, my dear little sister," Leslie whispered into Taylor's ear.

Soon Leslie and Taylor found themselves again in the club atrium. They paused a moment to admire a great floral display of classic pale roses. There were no salmon colored roses.

"Leslie, did you ever think about flowers. Do they like being cut and displayed for the momentary enjoyment of strangers? Or would they choose to chance the laws of nature? Would they choose to seed; a chance of life and a next generation? Do you think they would even try if they knew the odds?"

"Dear Taylor," Leslie responded in her most gentle tone, "it's true that flowers exist only to reproduce, to give life to seeds. They never see their offspring as we will see ours and even theirs. But they live out their lives with honesty and conviction worthy of our admiration. In as much as they know anything, they know this truth: theirs is the duty to attract admirers. Be they bees and hornets to spread their pollen and in so doing geminate the next generation. Or to attract the farmer to aid them in their life cycle so the farmer and we can enjoy the beauty of their splendor. They, by their attractive beauty, assure the farmer's assistance in their life's mission for many generations in the future. How are we not a natural part of the flower's reproduction? Are we not now "buzzing" about their beauty, attracted as any other pollinator?"

"But soon they will wilt and brown," Taylor replied, sorrowfully. "They will die slowly and in the end be thrown out into the trash pile for all kinds of vermin to devour! How can they be content with this future?"

"Their children are already cultivated. They have achieved their life's goal; another beautiful generation will come to pass. Their life is all that simple. Believe me, dear friend, they are content and fulfilled. To us comes a greater task, that of making understanding out of all we experience around us. To put it a more gracious way, to find the relative beauty in our lives and in all we experience." For the moment Leslie thought she saw a slight smile on Taylor's lips...

"Eeek!" a cry bust from Sandra Cox's mouth. "Eeek, Leslie dear, you have come! I knew you would not let us down. Can you believe it? We are all together again! Quick dearest, give me a hug." Sandra and Debbie Johns were in the atrium, coming directly for Leslie. She steadied herself in anticipation of a momentary collision.

"Sandra, Debbie," Leslie returned the greeting with somewhat less enthusiasm than which it was delivered, " how wonderful it is." Arms crossed between friends, purses shifted, Leslie almost lost her footing. A chorus of: "How long has it been? Where are living you now? Did you see...? Can you believe...?" and so on raged until Leslie had to step back or be consumed. Dressed in a brown silk pant suit and pale yellow linen blouse, Sandra reminded Leslie of her mother's favorite comment on others' dress: *"They wear gray when they cannot decide and brown when they can NEVER decide what to wear."*

"Leslie dear, you've got to tell us all about your new beau. It's been so long. You can't keep secrets from us."

"Why that's right," Debbie joined in, "we don't know a single new bit of gossip about you!"

"And it's unfair for you to share all the good stories about him only with Taylor," Sandra scolded. "Come on, let's get a table in the corner so we can talk freely and keep this confidential."

"Have you missed us?" Sandra asked Leslie as she seated herself at the head of the table. "Will you be staying this time? I swear I don't know why you ever left Charleston. Why, everything you could possibly want is here. Don't you agree girls?"

"Good friends," Debbie joined in, "handsome men, balls, parties, great restaurants, family, why I could not survive anywhere but here."

A waiter appeared with a pitcher of chilled wine and stem glasses. Sandra had placed the order before arriving. Leslie waited for the waiter to complete his mission. "Well, girls," Leslie leaned forward and spoke softly, as if to deliver a deep and dark secret, "there are handsome men everywhere in the world."

"Surely not as handsome as ours," Taylor responded, "and not as chivalrous, I'm sure."

"But tell us of your beau, dear Leslie," Sandra asked. "Is he as handsome as our men here in Charleston? Does he have hands as large as our beaus?"

"My Robert is a thorough gentleman," Leslie began. "He is chivalrous, from the best Palm Beach social circles, a successful business man, and loving and caring. My Robert is everything I would ever want."

"He sounds to be a perfect catch," Taylor added.

"How much money does he make?" Debbie asked. "Come on now, dearest Leslie, you are among friends. That means we want to know all about his financial statement; so we can make the proper associations, judgments."

"Can we hold him upside down and shake?" Sandra sarcastically interjected. "Or, how about placing him on a balance scale, for accuracy. Why we could weigh him against Debbie's dear husband Foster. Tell us, dear Leslie, who would tip the scale in the most pleasing direction, Debbie's beau or yours?"

Robert is from old Palm Beach money," Leslie answered, trying to hide her annoyance with the question. "He has inherited wealth, but believes a man needs to add to the family wealth, to prosper the future generations. His seed capital firm earns in the neighborhood of 120% on its investments per year." At that moment she was pleased she had remembered to wear the tennis bracelet.

"He sounds delicious," Debbie announced, "but what about, you know, the bedroom?"

Leslie smiled. "Which one?" she asked. "The mansion's water bed overlooking the Atlantic? The yacht transom cushion bed with stars overhead and the gentle rocking and slapping of the waves? Or perhaps the island retreat; complete with a private waterfall and lagoon? Tell me dear Debbie, which bed do you wish to hear about?

"Oh, I want to hear about the waterfall and lagoon," Taylor grinned.

"And have you plans for children?" Debbie asked bluntly. My Foster and I have a boy Josh and a girl Jamey, and he wants more."

"And he will get them, I'm sure, one way or another," Sandra added. "Tell me Debbie, where is dear Foster at this moment? I called him before coming, about the pre-nuptial and his girl told me he is out for the rest of the day." All eyes except Sandra's looked down with the remark.

"He can be a scoundrel, that is certain," Debbie responded after a long moment. "But he loves, and cares for me. I am prepared to wait for him to grow up." Debbie spoke confidently. "His silly meanderings are only that. He's wandering toward me, like a boat in a river that can change course a dozen times but inevitably finds its way to the ocean." Debbie was trying to be tactful, and somewhat discreet in the hope her friends would follow her suggestion.

"And what if he meanders a hundred times on his journey?" Sandra asked.

"Then I would be forced to cut off his rudder, so to speak, and sue him for everything he has I suppose," Debbie answered with an evil smile and giggled. "Look Sandra, here comes your Mark now."

"Lovely ladies," Dr. Mark Gardner said as he approached the circle of friends with a mixed drink in his hand, "a finer picture of feminine beauty could not be had anywhere else in the world than at this very table. How is everyone this late afternoon? Who are we roasting over the fires of idle, though lovely, conversation? Not me, I prey." He bent over and gave Sandra a peck on the cheek.

"Darling," Sandra muttered as he gave her the kiss. "We have been roasting my attorney, for now. But don't be concerned, dear. I shall protect you from the fires of feminine judgment. You are in good hands." Then she added in a loud and happy voice: "but don't be a prude dear, our friend Leslie, long gone from us has returned. Give her a Charleston welcome!"

Mark kissed her on the lips. Leslie was shocked, caught unprepared. Sandra turned red for a moment. The others sat speechless.

"Dear, don't go and tire yourself out now," Sandra warned good-naturedly. "Tomorrow is our wedding night and I have expectations." Everyone giggled.

"But I am yours, dearest," Mark answered. "Have I not made my appearance as requested?"

"Showing off again?" Debbie asked with a grin. "My but, he is a fine specimen. We were just having a discussion about the economy. Tell me, Mark do you make into the seven figures?"

"Hardly," Mark answered, "I must report that we general practitioners only get a small pittance compared to the earnings of a specialist, or on the other side, a surgeon. But it is still enough to get by with style."

"And that's what counts, style." Taylor interjected and poured herself another white wine cooler.

"And are you ladies ready for the big day?" he asked. "All preparations in order?"

"Right down to the ruffled necklines for my two maids-of honor," Sandra assured him.

"Ruffled!" Taylor yelled.

"Ruffled?" Debbie asked, surprised.

"What's wrong?" Sandra muttered with dread.

"I gave Mama Gena the order for a scalloped neckline," Taylor said.

"Mine was to be draped, you know so as not to expose too much," Debbie explained.

"Problem, problem, oh God, what a problem," Sandra began, "I can't have my two equal maids-of-honor in different necklines! And not in scalloped!'

"Draped makes me look old!" Taylor exclaimed.

"It must be ruffled, then," Sandra announced and reached for her cell phone. In a moment Sandra was talking to the elderly seamstress: "Yes, it's all wrong....make the ruffled...no, no,,no time....ok then, ten minutes." She hung up the phone. "Dears we need to go over to Mama Gena's right away for new measurements."

"And leave me without the company of my lady?" Mark complained. "My dear, soon to be wife, have you forgotten me already?"

"Don't be silly," Sandra chastised. "I shall leave you safely here with Leslie to watch you. Now you be good or I shall certainly hear of it."

Chapter 24   Dr. Mark

"It seems we are both now outcasts from the circle of ladies. Leslie, I know of my manly fault, my masculine reason for exclusion. But you what vice, what rude display or social transgression did you commit to be marooned here with me and the Chablis?"

Leslie chuckled. "Afraid I'm have been gone a little too long to be always remembered. Especially when matters as serious as necklines are the priority. But why aren't you angry, you dear man? You who have so quickly been ruled inconsequential, even if only for the moment?"

"Inconsequential?" Mark replied, raised an eyebrow and cast a humorous and helpless look over his countenance, bringing her hand in his to his heart. "It has always been my lot, to be forgotten and then only called for when my friends have forgotten something like a phone number, or have missed the latest gossip, need a ride to the garage to get their car, or have forgotten to bring money for the bill." He nodded at the pitcher of Chablis and grinned.

"Oh, how perfectly awful of me! I shall not allow you to pay for these drinks. Why you did not even partake." She pointed at the mixed drink in the double glass in Mark's hand.

"Not to worry," Mark answered. "I'm the best of husbands-to-be; well trained. I've already taken care of the bill. You see, I know my uses."

"No, really that's unfair. You are left alone."

"Unfair, why?" Mark asked, grinning.

"Well, because, because for several reasons… What's so funny?"

"You, everyone. I'm mostly the collector of complaints. Listen, have you ever considered how often you see your doctor?"

"Why is that important? I see him when I need to."

"When your'e sick, correct?"

Of course," Leslie answered. "When would you expect me too?"

"Oh, you're quite right, of course," Mark said, "But no other time?"

"What do you mean? Should I go to the doctor's before I get sick and then tell him to guess at my symptoms, those I don't have?"

"Well, in word, yes." Mark replied. "You, see dear friend, it is like these two drinks."

She was beginning to enjoy the word game. "How is it like drinks?"

"Well, you are drinking Chablis and I got scotch and something, correct?" he asked.

"Correct," Leslie answered. She stared at the drinks. Mark's did look slightly odd.

"And here I sit for all the womanhood of Charleston to envy for I belong to Sandra Cox, the soon to be Mrs. Dr. Mark Gardner. And yet, no one ever asks me for my advice. They only bring complaints, to my office that is, after they're sick. Why don't you ask me which drink is healthier?"

"The Chablis," Leslie answered loudly, trying to get his goat. "Really, Mark, is this why you became a doctor, to play word games in the afternoon?"

"Yes," Mark whispered and bent over the table as if to tell a confidence. "In a very direct, if somewhat obscure way, you have found out my secret. You see, there is a difference of health in the Chablis and scotch. But you didn't ask me. I suppose if you were my patient I would have to wait until you arrive at my examination table before we talk about the liver."

Leslie smiled warmly. For the first time she saw Mark as a doctor. No longer was he the boy she grew up with. "Is that why you became a doctor? To take complaints?" she smiled.

Mark paused. His eyes became soft, bright. "I suppose it takes an unnatural amount of idealism to become a doctor; definitely an almost unhealthy amount to be a general practitioner. It seems I spend half my day warning my patients, though I swear I try to make it sound like good advice."

"Do they listen?"

"Politely," he answered. "Then go about their business. Still, I do make some progress." Then, being the well-trained husband-to-be, he asked: "But what of you, Les. What have you been up to in that great world outside our little peninsula?"

Leslie hesitated. She wanted to scream in anger, cry in despair. She began to explain her last few years of life as a resume, starting with New York and ending at RRR.

Mark looked perplexed. "No loves? You're holding out."

"There is a gentleman," Leslie began and averted her eyes as she thought about Robert on Bimini. "My Robert is the finest of men. Gentle and successful."

"And the future?"

"I have no plans."

"Don't lie to your doctor!" Mark demanded, teasingly. "Les, you can't keep a secret from me. I know you didn't return to us because of the wedding. It's wonderful you are here, but it is not your agenda. It's an affair of the heart, isn't it?"

"Please, dear friend, don't press," Leslie asked in a soft voice.

"Yes, indeed," Mark answered moving his chair close to Leslie. He gently touched her hand. "Well, you don't need to explain yourself to me. I have known you were a helpless romantic since grammar school. You love so much, it is a wonder anyone could love you enough."

"We do love each other, of that I'm certain. As certain as I know the sun will rise in the East to begin our next day."

Mark paused a moment in thought. "Then it's what happens next, that's the dilemma. And I bet it's a big one!" he answered. "Marriage?"

Leslie flinched. "No."

"But, still, you wait. You've always possessed a waiting love." Now his face became serious. He whispered: "Fortunate you are, unlike me. I have the wisdom, and strength to chance giving my great love for a lessor love in return. But you stand resolute with your's, waiting.

A look of shock overcame Leslie's face, though she tried to mask it with a smile. "Don't be silly, old friend. Why Sandra loves you deeply." She patted his hand.

"Certainly, she does. As deeply as she's capable of loving. For that I give her my love in return. We are like two buckets standing together, one is larger, both filled to the brim. No one faults the smaller bucket for being smaller. But no one expects the larger bucket to be able to empty its' contents into the other. No one expects that. No, they just wonder what the larger sees in the smaller. They never realize the great beauty in the smaller bucket also; that of true love in as much as it can hold. The smaller is truly committed, holding all it can."

"So there's no dilemma in my life, dear friend," Mark assured her in the gentlest of voices. "I have my patients to catch the remainder of my water of love as it spills out of my bucket. Really the best thing for a doctor, you know. We need extra buckets around us, more than others."

"You aren't an idealist, Mark Gardner," Leslie whispered. "You're another hopeless romantic. Bless you." She leaned over and gave him a peck on the cheek.

Mark blushed. "But now, what are we to do with our other hopeless romantic at the Chablis table?"

"The Chablis and scotch table."

Mark grinned. "I will tell you a little secret, if you promise to keep it until your dying day."

"To my death bed," she promised, grinning. "Now out with your, deep, dark secret that is not fit to be repeated.

"White ginger ale, ice and a twist."

"What?"

"The Chablis and ginger ale table, that's us," Mark whispered. "I never drink. It clouds up the senses. So the joke's on me, I'm always aware of our pitiful plight as human beings. We love too much and too little all at the same time, and I'm the only one that's aware of every gory detail in our mad pursuits. It would be a sobering experience if I wasn't already sober."

"Truly noble, if done for the right pursuits," she answered, thinking of Robert.

"Is it possible you are the victim of a treachery?" Mark asked. "Your words have a sound like a woman scorned. Who was it, dear?"

"I think I'd rather believe in an ambiguity, and uncertainty in the matter. It seems the easiest way. Rather than confrontation: avoidance and plausible ambiguity?"

"In other words, mind my own business," Mark answered. "I'm right, aren't I? I was right about the romantic problem. Come on now, no one could believe you'd possibly return to Charleston unless for some perilous reason, definitely not for Sandra's marriage. Love us as you do, you could never convince me of that."

"The problem is far away, and I think that's the way I want to keep it."

"But he can never find you here," Mark warned.

"Good for that."

"No, no, this just won't do, Les," Mark announced in a loud voice. "You need put your foot into it, both feet.

"My feet are happily set in Charleston."

"What about your lips, fingers, heart? I don't believe they belong so far away from your problem." Mark replied sternly. "Nothing will change as long as you are here. The problem won't go away and neither will the pain."

A tear traced down Leslie's cheek.

"The point is, Les, you must jump into it with both feet and everything else. You have a lot of love to give. Perhaps your waiting time is through."

Leslie threw her fists in the air: "Love is a game of competition. I don't want to play. Robert loves me. I am sure. Yet, he lies. This love is all too painful. He has someone else, I know, and yet, I know he couldn't. It's not in his heart."

"Then there must be more to this story. It is unbalanced. Dear Les, life in the end is always balanced."

"Men!" Leslie shouted. "Oh, Mark, I didn't mean you."

"But, I am."

"No, you are different. Robert is different, or maybe not."

"Time to find out. Its time Les, to go home. I'll drop you at your mother's if you like."

* * *

The short four block ride in Mark's car was uneventful. Sheltering small talk prevailed. Leslie didn't smell the Atlantic or the wax myrtle. Her mind was lost in Palm Beach. When they arrived at her mother's front drive there was a limousine parked beside the hyacinths.

Leslie stepped out of the car and closed the door. Then she tapped on the window. Mark opened it and reached over. She placed her hand under his chin. "Close your eyes, Dr. Mark Gardner," she commanded. He obeyed. She bent over and kissed him on the forehead. "You are a friend and a gentleman. God Bless," she said, and walked away.

Chapter 25 Roots

The limo driver was wiping the limousine's the rear doors with a cloth as Leslie passed the iron gates and walked up the brick drive. "Evenin' Ma'am," he said as he tipped his hat.

Leslie cringed at the word 'ma'am.' "It's a fine evening, right for walking and visiting, I say," she responded.

"That it is Ma'am, a fine evenin'," the driver replied. "If you be Miss Leslie, you be savin us all a lot of drivin,." He looked anxious for the answer.

"I am, but of what concern is it?"

"Best be gettin' into the house promptly," he suggested. "Before they all burst. It's a regular war meetin' goin' on in there."

Leslie closely examined the driver's face, looking for some telltale smirk to give away a practical joke, but there was none. She looked over her shoulder as she passed and jokingly said: "I shall, but do call the police if you hear gun fire." But the driver didn't smile. He just stopped rubbing out marks on the limo and stood erect, as if listening.

As she opened the leaded glass front door a familiar voice came from within. "Why dear Bev," Leslie called out, "its great you have come to visit us." She walked into the foyer, turned right and into the formal parlor where she found Bev, her mother, and Cele all sitting on the edge of their chairs, talking 'a mile a minute' as Cele was fond of saying. Though no one was listening. They had not even heard her enter the room.

"What's this?" Leslie called out to gain their attention. "Why, you are all sitting around like hens making such a racket. Bev, why what a fine, though unexpected..."

"Robert's lost at sea!" Bev blurted out and waited for Leslie's reaction. The whole house fell instantly silent, waiting. Edith and Cele grabbed each others' hand and stared with worried frowns on their faces. Only Bev, after a moment's hesitation, stood and rushed to Leslie's side.

"Oh Leslie dear," Bev cried, "I'm sorry." She wrapped her arms around Leslie and almost took the air from her lungs. Bev began to sob, her tears fell on Leslie's shoulder.

"Wait, wait, begin at the beginning," Leslie said. *Robert is resourceful and cunning. He quite possibly could have orchestrated the disappearance for good reasons. I am not going to fall apart, not yet anyway.*

"Tanny and he decided, oh I don't know why, to cross the Stream last night in Tanny's second boat, the Boomer, and they haven't made it to port," Bev blurted out.

"Well, there could be any number of reasons for their apparent disappearance," Leslie responded calmly.

"They haven't disappeared, not yet dear, well not until about ten hours ago," Edith added. Leslie looked confused.

"The Coast Guard dispatched a rescue boat after picking up a distress call," Bev explained as she sat down. Bev starred off into the distance. "But the ocean is so damned rough, with the storm and all, well, they haven't been located." With that, the three matrons sat quietly and waited for Leslie's response They knew what it would be. Cele reached for the box of tissues.

But Leslie didn't cry out. *I'm expected to fall to the floor in an agony of worry. I know the scoundrel better than they.* Instead, she crossed the parlor to a telephone table that had resided next to the French doors for fifty years, picked up the headset, and began to dial the rotary dial. The three ladies looked on in amazement at the apparent control of emotions.

"Let me check on something," Leslie told the ladies in waiting. Soon Leslie heard the familiar voice on the answering machine, her own. It began:

Robert is not in his office and the caller should press nine if they would like to speak with a secretary.

Leslie's face paled. *If Robert had planned the disappearance he would have disabled the recorded message, standard operating procedure at RRR, and it would have enhanced the effect. He could be sitting at a bar right now, waiting for the opportunity to complete his plan. But still,* Leslie thought, *ten hours is a lot of time at sea without a rescue. The Coast Guard should not have taken so long to pluck him out of the water once they received a call for assistance. And ten hours is more than enough time for Robert to get to a phone and disable the recorded message.* The recorded message was working. Robert had not disabled it. He was definitely not in control of events. Of that she was certain. Leslie returned to the three ladies.

Bev knew the answer by Leslie's face. She did not want to hesitate any longer. "Leslie dear, I'm afraid that is not all of it," Bev gently spoke. "Our very own Mr. Jessup has not turned up in Hong Kong as planned. Actually, he is nowhere to be found, the scoundrel."

Leslie hesitated a moment, taking in all that had happened. "Thank God you came back when you did," Edith exclaimed, breaking the silence. "We were about to go out looking for you."

"We called the club, but they say you girls left," Cele added.

"We've been talking," Leslie responded, still in shock. "Just talking,"

"Well, let's go girl," Bev announced, "we need you at home."

"I am at home," Leslie answered and for a moment she wished she had never met the outside world with all of its problems, the world outside Charleston. "I came home for a reason. I guess I could go back though, for a while."

"Child, what you talking about?" Cele asked in a scolding voice.

"Leslie dear," Bev asked, "what else is the matter?"

"That Robert," Leslie blurted out. *Trouble with the Atlantic Ocean is not large enough for him.* "I found his secret, found where he keeps it, the scoundrel."

"Where he keeps it?' asked Bev.

"The scoundrel?" asked Edith.

"His secret?" demanded Cele.

"You didn't know about the south of France?" Leslie asked Bev. "Can he ever keep anything from you?"

Bev shook her head. "I told him to come clean, fess up, tell you what's what, the coward. It just goes to show how much it still hurts. He can't deal with it."

"What about the south of France?" Edith and Cele asked in unison.

"He keeps his wife in the south of France," Leslie announced and bit her lip.

"The scoundrel!" Edith exclaimed, "Toying with my daughter's affections."

"Let's get my prunin' shears," Cele announced, "and trim him some."

"Keep her?" Bev shouted as the lynching party began to form. "He doesn't keep her anywhere. Leslie you have to be told. That Nora is a witch. She was a monster before the kids, and before the car accident."

"Kids?" Leslie yelled. "Kids?"

"Car accident?" Edith and Cele asked in unison.

"Oh boy," Bev whispered. "That Robert owes me big for this one. Sit back ladies, and get out your tissues and hankies. What I'm about to tell you is going to hurt. Our dear Robert is not all-powerful, not always in control. He is human and like all us humans he has weaknesses. Unfortunate for him, he found the one woman in the world most suited to making his life miserable."

"Nora, in the South of France," Leslie interjected. "I had the unpleasant duty of returning her call last evening."

"Hush up girl," Cele ordered, "we want to get to the bottom of this mess." Cele clutched the box of tissues.

Bev began: "They were pushed together, really, both were too young for marriage. And her drinking increased from the beginning. Nora never had any self-control. She always got what she wanted. She had always been the center of her parents' lives, the center of attention. Nora could not adjust to married life, especially when the twins came. Sometimes I believe Nora actually resented them. They were so very beautiful. Here let me show you." Bev reached into her purse and retrieved her cell phone. "Two identical twin girls, here about three years old. They loved to hug each other. They loved posing for the camera. They had Robert's dark hair and strong chin, and their mother's green eyes."

Bev teared at the sight of the photograph. She could not speak for a moment.

"The car accident?" Cele asked.

Bev swallowed hard and continued. "Robert blamed himself. That evening he was at one of our non-business, business parties. Nora stayed home with the twins. That Nora, drunk as usual and angry for being left at home, found the car keys Robert had hidden..."

Bev paused a moment to catch her breath.

"She hit a tree, the car rolled, and of course, she survived. Nora was wearing a seat belt. But in her drunken stupor, she hadn't bothered to strap the girls into their car seats. One was thrown through the windshield, her lovely face destroyed. Robert came upon the accident while returning home from our party. He was the first on the scene. He found Veronica where she was thrown by impact, in the woods next to the car. Alexandra cut and bleeding, was pressed against the windshield. Cuddling his daughters almost lifeless bodies in his arms, he phoned for help. He would not release his hold on his babies until the ambulance arrived at the hospital. Two of the most beautiful babies, three year olds just starting school, big dimply smiles..."

Bev choked. "They died in his arms. Nora blamed Robert. At the funeral Nora screamed for Veronica and Alexandra. She shouted out: "murderer," cursed Robert, struck him in the face, and collapsed on two little white coffins. She kicked and screamed, and crashed flower bouquets to the floor as she clung to friends. Through it all Robert sobbed and held two little teddybears to his chest. Ones found at the scene. And, of course, she drank. By then it was hopeless, really. The marriage was doomed. Robert has always blamed himself. After the funeral, Robert put Nora in a clinic to sober up and he disappeared for weeks. When he returned, he never smiled. It was all work for him from then on and she was gone to the south of France."

"He should divorce the monster," Edith suggested, trying to protect her daughter's feelings.

"He can't," Bev continued to explain. "He can't. He somehow blames himself for Nora's drinking. 'If I had gotten her help earlier ,had been more understanding, comforting. If I had hidden the keys better,' he once told me."

Bev had finished. She sat silently as the ladies looked at the picture of the twins.

"He could have told me. He should have told me. I can be trusted to understand. I love him. If he had, I would have never come back home." Leslie swallowed a cry. "I could be there with him now."

"Home!" Cele exclaimed, "girl, you never done come home. You just visitin here in Charleston. Everybody knows it but you!"

"It's true, dear," Leslie's mother said. "We all have seen you've changed, grown, just as you should. You don't belong to Charleston anymore. Oh, you did once and the little girl in you still does. But you've grown into a new woman somewhere else. That is why I hadn't wanted you to go. I knew this would happen. You would adjust to and then master your new home. I knew you would, after all, you are my daughter."

"It's roots, remember?" Cele asked.

Leslie nodded yes. "Bloom where you root," she said. She remembered well the first of many lessons in sociology given her by Cele.

"So just why is it we are all blooming and rooting?" Bev asked rather impatiently.

"Let me explain, dearest friend," Edith began. 'Bloom where you put down roots,' is a quote of Dr. George Washington Carver."

"A black man," Cele added.

"It is nature's plan that you live and prosper where you are, it is a philosophy," Edith said. "We are to prosper by nature's laws where we are rooted.

"He decided to stay in the South where he was needed," Edith added.

"Where he was rooted," Cele stated with emphasis.

"But, now my roots are with Robert." Leslie placed her hands on her hips. "Bev, how quickly can we get to the airport?"

"The limo's waiting outside and a chartered jet is waiting for us there. I wasn't going to leave without you. We can be back on our island in two hours."

"Fine," Leslie announced. "Mother, will you be kind and arrange for my car to be shipped to me? As for Sandra, a simple phone call and message left on her answering machine will do. She'll no doubt feel victorious thinking she has run me off. No matter, let her enjoy her illusions. Mark I'll understand, I know. As for dear Taylor, well, Cele, would you kindly explain the matter to her, and gently. For Taylor, more than the typical 'called away on business' statement will be necessary." Leslie paused, then said: "She is so very fragile."

"Then you must leave now," Edith commanded and began towards the door. "We will get together again, and soon. But first take care of your Robert."

"And we expect to see him on your arm as a husband next time we meets," Cele warned. "I'll git your things while you say your goodbyes to your mother," and she was gone out of the room.

"The time together was much too short, dear daughter," Edith whispered in Leslie's ear. "But I want you to go and get that man. And remember, if you can, to be just a little more like me than your father. Dear man that he was, he took much too much gruff from people, especially me. You stand up for yourself, and your love."

"I will mother," Leslie whispered back. Now she knew what had been wrong all these months, and she knew what to do.

"There, then," Edith announced. "Off with you. Your adventure awaits on a far-off island."

"No mother, it's not like some desert island lost in the ocean, mother," Leslie teased. "We have plumbing and such things. We are civilized."

"But too many Yankees, remember," her mother answered, grinning.

While Bev got organized, Leslie took a small walk about the house and grounds before leaving. She knew her room would stay as she left it. She imagined that someday she would have Robert in her bed, that bed. She walked out back to get a compact from her car, past the garden.

Still, it won't be the same, she thought. *There will be new flowers blooming next season. And the old flowers, like the little girl that once played here, will be gone forever.*

Chapter 26   Damn Yankees

With fear and duty, and the unknown looming on the horizon; both women looked for a release from threats, if only temporary. Bev began:

"Damn Yankees," Bev muttered as the limo sped toward the airport. "Damn Yankees. Damn Yankees. AR, AR-HUH!"

Leslie chuckled. "She knows you are a Yankee," she explained, "but, well, that's Mother's way of accepting you into the family, sort of. Hah-hah-hah!" Leslie laughed out loud. "I would bet you would not like to hear her comments if she didn't approve of you."

"Damn Yankees? Why does she always have to place the prefix? I think she's itching for another Civil War."

"You mean the War of Northern Aggression. I suppose Mother would like nothing better, excepting a different outcome. But no matter, she likes you very much." Leslie hid her grin behind her hand. "Please take pity on her, I sometimes believe she suffers from some birth defect, unknown to the outside world, but very evident through several generations in the South. That defect of not being able to form the word Yankee without a 'd' and an 'm' immediately preceding the 'y'. Though I've been spared the affliction, no doubt because of my father's Yankee blood. There, you see, I can say it." Leslie grinned. "No damn!"

Bev sat silently for a moment. Sitting quietly always put a strain on her constitution and right then it was very evident. She said nothing, but her closed mouth quivered. First one way and then the other, she moved her lips sideways as if words were trying to escape and it was all she could do to restrain them. She blinked her eyes repeatedly. After a moment, Bev found the ability to speak civilly. "You say she likes me?"

"Certainly, Leslie answered, teasingly. "If she didn't she would have said 'you damn Yankees,' and not 'those damn Yankees.' So you see, she approves of you. It probably has something to do with the latitude of Palm Beach. It's to the South, you know."

"Well, she's a fine woman, but I am a Yankee," Bev responded. She was not amused and that made the fun all the better for Leslie.

"Yes, dear friend," Leslie added, "but you are not damned. Be happy for that. Mother has found similarities with you. Her birth defect's nothing she can change. But with you, they are 'those' damn Yankees. Believe me, that is quite an accomplishment. My very own father was vacillated between, 'you' and 'those' his entire life." Leslie was having great fun with Bev.

"So its Palm Beach then," Bev asked jokingly, "that's saved my soul?"

"yes. " Leslie answered, "The fact that Palm Beach is technically in the South has earned you a reprieve from condemnation. She simply holds out some hope for you, considers you worthy of consideration, and found in you some redeeming value. Because she believes you are, at least at times, affected by a few remaining gentle people of the South who may still be residing in Palm Beach."

"Something good has rubbed off, huh?" Bev asked.

"Exactly, though it's not the way she would put it in social circles," Leslie answered.

"And she decided to ignore the fact I am from New York?" Bev asked. "I traded Manhattan for Palm Beach; one island for another."

"She can overlook details when she loves someone," Leslie responded jokingly. "Remember my father was from Manhattan. I believe mother has elevated you to his level, taken you into her heart in her own unique fashion. But be careful, dear friend," Leslie cautioned. "It can be a slippery pillar at times."

Bev stared at Leslie for a long moment and then began to laugh out loud. Leslie joined her in the laughter. The friends hugged each other.

* * *

One half hour from Leslie's mother's house they were airborne. "Our twin engine Lear jet will be approaching Palm Beach International Airport in 40 minutes," the captain informed upon their departure. He made a brief mention about a storm he wanted to avoid. "We will fly well inland, staying over land most of the way. We will have a great view of Disney World out of the port windows," he had informed them. "But please keep your seat belts on loosely during the flight, we may experience some turbulence." As it turned out, he was right.

Leslie strapped herself in opposite Bev as the plane taxied. The possibility of bad weather made her uncomfortable, so to hide her concerns she began to work. "We need to take an assessment of the situation," she told Bev as the nose of the jet lifted off the runway. Bev was equally willing to avoid talk or even thought about the pending flight. She knew about the storm from the flight up. Even before she left, plans were underway to shut down the airport if the storm continued to develop and approach the Palm Beaches. "We may be taking the train back," the pilot had kidded. Now they were flying at 33,000 feet and 600 miles per hour toward it.

"Assessing is simple," Bev answered with an angry tone in he voice. "Simply keep your first three letters and flush the rest. That is what he deserves."

"First three?" Leslie asked.

"Yes," Bev replied. "A-S-S, that is what he is, that Jessup. I need to introduce him to some of my Jewish friends. He needs a bris. You know, the circumcision ceremony. But I want to make it a very close one, if you know what I mean. That skunk has called my friends and told them Robert is not handling the wool deal honestly. I never liked the man in the first place. Any fool as old as he who thinks he is God's gift to women is not to be trusted. His thinking processes are as fouled up as Tanny's machinator."

"What dear, is that?"

"You remember Les, that supposed to be 'romantic' sail on the square-rigged yacht, wind power only. But the toilet didn't work. Don't you?" Bev asked.

"Oh, how could I ever forget," Leslie answered. "We became very authentic 19th century on that over-night, over-the-rail, sail."

"Yes, the machinator was jammed," Bev explained. "The thing-a-ma-bob that grinds up the waste from the toilet before it pumps the stuff through the bulkhead and into the ocean for disposal. We had to hang over the side with toilet paper in hand or explode!" Both women laughed.

"So you knew Jessup, before RRR I mean?" Leslie asked.

"Afraid so," Bev answered. "I always thought him only semi-talented. He's the kind of lawyer who's almost smart enough to pull it off, to fulfill promises, but only almost. He simply had to fly down to Palm Beach first class once a month, review contracts, and sometimes carry a certified check back to Manhattan. I told them to find another firm, but doctors, well you know. Sometimes their wives are in charge of family investments. Jessup got lucky. He bought a firm and within one year a sizable probate gave him introduction to the bereaved family's friends. He can make simple stuff look complicated. I'll give him credit for that. He made himself look good. Crap, how hard is it to liquidate bearer bonds anyway?"

"So how did he get to RRR?"

"I told my friends about Robert. They insisted Jessup take them to RRR and he definitely did not like that. So you see, Jeffery and I are the keys to his success and continued control. As long as he wants the business he must deal with us; hence the false affection for us."

"Unless he can tarnish the RRR reputation and in so doing cause you to lose credibility with your Manhattan friends," Leslie stated emphatically.

"Creating an accounting crisis, or worse a scandal, would certainly give him the opportunity to steal away the New York interests' business."

"And I doubt it wouldn't be any time at all before there would be another disaster, one that would about wipe out the assets of his new company," Bev added.

"He has the correct accomplice, the perfect patsy: Sykes."

"Funny, though isn't it?" Bev remarked. "He's smart enough to begin this swindle and stupid enough to believe no one will catch on. There should be a special name, title, for such a semi-competent con artist. A clumsy robber of retirement savings, even widow's and orphan's funds."

"There is," Leslie answered. "According to my mother they are called carpetbaggers. One hundred years ago, no citizen was fooled by their charades. Not for long. Only the force of an occupying army could cover their crimes. It's called the Reconstruction."

"A Damn Yankee?" Bev asked.

Leslie nodded and shrugged her shoulders.

"But have no fear, this Yankee will fight him!"

"True friend," Leslie replied, "your support is invaluable and unquestioned. But, if dear Robert is lost at sea, then there is no RRR. I believe it is a safe assumption that Nora would not fill his shoes. I'm afraid RRR would become a non entity. "Jessup would steal the investors, and rob them. It would be the end."

A can of soda flew from Leslie's tray and bounced cross the cabin. They tightened their lap belts. For a moment they stared at each other, hesitant to say what was on their minds for fear of it becoming true just by speaking. *Robert is still out in this mess. Worse, Jessup is responsible for Robert's disappearance.*

Chapter 27   Palm Beach

The flight was a painful chore for Leslie. Bev decided to use the time in flight to educate her about Robert. Leslie listened to Bev's regaling of Robert's estranged wife. "Her drinking began long before their marriage, Les dear, so don't think that charming boy was in any way to blame. More to blame I'd say was Bobby's mother. With all good intentions, she pushed those two together." Leslie listened. With every detail pains shot through her heart.

So Bev blames Robert's mother for the bad marriage, Leslie thought to herself as the plane sped across the early evening sky. *If only partially true, Robert would never admit it to himself. He would certainly blame himself all the more to protect his mother from criticism. A loyal and true hero and victim.*

"That Robert," Bev continued, "is such a chivalrous man. He always takes responsibility when women are concerned."

Leslie mind raced back to their so very special night aboard his yacht. The night they spoke of marriage. *Robert's apology had been so mysterious.*

"Of course," Bev went on, "that requires his total control of every situation. He will always make certain he is in control. He does not take chances if they can be in any way avoided, not after the accident. You are so deeply in love. He is a true Southern gentleman in your eyes, chivalrous, cautious with his affections, caring. But I must admit that after meeting your mother I cannot see you being satisfied with only that."

"Only that?" Leslie asked, surprised. "Isn't that perfection?"

Bev let out a huge laugh. "Leslie dear, you would not be satisfied with a man who plans your every move, who believes it is his masculine responsibility to keep all evil things from your delicate mind. You, my dear, want to be in control of your own destiny, like your mother. Or, perhaps you are somewhat modified by your father's influence. Perhaps you regard marriage as a partnership of responsibility?"

Mother had always considered father to be the junior member of the marriage, though her father had always wanted an equal partnership. Mother had always used the 'damn Yankee' character fault to gain control of every issue. Father had simply ceased arguing and ceded control to the 'grand dame' of society. In my mother's eyes, Leslie's father could never be the complete Southern gentleman.

"And that's why you ran off to Charleston," Bev continued, "to get a bearing on your life, right?"

Leslie did not answer.

"But what you found there was an imperfection, I'm guessing. You see Leslie dear, there is no perfection, so no one can achieve it. Not even a perfect Southern gentleman. What you want is a complete and open partnership."

Leslie nodded an agreement.

"And wowh! When Robert kept you out of the loop on the wool matter," Bev finished, "you were furious. It wasn't the Nora phone call that drove you to Charleston. That was only an excuse for the quick decision. You're a woman of the 21st century."

"And here we are, coming to his rescue." More than Jessup, more than the high seas, Leslie was angry with Robert.

The pilot had invited Leslie and Bev into the cockpit for the view. But Disney World was covered in clouds that swept in from the northeast Atlantic in a wide arc and turned southeast somewhere over Orlando. "It doesn't look good for a Palm Beach landing," the pilot announced as he surveyed the giant swirl pattern of clouds. "That cloud structure could mean the storm has intensified."

"Jeffrey is home alone, right on the beach!" Bev exclaimed. "Perhaps Robert was found by the Coast Guard. It's been a long time." She was trying to lighten the moment but both women knew the difficulty of finding a small boat in a rough sea.

As if on cue the pilot announced: "those look like feeder bands. I bet we are getting our first tropical storm of the season. We may want to set down in Vero Beach."

"No, not a chance of that," Bev ordered. "We have people we must reach and a business emergency. Were going!"

The jet had already begun its' slow descent into West Palm Beach when the pilot radioed the control tower. "They're telling us to wave off," he said. "Want to send us north and out of the way of the storm."

We're going to Palm Beach," Leslie answered with force in her voice. "Send them a message. Say we can't hear them clearly, that we are on approach to runway 90 left. Click the mike a few times. They will be too busy readying for the storm, and after the cleanup will keep them occupied.

"Here we come," the pilot said. "Lear jet flight 3761, Charleston to PBIA on approach to left 90 at six thousand feet.... requesting emergency landing instructions. We're having some trouble with reception…. Say again." He listened into the headphones a moment and then announced: Cleared for emergency only. We'll be the last plane into PBIA and it is going to be a rollercoaster ride. We'll have a 40 knot shear wind so I'll be landing with the nose aiming at the terminal, not the runway. Don't get scared.

"By the way," the pilot commented, "she has a name now."

"Who?" Leslie asked.

"Why the storm, of course," the pilot answered. "Ladies, meet Agnes," he said as he pointed out the windshield. Ahead loomed a deep, dull gray wall of water mixed with turbulent air. "Better get back to your seats."

"Final approach, tighten those seat belts back there," the pilot's voice warned over the intercom.

"Do you see the airport?" Leslie asked into her microphone.

"I should, except for Agnes," was his reply. Then he added: "I think it would be a good idea if both of you place a pillow on your laps and rest your head there. It is going to be bumpy."

They did so just as they heard the landing gear set in place with a thump. *A reassuring sound,* Leslie thought. In a moment they were being bounced down the runway. Leslie looked up to see if Bev was all right. Her head was buried in the pillow as ordered. Leslie held her neck tight against the violent snaps and thrusts of Agnes. She looked out the window to see only a darkening sky and flying horizontal rain as evening approached. No lights could be seen and no Robert. The nose touched down and then the reverse thrusters came to life. "We're home," Leslie said softly.

Bev looked up and smiled: "Yes."

They taxied to the south side of the field, to a waiting hanger. "Just in time," the pilot announced. Here is something you'll never see again," as he taxied down the main landing strip. "No one else is coming or going. We and Agnes have the whole damn place to ourselves." Ground crew directed them into the hanger. The pilot did not wait for a truck to pull him in. He taxied into the hanger, jet engines roaring.

By the time Leslie and Bev were down the ramp and into the waiting rental car, the ground crew had already anchored the jet. "They want to get home fast," Leslie remarked.

"So do I," Bev announced as she turned the car's key. It took only a minute for Bev to get through the fence gate and on to Perimeter Road. "I know a short cut, watch this," she said as she turned 180 degrees and jumped the grass strip between Perimeter Road and Congress Avenue at the East end of the airport. The car jumped and bottomed out into the deep drainage swale before clearing all obstacles.

"Don't stop for lights," Leslie instructed. They sped east on Southern Boulevard toward the island. A policeman stood in the road at the causeway ramp to the southernmost bridge to Palm Beach. "It can only mean they are opening the bridge for the storm."

Bridges to coastal barrier islands are left open during storms to facilitate navigation, but it closes those islands to automobile access for the duration. The crossing gate was down. The policeman waved them off with a red flashlight. The bridge was beginning to raise.

"Jump it," Leslie yelled.

"I always wanted to do this," Bev answered and drove the car past the jumping policewoman, through the wooden guard with a smash and onto the metal bridge. The car bottomed out but Bev held control. Over bridge and onto the pavement they went before the policewoman could turn to get their license plate. "Woo, woo," Bev shouted. "That was fun."

Soon, Bev pulled the car through her gate and directly across the lawn to the front door. The car bumper hit the Coquina steps and they came to an abrupt halt.

"Now that was fun," Leslie announced. "Too bad we don't get more hurricanes." Both women laughed.

The wind was by now blowing so hard that they could not open the windward door. Instead both women exited the car from the leeward side, the wind almost pulling the door out of Leslie's hand. They made a fast run for the portico. Leslie pounded on the door while Bev searched for her keys, both women yelling. They were drenched with rain.

Momentarily the door opened. It was Jeffrey. They rushed in, Bev into his arms.

"Was beginning to become a little concerned about you," Jeffery said. "Heard you were flying in his weather. Taking chances on my account?" He asked humorously.

"Dearest man, I could not leave you alone here on the beach in a hurricane," Bev answered, and gave him a big, wet hug.

"Oh, but you needn't be so concerned, my dear," Jeffrey answered in a flippant manner. "We have a house guest to look after me. Mr. Jessup arrived a while ago and I am afraid is now marooned with us, at least for the duration."

Both women were shocked, speechless. Jeffrey winked and nodded behind he door with his head.

"A wet good evening to you ladies," Jessup said with a large smile. "By the looks on your faces, I would guess I've completely surprised you."

Chapter 28   Anges

"I was visiting friends on the North end, well trying to," Jessup announced. "They weren't home, darnedest thing. Seems they scooted out and over to the mainland for the storm. Imagine that! A little thing like a hurricane and they skedaddle, just like that, hah! So I got to the middle bridge and it was up and the cop said it was going to stay up, just like all the bridges, until the storm blew itself out. Now can you imagine that, I ask you? It wouldn't happen in New York."

Leslie and Bev stood frozen for a moment, listening in disbelief to the words of their enemy. Unready to answer, they let him go on.

"Can you?" Jessup continued. An air of sarcasm entered his words. "Just like that they close, or I guess the correct thing to say is they open them and don't close them, let them down I mean. So I'm stuck on the island. But then I remembered my old friends the Millers and thought it would be bad if you two had to go through this storm all by yourselves."

"Mr. Jessup found me in the pantry, dear." Jeffrey began to explain. He gave Bev a look that warned her not to attack, not yet. "I didn't hear the door bell, with the wind and all. I must have left it unlocked." Jeffrey smiled a phony smile and winked.

"I had to go looking for him, wouldn't have ever guessed he'd be in the pantry. What happened, help run off?" Jessup did not hide his contempt for Palm Beach.

Bev came out of her trance. The thought of Jessup roaming her home was too much for her, but she bit her tongue and said scoldingly: "Of course they want to be with their families, there is a hurricane coming." Bev paused, remembering that Jessup could be dangerous. Then she added: "I'm glad to see you here. No one should be out in this weather," thinking that at times like this caution is the better part of valor.

The Baccarat crystal chandelier above their heads blinked off for an instant and then regained its' reassuring bright glow. Everyone looked up and paused.

"Of course, of course," Jeffrey said to Bev. "But the two of you are drenched to the bone. We can't have that." He reached his arm around Leslie and nudged her in the direction of the staircase. "Get into the bedroom and get some dry clothes on. Leslie, try on my garden clothes. The jeans may be a little tight around the hips, but the waist and length should be fine. In any case we want sturdy clothes on during the storm. Jessup and I will meet you in the kitchen after you change. Come along," he said to Jessup and they left Bev and Leslie in the foyer.

As Jeffrey and Jessup walked toward the kitchen, Jessup announced again: "Leave the bridges up! Can you imagine that, in a city? That would never be tolerated in New York. People wouldn't stand for it!"

"Damn Yankee," Bev muttered under her breath.

Leslie giggled. "Why dear Bev," she said pretending to be shocked, "have you become a Rebel?"

"He is a low snake, no, he's lower than snake, lower than snake spit," Bev whispered. "I don't want him in my house, especially when I'm not at home." Bev's face was reddening with anger.

"Don't despair," Leslie answered. "Let's go get in some dry clothes. It's a blessing, in a way, we now know where he is and can keep an eye on him, though I'd prefer he was in a Chinese jail."

"He has been roaming my home, damn it!" Bev repeated, alarmed. "And we can suppose he has not found whatever he was looking for, otherwise he would be gone."

"We know what he is looking for," Leslie reminded Bev. She didn't need to say what they both feared: Jessup would not leave until he got the wool sample.

* * *

The master bedroom became bathed in white light as Bev entered and passed her right hand over the doorknob. "Another one of Jeffrey's passions, gadgets," Bev remarked to Leslie. "He can't have just a door knob and a light switch. Everything must be automated, impressive to his golf buddies. He actually goes to those home improvement shows and fills out those damn cards. We have salesmen in here all the time!"

The room displayed tropical touches set against an eggshell white silk wall treatment. The contrast between verdant green, powerful tropical flower pastels, and the muted white of the walls created an oasis effect. The room seemed to be detached from the rest of the house, *as if you pass over a stream or through a time portal to enter*, Leslie thought to herself. *Detached from the reality of this world.* It was Leslie's favorite room in the house. "The perfect place to escape the world," she muttered.

"Watch this," Bev announced. She walked into the center of the room and announced in a clear voice: "Morning!" Instantly a huge wall mural sprang to life. Depicting a green meadow in the Alps, and it began to move.

"Oh," Leslie gasped, surprised.

"You haven't seen nothing yet," Bev warned her. The mural scene followed an Alpine stream, down and down, over granite rocks and under evergreens until it crossed under a stone bridge and entered a village. The scene stopped there, paused. "Well, how do you like it?" Bev asked. "It's Jeffrey's new toy. It's programmed with 150 scenes for him and another 150 for me."

"Quite impressive," Leslie answered. "How does it work?" Leslie knew her friend wanted her to ask.

"Jeffrey had to have it after he heard a rumor that that computer tycoon had one in his parlor, you know that Bill somebody." Bev explained. "Only

Jeffrey had to do him one better, put romantic stuff in it, and program it. So we just had to put it in the bedroom."

"Ok, let me see," Leslie asked, now she was hooked. She had forgotten about their unwanted houseguest.

"Not that easy, dear," Bev said. "You see it is programmed specifically for Jeffrey and me, or each of us. It has sensors like infrared for body temperature and low frequency microphones that pick up our heart and digestive sounds, and stuff like that. It can read our feelings. If we are excited, or sad, or whatever, it will display the scenes we best like when we are in that particular mood."

"Let's see it work."

"Ok, but let me warn you, what it is going to display is beyond my control." Bev warned. She stood in front of the mural and said "Bev." The scene dissolved in a swirl of color. The palette turned dark and a small figure appeared, slowly growing larger. Trees appeared around the scene, dark trees; dark woods with a path in the middle. In that path, a rider was approaching at a gallop. In a moment the rider and horse passed over the viewing position, throwing sparks from the horse's hooves.

Leslie felt trampled. She gasped: "What were you thinking about?"

"Jessup," Bev replied. "We better get dressed. The bastard is downstairs and I want to keep an eye on him." Bev reached into Jeffrey's bottom drawer and produced a pair of jeans and an old linen long sleeve shirt. She tossed them on the bed. As if to remind them, the wind gusted and rattled the French doors.

"Better let me borrow a pair of tennis shoes, too," Leslie asked. "I don't want to be walking around barefoot if a window breaks. It will take hours for mine to dry."

The women took turns using the bath to dry off.

"I am not going to bother with my hair," Leslie announced from the bath. "If Agnes doesn't like it she can go somewhere else." She knew humor was a healthy way of handling stress and she was concerned for Bev's mental state. The mural had disturbed her, Leslie was certain.

When Leslie emerged from the bathroom Bev was already dressed. She hadn't bothered to dry her hair. She had just combed it. It hung straight down to her shoulders and Leslie realized for the first time that Bev was aging. Bev was stressed out.

"Let's go see what that snake is up to," Leslie announced. As she left the bedroom Leslie noticed the mural had returned to the Alpine stream scene. The friends descended the staircase.

* * *

"What you do is turn it slowly, no the other way," Jeffrey was saying to Jessup as Bev and Leslie entered the kitchen. "No, more slowly" There on a stool stood Jessup, reaching up and over the window with a crank in his hand. "That's it, now tighten"

Jessup let out a groan as he pushed the handle. "Look, that's got to be enough," he said. He climbed down from the stool and brushed imaginary dust from his pants. "You should get someone to repair that for you."

"Mr. Jessup was just helping me shutter up for the blow," Jeffrey offered. "That last one was stuck." The ladies grinned.

"Really don't see what all the fuss is about," Jessup said as he brushed his slacks with his hand. "You act like children. It's only a storm."

"A storm you say," Jeffrey interjected. "Why in 1928 a storm came through Miami Beach and blew out all the walls on the hotels, left three feet of beach sand in the fourth floor rooms. Back in 1936 over 600 people died in that one down in the Keys. They are more than just storms."

At that moment, a crash was heard outside. Everyone ran to the front door. Leslie opened it an inch and all peeked out. A white oak had crashed to the ground and onto Jessup's rental car. Now a gash three feet deep and four feet wide stretched across its roof. "We can expect more of this," Leslie warned.

"Look," Jessup said, visibly shaken. "If it gets that bad no one should ever live here. You people are crazy. It just makes no sense. Why do people move here?"

"We tell them it doesn't snow," Jeffrey answered smiling, "it's the truth. They never ask about hurricanes and we don't tell them until after they buy. It's our little secret." Jeffrey was enjoying tormenting Jessup.

"I've had enough of this silliness," Jessup announced. "I need a drink."

"We'll all join you," Bev said. The wind was now howling through the cracks around the windows. "That's going to get louder."

Jeffery reached into a bottom cabinet and produced a bottle of rum. "Get some coke from the fridge and a few glasses, dear," Jeffrey asked Bev. "There should be ice in the freezer. We should enjoy refrigeration while we can."

"Why, is the storm going to blow down the refrigerator too?" Jessup asked sarcastically.

"No, but it could blow down the power lines," Leslie answered. She moved to Jessup's right and grabbed his arm. "You're not frightened, are you?" she asked.

Jessup pulled his arm away. He knew she was trying to insult him. He reached in his slacks pocket and produced a white handkerchief. "Something in my eye," he said. "Could you help me with it?" he asked Leslie and moved to her.

"Help yourself," Leslie replied and stepped back.

"What's this?" Jessup exclaimed looking at his handkerchief after wiping it across his eyes. "Looks like bright dirt."

"Sand," Leslie answered, "beach sand. You've got beach sand on your face. Haven't you ever been to the beach before?" she asked. "It's all over the place and it's going to be all over us before this storm is over."

Bev poured the drinks. "Mr. Jessup," she asked, "we thought you had returned to New York. What caused your delay?"

"Forgot something, or rather misplaced something," Jessup answered. "It's embarrassing, really. Bev remember those little balls of wool, you know, from the board meeting? Well, I seem to have misplaced mine. Thought I left them at my friend's house, but well you know, they are not at home. I don't suppose you could lend me yours, could you? I wouldn't want to return to New York empty handed."

"Why don't you get another from Robert?" Jeffrey asked. He did not know about the boat.

"Not possible," Jessup replied. "He seems to have disappeared from the face of the earth." Leslie did not like his choice of words. Neither did Bev. "It's like the ocean has swallowed him up." He noticed the expressions on Leslie's and Bev's face and added: "But don't be concerned. He is probably judging a Bikini contest on some small and private island." Jessup watched for their reaction. Leslie didn't display anger at his comment. Bev said nothing. Jessup smiled. He knew they knew.

* * *

Slam, slam, there was a pounding at the front door. By now the winds were over 75 miles per hour, hurricane strength. "My God, some poor soul is out in this monster storm," Jeffrey announced. "Quick, let him in!"

Leslie, Bev, and Jessup ran to the door. Slam, slam, came from outside. Leslie pushed open the door against the wind. A stream of horizontal water flew in and with it a man was tossed through the door. After him, another came running.

The first man slipped, and fell to the marble floor. The second entered and kept his balance. He placed his right foot on the back of the stranger lying on the floor. "Now don't move a muscle, if you know what's good for you," the standing man ordered. It was Robert.

Jessup looked angered. Bev screamed for joy and yelled: "Your alive, my dear boy, your alive!"

Leslie rushed to him and wrapped her arms around his neck. "My dear, I made it back to you, I promise I always will," Robert whispered as he hugged her.

Leslie tightened her hold around his neck. "You must never leave again," she whispered in his ear.

"I promise I won't," Robert answered. Then he let out a yell: "Eouh! That hurts!"
Leslie had increased her squeeze around his neck.

"And you WILL NOT keep secrets from me, you hear me!" Leslie warned.

"Alright, alright," he promised, "here, look what I've found sneaking around the garage. "It's our very own Mr. Harvey Sykes. Say hello Harvey." Robert pressed down on Harvey's back with his foot.

"Aah, cut it out, you can't do that to me!" Sykes cried out.

"Oh, I think so," Robert answered and pressed again. "You think we forget so quickly? And what are you doing here? Not stealing company secrets here. So what?"

"Aah, Jessup do something!" Sykes asked.

"Good evening Mr. Jessup," Robert said. "Good to see you again. Has everyone been waiting long? I was a little delayed, something unforeseen. You know what it's like, right, Mr. Jessup?"

"Glad to see you made it, to our little party, but what of Sykes?" Jessup asked.

"Get me up!" Sykes yelled.

"I would ask more politely, if I were in your position," Jessup told Sykes.

"Promise to be a good boy now?" Robert asked Sykes.

"Yes, yes, anything you say," Sykes promised. Robert removed his shoe from Sykes's back. Sykes got to his feet.

"Really, that wasn't necessary," Sykes complained.

"Nor your scurrying around my home," Bev accused.

"Wasn't scurrying or anything, just looking for Jessup." Sykes explained. "Besides, I don't have to tell you anything."

"I'm your boss, and if you don't want to be unemployed you will explain yourself," Robert ordered.

"Just be happy I don't have you arrested for assault," Sykes answered as he attempted to brush off water from his suit with his hand. "More than that, I choose not to say. And as for working for you, I should think I will not after the way I was assaulted. I may sue you for injuries sustained, though."

"What injuries?" Bev asked angrily.

"My attorney will find some," Sykes answered as he brushed his coat.

At that moment the lights failed.

"Oh, great what now?" Jessup asked. "This hurricane business is really getting in my way."

"The phones will be out too," Bev said. "Jeffrey, bring a flashlight." The portico slowly began to glow with the bouncing light from Jeffrey as he approached.

"I have candles out on the breakfast table," Jeffrey informed all. "We better get them lit. There is one for everybody." They made their way to the kitchen and the breakfast room beyond, Robert pushing Sykes all the way. Jeffrey lit a candle for everyone.

"Looks like we are going to be here all night," Robert announced. "We late arrivals are going to need some dry clothes. Bev, can you help us out?"

"Leslie, you take care of Robert, I'll get something for Mr. Sykes," Bev replied. "Can't promise you much Sykes. You are much bigger than Jeffrey, more my size. How would you feel about a nice pant suit?" Sykes grumbled. By now the roof tiles were vibrating like some slow moving train. A dusting of sand, blown threw cracks in the door and window frames, was evenly distributed throughout the ground floor.

* * *

Leslie brought Robert to a guest suite while she went to find some dry clothes. He lit a candle in the bathroom. The water was still hot so he decided to take a shower. She found him there when she returned. Leslie watched him as he bathed. *He appears to be so strong, confident, yet he could not tell me about the twins; about Nora,* she thought as he washed his chest. Leslie felt tears in her eyes. *I wonder if I could have lived with such a secret.* Leslie ached for him, ached for his pain.

"That damn Sykes," Robert began, talking to Leslie through the glass shower door. "He was poking around a window, with a screw driver in his hand! The bastard intended to break in."

"What did the creep want, do you suppose?" Leslie asked back. She reached into the shower. "Want me to do your back?" She wanted to stay close to him. If he were to be lost to the world again, she would be with him. "That reminds me," Leslie remarked, looking at his glistening body, "Weren't you lost at sea?"

"My dearest," Robert turned and looked deep into her eyes, "Luck was with us the entire time. We, Tanny and I, were out of gas. Someone stole it in Bimini. We drifted for a while until the Coast Guard found us and gave us gas. Tanny dropped me off at the north end pier and the police were kind enough to drop me here, and just in time to find Sykes. Nothing much to it, really. The worst is over now,"

"The hell it is," Leslie replied as she reached behind him and turned off the hot water.

"Yeow!" Robert shouted out at the sudden chill, "What's that for?"

"For the south of France," Leslie answered and folded her arms in defiance. "You know, Nora. How is she?" Robert paled. Leslie wasn't sure it was because of the water temperature, or her question, or both. She hoped both. He froze, afraid to ask for a towel, he turned off the cold water and stood there, dripping.

"I meant to tell you," he said softly. "A thousand times I meant to tell you. But, it's complicated."

"You mean it's something you were to handle yourself, without any help, don't you?" Leslie yelled.

"It's my duty, my fault," he hesitated as he spoke, "my fault you did not know."

"And what of your professed undying love for me?" Leslie answered, becoming angrier. "Why do you think only you can be trusted with such a responsibility? Are you the only one who cares for another? Really Robert, if you are to be mine, then I own your situations, all of them. I shall not be excluded. Do you hear me Mister Robinard?"

Robert reached for her but she withdrew and threw him a towel. "Dry yourself mister, you're dripping." Leslie said with complete authority. *He does look good dripping by candlelight,* she thought to herself.

"Dearest, I tried to tell you, but, well it is a terrible thing..." he began.

"I know all about it," Leslie answered. "Dear Bev informed of that horrible Nora, but what about you? You could not trust me with the truth! How can we live our lives without sharing all truths? Bobby, I am beginning to wonder if I can trust you!"

"Oh, you can, you can, trust me I mean," Robert answered. Then he added: "Did you just call me Bobby?"

I shall call the man I intend to share my genes with anything I care to," Leslie announced. Robert began to say something, he took in a breath as if to announce a rule, but Leslie wrapped the towel around his butt and pulled him toward her. "Hush," she ordered, "and come here." She pulled him to the bed. He gladly fell upon her, unquestioning.

"This is how it is going to be," Leslie told him as she maneuvered under his weight. "I share in everything. We are going to marry as soon as you believe you can. We are going to have an agreement, you and I Mister Bobby, a binding one." And with that she grabbed him. "You are mine."

"They were my d…" Robert began to say: daughters, but Leslie simply put her index finger to his lips and silenced him.

"I know, dearest," she whispered. "You are a good man," she said looking into his eyes. Robert bent down. All energy fell from his body. He put his head upon Leslie's breast and softly began to sob.

"What could I do?" Robert asked. "What? The police impounded the car and covered it with a yellow plastic sheet."

"Don't talk about the pain, dearest," Leslie directed tenderly into his ear. "Speak only of the good times. Remember them like that."

Robert sat up in bed. "They were twins, did you know?"

"Yes dearest."

"Identical in every way except one. They both liked to draw. Alexandra would stay within the lines but, Veronica never did. Veronica would draw right off the paper and onto the bed sheet, or wall, or floor, or whatever. It made it hard to display their creations. Might have to hang a bed sheet or cut up a floor to rescue Veronica's creations." He laughed between sobs. "Alexandra had her ballerina doll, bigger than her. She would delight in it and dance evenings for our entertainment. Veronica had a monkey doll, bigger than her that hung its arms around her neck. She was never without it." Robert took a deep breath and continued.

"Did you know police save everything from a car wreck?" He asked again. "Personal items must be collected by the nearest of kin. Nora was in hospital. Under the yellow plastic, on the rear seat I found the ballerina doll, torn and soaked with mud. As I left with what remained, an officer presented me with a yellow plastic bag. 'Found by the tree,' he said. Inside was the monkey doll, torn and blood soaked."

"Have you ever been to Ireland?" He asked Leslie. "It is a beautiful island. Meadows and small villages abound. Winding country roads, manor houses, horses and sheep. Kids like sheep. I always had wanted to take Alexandra and Veronica there. We decided to wait until they were older, so they would remember it. Older..."

"That would have been a wonderful vacation," Leslie answered. "Would you still like to go?"

Robert didn't answer. He looked deep into her eyes. "I wrapped the dolls in linen, put them in a box and brought them out by boat into the Atlantic, to the Gulf Stream. I set them free." He sighed. "I like to think they found their way across the Atlantic to Ireland."

Robert folded into Leslie's arms...

* * *

In the almost total darkness of a house lit only by a few candles, the roar of the wind outside took on gargantuan proportions. One moment something could be heard dragging across the roof, like a giant claw. Next there was banging on the front door, and the air currents inside the house moved, well, in an unnatural pattern. Or at least it seemed to Jessup.

"How long do these things go on?" he asked Jeffrey as they both stood over the natural gas fired kitchen range heating some water for hot tea in a pot. The glow of the gas flame added an additional eerie value to the moment.

"What goes on?" Jeffrey returned his question with another.

"The damn hurricane, of course," Jessup responded, "what the hell else did you think I meant." Jessup was beginning to loose his composure, to Jeffrey's great delight.

"Relax, old boy," Jeffrey falsely comforted Jessup. "These things usually blow themselves out in a couple of hours."

"Well, it's been longer than that!" Jessup exclaimed. "What the hell…"

Jeffrey interrupted with a lie: "Of course, they can grow, after they hit land, you know. The Seminoles used to say the land angers the storm god. Kind of gets them worked up. That's why there are storm surges."

"Storm what?" Jessup asked as he looked down at the boiling pot of water.

"Surges," Jeffrey answered and joined Jessup in the observation of boiling bubbles.

"So what the hell are they?" Jessup anxiously repeated his question.

"Oh, quite obvious, old boy, I should say," Jeffrey took his time in answering. Jessup was beginning to show beads of perspiration on his forehead. "You see, a hurricane is a lot like this boiling pot of water. It has a tremendous amount of energy collected into a small space like this pot to the rest of our kitchen. Well, the energy has to go somewhere. You can hear it outside trying to bust loose right now. But, you see, it also goes up with great force, like the bubbles in the pot." Jeffrey stopped speaking.

"So, we just shut off the range," Jessup said in a sarcastic tone. He was not buying what Jeffrey was selling. Not in his mind. Not for a minute.

"Thats all well and good, old boy," Jeffrey continued, "but you see like in the pot, when the bubbles of boiling water go upward and leave the pot something must come in and take their place, nature abhors a vacuum. So air replaces the bubbles and the water goes down." Jeffrey could tell Jessup was losing his interest in his science lecture so he added: "so soon we may have salt water around our knees, old boy," and waited for Jessup's reaction.

Jessup did not say anything at first. He just added perspiration beads to the collection on his forehead. "Ok, why salt water, Jessup asked. "You going to tell me it's raining salt water?"

"Not at all old boy," Jeffrey answered, "but that vacuum is going to draw up the ocean. Not that we will be swimming in it, but it could get worse. Especially if you add to that the wave action." With that, Jeffrey bent over and dragged his left index finger across the lower portion of the cabinet and brought it to his mouth and tasted. "Salty," he told Jessup.

"Bullshit!" Jessup shouted, but he took his own finger and sampled the cabinet. It was salty. Jessup's eyes got big.

"Water is ready, get the cups old boy," Jeffrey instructed Jessup. "The cups," he repeated. Jessup seemed to be lost in thought. Jeffrey smiled.

* * *

"Ow, what was that for?" Sykes yelled at Bev from inside the bathroom.

"Oh, sorry," Bev answered as she again thrust the long handle of a broom, suspending a pair of bib overalls through a crack of an opening in the bathroom door. "Here grab it, you slimy, sneaky snake. Grab the bib overalls or I swear I'll throw you out into the storm." She was dressing Sykes in some of her gardening clothes. "Save your shoes, varmint."

Sykes was dressed only in one of her old sweatshirts, dodging Bev's broom handle unsuccessfully as another thrust jammed into his floating ribs. "Cut that out!" he begged.

"Now you ask for mercy," she shouted. "Tell me what you were doing at my window with a screwdriver!"

"My job," Sykes answered, "and damn it, stop jabbing me. Jessup said we needed something in a Chinese box. There had been a mix-up and of course Mr. Robinard was nowhere around. We had to do something and quickly, or else the New York partners would be angry with the mix-up."

"Oh sure, you were just helping out, were you? Well what about a phone call? Bev asked and prodded into the bathroom again.

"Jessup said you didn't answer." Sykes responded with some pleading in his voice to be believed.

"And you called Miss Devereaux, too?" Bev rebutted. Sykes did not answer. "She is Robert's second, or have you conveniently forgotten? Really, Sykes, you are beginning to piss me off," and she jabbed into the bathroom again.

Robert and Leslie lay silently together, arms, and legs intertwined; without words, all secrets revealed. Robert moved to get up. Leslie held his arm above the elbow. "What is it she asked?"

"The wind has died," he answered, rose and walked over to the window. He turned the crank and raised the hurricane shutter. Slowly the spectacle of the storm was revealed. Leslie joined him at the window. Out of total darkness came distant strikes of lightning. With each explosion of light they could see walls of violent rain and wind. But where they stood all was calm. Caught in the middle, the eye of the storm, surrounded by danger, there was no wind or rain. Above stars twinkled in the night sky. "For the moment," Robert whispered, "we are safe. But it encircles us."

Leslie looked at her man, naked, illuminated by dangerous lightning, and felt sorry for him. "Don't be concerned," she whispered as she pulled his arms around her. "Danger is all around us, even under this roof, but at last we are truly together." She led him back to the bed and fell upon him. "You are mine," she whispered.

Together again, they swirled into each other as Agnes swirled around them. "I must have you," he whispered, "I must have you, all of you, for my very own." He kissed her lips, her neck, her breasts, and followed her tensing body down to her center of passion. Deeper and deeper they folded into each other.

The single candle danced wrappings of light and shadow about the room creating a new reality, a new dimension that swallowed them up and covered them in a protecting sheet of soft darkness, if only for now.

Lights flickered and then held. "Hooray," Jeffrey shouted, "we are again in the twenty-first century!" Sykes and Jessup looked at each other, concern showed on their faces. "Soon the bridges will be operating and we can get on with our lives," Jeffrey added. Bev noticed Jessup was becoming anxious and she was anxious to see him gone.

"How soon" Jessup asked, "before we can get off the island?" He wondered if he could get off the island before police could get in. He had business to attend to.

"With luck an hour," Jeffrey answered.

Jessup's face reddened. "Do you think the roads are passable?" he asked and then added: "Maybe we should have a look outside." The group, less Leslie and Robert had spent the last three hours in the kitchen sipping first tea and then red wine. Gradually, the howling wind had died down. But the humidity had stayed. Everything had been penetrated with moist salt air; clothes, upholstery, hair and eyes. And sand too. It seemed to be everywhere in a fine dusting that now stuck to everything and everyone.

"Yes, it's about time," Robert said as he entered the kitchen with Leslie on his arm. His clothes had mostly dried during the night on the back of a chair. "Now that we are emerging from the tempest," Robert continued, "I think it is time for you two to explain yourselves," he said to Jessup and Sykes.

"Look, I was just following orders. It was all a misunderstanding. You didn't have to kick me!" Sykes exclaimed.

"I could have had you arrested." Robert answered. "Didn't you notice it was the police who drove me here? I told them I wanted to handle you myself."

"So that's how you so miraculously appeared at the door." Jessup quipped.

"At the window," Robert corrected, " the one Sykes was breaking into."

"I had my orders…" Sykes began.

But Jessup interrupted: "Quiet you fool. Can't you see this scoundrel is trying to frame us?" He looked at Jeffrey and Bev, the only hope he had to save his skin and he knew it. "This Master Robert has deceived my clients, given them a false report, and sample. Fortunately, before I delivered the wool to the investors I had it analyzed chemically. Master Robert," Jessup said sarcastically, "do you have the guts to tell them, or should I?" All eyes turned to Robert. Bev winked. Jeffrey moved slowly toward his golf bag behind the kitchen door.

"Happily," Robert answered. "You and Sykes have been stealing from the company, first cash and now ideas."

"Liar!" Sykes yelled. Jeffrey grabbed a nine iron from his golf bag.

"Gently, gently, Mr. Sykes, for our sake," Jeffrey warned, or I shall be forced to use this and I am sure you would want me to be gentle in such a situation on your head."

"Funds were transferred from RRR's bank accounts from your computer, we have the evidence." Leslie interjected.

"But I never, I swear," Sykes began and then paused. His face became illuminated. "It was you?" he asked turning to Jessup. "It was you," he stated pointing a finger at him. "I trusted you. You said that Jason was a thief. I should never have given you access, you..."

"Enough!" Jessup yelled. He pulled a revolver from his pocket. "This twisting of lies will stop. You didn't have to give me the codes, you're as guilty, but nobody is guilty, for you see I was protecting my clients' interests. You were going to cheat me out of the wool deal, cheat my clients out of the deal. I have proof. The stuff you gave me was just dyed. Now I want the real stuff." He raised the revolver and pointed it around the room. "Bev," Jessup ordered, "get me that sample!"

"I don't know what you mean, you scoundrel," Bev answered defiantly. "You can go to hell!"

Jessup's face flared with anger. He raised the revolver and put it into Bev's face. Everyone flinched.

"You dirty rotten snake!" Sykes yelled and made a move for the weapon. Jessup turned and fired hitting Sykes in the left shoulder. Blood poured out of the wound and he fell toward the floor. Robert and Jeffrey caught him and eased him down Jeffrey holding his head. Leslie ran to Bev and they held each other. Bev passed something to Leslie. Robert moved for the gun but Jessup again put it to Bev's head.

"Calmly, now folks," Jessup sneered the words from his mouth. He felt all- powerful. "Bev, dear, I want that little box of wool, now. I won't be tricked into a visit to Hong Kong looking for a needle in a haystack. You have the wool, the real stuff. Not the dyed crap you gave me."

"You can go to hell," Bev answered, and Jessup pulled the hammer back. Robert made a move for Jessup but he turned the weapon on him before Robert could reach Jessup's hand.

"Rethink the situation Master Bobby," Jessup warned. "I will blow you away if I must. Then he turned to Bev: "Get me the wool or I will put one in Bobby Boy here."

Jessup's back stiffened. He had not noticed Leslie moving behind him, an object clenched in her hand. A sensation like a prodding, followed by a slight pain from his middle spine found its' way to his brain and his face changed. Leslie was behind him with a 25 automatic in his ribs.

"Don't even cough, Mr. Jessup,' she announced. "Or I shall be required to employ skills my dear Daddy taught me on summer evenings when we would practice plucking cans from one hundred feet." She pushed the barrel tighter into his middle back. "Now I wish you to raise the barrel to the ceiling and Robert will relieve you of your weapon."

"Where'd you get a gun?" Jessup asked unbelievingly.

"From me, you damn fool," Bev answered. "And before you ask the obvious question, none of your business. A lady does not divulge such information. It is sufficient to say it had good company with a certain ball of wool."

Jessup began to look sick. "But you forget, ladies," he said, "I have a reputation for pulling a trigger into a chest cavity, while you Miss Devereaux, well, you pull triggers into empty cans of green beans. I seriously doubt you would place a bullet in my heart. Now everyone, tell Bev here to produce the wool, or else." Jessup smiled a confident smile.

Leslie's hand trembled. *Jessup is right,* she thought, *I could not kill him, but…*

She slid the barrel down his back until it arrived at his crotch and pressed. "You are right, Mr. Jessup," she said, "I am not cut of the same cloth as you. But be assured I would not hesitate to transform you into a genderless villain." She pressed the barrel hard into him.

Jessup gave a squeak and raised his gun to the ceiling.

Chapter 29 Leslie

The stack of papers arrived by special currier four days later, by plane, from the South of France. Leslie placed them on Robert's desk after careful review with instructions to sign them immediately. Crews were still drying carpet with tremendous vacuums and fans but business had returned to normal. Hurricane Agnes had left town and as storms go she had not been too bad. No bridges out, but lots of trees were down and everything was wet.

Robert would find it hard to tell his mother, Leslie thought as she placed the notice of divorce next to the picture of the twins on his desk. Nora was divorcing him, in France. There was nothing he could do about it under French law. She was claiming abandonment. *Perhaps he abandoned her when she moved to London or Trieste*, Leslie thought.

Sykes had been spared. He had been duped, as Robert said: " once fooled, twice smarter." And Jason was spared the pain of prosecuting Laura's family. He requested a transfer.

At lunchtime Leslie paged Robert and insisted he take her to lunch at the Forbidden. He arrived promptly, and as they left the building and were in the parking lot they passed Jason running in.

"What's up?" Robert called to him as Jason passed.

"Got a hot date," was Jason's reply, grinning, and he bounded over a planter with an easy stride.

During lunch on the front veranda, among talk of color changes in the office, modifications of Robert's family estate, lists of invited guests for the wedding, and the thousand things that Leslie knew needed changing in his life.

Together they sat, in the bright shade of a late spring day, at last content. When orange sorbet arrived for dessert, Leslie took Robert's hands in hers for a moment and pulled his attention into her eyes. "You know," she said. "Twins run in my family, too."